Briarwood Publications, Incorporated

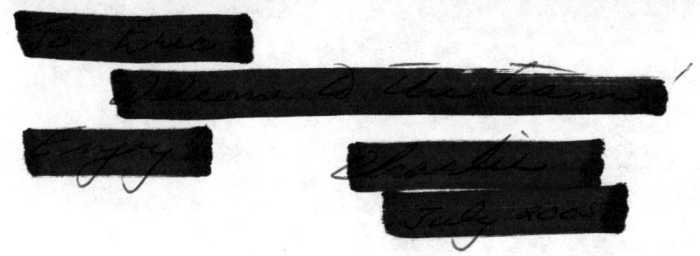

Shades of Murder

Charlie Hudson

Copyright © 2002 Charlie Hudson

First Published 2002
Briarwood Publications & Sassy Cat Books Inc.
150 West College Street
Rocky Mount, VA 24151

All rights reserved. The use of any part of this publication, reproduced, transmitted in any form or by any means, electronic, mechanical, photocopying, recording or otherwise, or stored in a retrieval system without prior consent of the publisher is an infringement of the copyright law.

CHARLIE HUDSON
SHADES OF MURDER
ISBN 1-892614-40-5

Manufactured in the United States of America

Printed by
Briarwood Publications, inc.

Acknowledgements

While I fictionalized a number of places in Shades of Murder, I want to thank Diver's Alert Network (DAN) for their technical information and for allowing me to use their name in the clear. DAN, as explained in the book, is a valuable organization that provides great support to the diving world. My thanks also to the Nags Head, N.C. Police Department, particularly Sergeant Kevin Brinkley and Earl Murray, for their time and technical assistance.

And what's a book without the right cover? The photograph for this one is the work of David (Dave) LaMay, an avid diver with an eye for composition Cynthia Campbell Reardon, a diver as well as graphics artist, is the one who put it all together.

As always, a big thanks to friends and fans who have waited for the second book and the second book would have taken much longer had it not been for the loving encouragement of my husband, Hugh and son, Dustin.

Author's Note

A quick word to the diving community. I respect those who free dive and even though this is a work of fiction, I want to explain that the theory described late in the book (no reading ahead) was not just writer's fancy. As of the publication of this book the theory has either not been pursued or the follow-on study has not been entered into the major diving information databases. Happy diving with or without tanks and kick back after the dive and read a good book. And non-divers, give the underwater world some thought – it's a wonderful sport.

Chapter One

Bev Henderson raised her eyebrows in question when Jim Osborn pulled into the mouth of Jackson's Marina and edged the unmarked car close to the ambulance. They should have been seeing a limp body waiting for the Medical Examiner rather than a man on a stretcher with a respirator covering his nose and mouth. Two paramedics jockeyed the gurney to lift it into the vehicle.

"Shit, they must have given us the wrong code. It doesn't look like the guy's dead yet," Jim said when they got out of the car and surveyed the scene of uniformed police keeping the small crowd back. Someone called out his name in recognition and Jim lifted his hand to acknowledge them.

Bev didn't respond to Jim's comment – she'd taken the call, but whoever had called the station might have been excited and given the wrong information. She walked over to the ambulance, slipped her sunglasses halfway down her nose and waited until the patient had been secured. The younger technician remained inside and was talking into the radio as Don McNeal, the older of the pair, jumped to the ground and gave a quick thumbs down signal when he saw her.

"No way on this one, Bev," he said as he closed the rear doors. He jerked his thumb toward a Marine Patrol boat docked at the closest slip. "They kept up resuscitation on the way in and we'll get him to the hospital, but I'm willing to bet there's been no brain activity since they started. They've got the details for you; name, age and so forth. I could be wrong, but I figure they should have time of death posted by the time you finish here. You need anything from me?"

Bev shook her head, swept her hand toward the cab and stepped aside to let him scramble into the driver's seat. He hit the siren and pealed away.

So whoever reported the drowning probably hadn't been too much in error. Bev could hear Jim's voice behind her and she knew he would join her when he got ready. She shoved her glasses back into place and turned to focus on the activity closer to the water. A blue hulled civilian boat with the name *Dare Devil* painted in large white script was next to the Marine Patrol boat. A distinctive red flag with a white diagonal bar hung from the antenna of the civilian boat to indicate it was outfitted for scuba diving. She assumed that the three men who were standing nearby were probably witnesses based on their diving attire and the fact they were inside the area allowed by the police.

Bev tapped her leather notebook against the side of her thigh and looked at Jim when he paused beside her. She wondered if he would want to proceed since a death required a full investigation while an ordinary accident could be handled by the senior uniformed officer on site.

"The guy did look pretty far gone and Mac didn't think he'd make it," she said quietly. "I told him to go ahead and we'd get the info from the patrol. You want to talk to everybody as long as we have them here or wait for the official call and then try and round them up?" It made more sense to her to continue, but if Jim wanted to get bureaucratic, it wasn't worth arguing about.

He rubbed his left eye and sighed. "We might as well get started and call the hospital in about twenty minutes. If the guy isn't really dead, we won't have wasted much more time than if we have to track people down later. You want the Marine Patrol or the other three?"

Bev was glad they were on the same wavelength and she studied the trio before she made her selection. The two young men standing next to the dive boat were still wearing shortie wetsuits with the top portion pulled down to their waists. The older man speaking to them was clad in a pair of red swim trunks and a navy blue T-shirt imprinted with a red, white and blue logo of the Adventures Below Dive Shop. Air tanks and other equipment formed an untidy semi-circle around them.

"I'll take the dive buddies together and then the other one unless you get to him first," Bev said as Jim took his pen from the front pocket of his shirt. "They look a little peaked and I can probably get a better story from them while they're rattled."

Jim nodded and turned toward the waiting patrolmen. Bev pulled off her sunglasses and smiled sympathetically at the divers. They were about the same height, but the sandy-haired one had broad shoulders and maybe thirty pounds over the redhead. Neither one of them looked older than their early twenties and both wore the awkward expression of not knowing whether they should be thrilled with the excitement around them or subdued because of the circumstances.

The man in the T-shirt stepped between Beverly and the two men and extended his hand. "Detective, I'm Tom Farmer," he said. "The dive shop is the next building over. I have an office as well as a classroom if you want to use that to talk to folks."

His brown eyes held no awkwardness nor did his deeply tanned face show any sign of shock, but if he was the seasoned ocean-goer he appeared to be, then in all likelihood, this was not the first time he would have seen a drowning victim.

"Beverly Henderson," she said and took the offered hand. She preferred to go by Bev, but she used her full name for professional discussions.

The man shook hands with a firm grip and the calluses on his fingers were of someone accustomed to manual work. "You're the boat captain, I gather."

He nodded. "Boat captain, primary owner of Adventures Below, and I was acting as safety diver. Greg, Greg Wiley, that is, is a part owner and was on a free dive when he started having problems."

Bev saw no reason to say she wasn't familiar with what

he was talking about because she'd find out soon enough, but she did notice that Farmer was blocking her from the other two men. It could be that he was a take-charge kind of guy or maybe he was trying to divert her attention so she would speak with him before the others. She'd only worked a couple of water related deaths and if negligence was involved, the odds were it would be the captain's fault. If that was the case, Bev was hoping the three men hadn't had time to put together a solid story.

The waiting pair shifted uncomfortably as if trying to decide to approach or stay still. She held her hand forward to indicate they should hold on for a minute.

Bev was eye level with him and held his gaze as she replied.

"Well Mr. Farmer, I'll obviously need to talk with you, but I'd like to go ahead and interview these gentleman first," she said firmly. "I appreciate the offer of the shop, but it will be easier if they can walk me around on the boat while we talk. That will help me get a better picture of what happened."

"Certainly," he said quickly and gestured toward the boat. "I've got some soda and beer iced down if you'd care for anything. The ice chest is starboard side."

"Thanks, I'm fine," she replied.

Farmer grabbed the dive gear sitting on the dock and indicated he would return shortly. Bev crooked a finger to the two young men who came forward in response.

The pair had the familiar look of tourists with pale skin and irregular splotches of red where they hadn't applied sunscreen. They introduced themselves as Justin Bibbins and Wayne Matson, their flat accents a likely product of the Midwest. Bev motioned them to board the boat and they sat on the edge of one of the two fiberglass benches. Bev liked the look of the boat with its extended forward area and racks behind the benches for the air tanks – definitely a cut above some of its neighbors. The sturdy white ice chest Farmer had mentioned was stowed neatly in place. A green towel had been left behind and snaked in a wet curl near Matson's foot.

Bev took the bench across from the two, laid her sunglasses down and opened her notebook. She entered their names and smiled to put them at ease. "I'll try not to keep you too long," she said. "I know something like this can be unsettling, but I need you to think about the sequence of things that led up to the accident and what you saw from then until the time you got here. Okay?"

They both nodded and seemed eager to begin when Jim walked up and rested his wide foot on the edge of the boat. Bev poised her pen.

"Bev, I checked with the hospital after I finished with the Patrol guys. The victim, Greg Wiley, was declared DOA and we'll get the exact time of death when we go by. I'll go ahead and do Farmer and then we'll catch the other end."

She brushed away a strand of hair that had escaped from her French braid. She wasn't surprised at the news nor the fact that Jim had finished his interview – the patrolmen were experienced enough to rattle off the kind of information that was needed and they didn't usually hang around.

"Got it," she said and pointed down the pier. "Farmer took the gear to the shop and should be there."

She turned back to the witnesses as Bibbins gave a low whistle. "Man, I didn't think Greg would make it, but you know, that's a real bummer."

Matson, the slender one, was sweating, although it was difficult to tell how much was the strain, the warm April sun, or the result of the beer she smelled on his breath. He was coherent though and she proceeded with the basic questions of departure time and the location of the dives.

"Well, you know, we were just out to go diving," Bibbins said. "We got certified last year and this was our first chance to come to the Keys. It was pretty awesome diving you know, I mean before what happened." He looked to Matson for confirmation and he grinned in agreement.

"Oh yeah, it was great and since we didn't have a whole lot of experience Greg went in with us on both dives. He really knew the area and showed us a bunch of cool stuff – found a couple of eels and a nurse shark too."

"Did Mr. Farmer go in the water at all?" she asked.

Bibbins shook his head. "No, he stayed on board and then he said they didn't have an afternoon dive booked and asked we if minded staying out for a while so Greg could get in a free dive. We didn't have anything going so we said it was okay."

Matson jumped in. "Oh yeah and Tom wanted to make sure we'd be okay on the boat because he said neither one of us had enough dives to be in the water with Greg. He had to be the safety diver, I think he called it." He inclined his head toward Bibbins. "We were anchored and he took the wheel, to well, you know, I mean it seemed kind of cool."

"It wasn't like I was doing anything," Bibbins said quickly. "And my uncle has a boat, so it's not like I've never been around one. Oh, and I wasn't drinking yet either. I was going to wait until they came back on board – Tom said the dive wouldn't take long."

"Sure, that's not a problem," Bev said soothingly. "By the way, had Mr. Farmer and Mr. Wiley been drinking?"

"No, just me," Matson said. "I mean everything was fine, you know. Greg was like in great shape and he didn't seem to be like tired or anything. I mean, I wasn't watching exactly until I heard him holler and then it was like everything was happening all at once." His voice had risen slightly and a line of sweat trickled down the side of his face. He swiped it with his forearm.

"Heard who holler?" Bev asked. "Mr. Farmer?"

"Uh no, that was me," Bibbins said. "I'd seen Greg go down for his dive and then I was looking around and then gee, I don't know how long, maybe five minutes or so, Tom was pulling Greg up. I thought he was okay at first and then, man, he was all limp and Tom put him on his back and was giving him mouth-to-mouth right there in the water and all. I was going to jump in so I called out to tell him, but he yelled for me to radio for help, so I got on the radio and called for the rescue guys, I mean the Patrol guys, and told them as much as I could," he said in a rush. "I mean, I had to read off the location and stuff."

"Yeah and when Tom got close enough to the boat we helped pull him – I mean Greg – on board and got Tom out of his gear while he got the oxygen going. I mean he knew what he was doing so we just kind of stayed out of the way," Matson added.

Bev squinted her eyes slightly. "When you said Mr. Farmer *was pulling Greg up,* do you mean you could see them or you just saw Mr. Farmer?"

Bibbins paused for a minute and frowned. "Uh well, Tom was just below the surface, I mean I could see his bubbles and all and he was waiting for Greg to come back up, so I guess I couldn't exactly see Greg. Tom must have dove down a little because he was out of sight for maybe a minute and I guess he must have seen Greg was in trouble so he went and got him. It wasn't very long though," he finished and looked to Matson again. "I mean, it didn't seem very long."

Matson shrugged. "I don't think so, but like I said, I wasn't looking in the same spot as Justin. And I'm pretty sure the Marine Patrol guys came fast."

Jim would have gotten that information and Bev spent another ten minutes with the two men. It was possible that they were delivering a smooth lie except that neither of the two struck Bev as accomplished actors.

Both men were on vacation from Omaha and planned to stay for another few days. Bev handed them her business card, thanked them for their cooperation, reminded them to call if they thought of anything new and requested they not return home without notifying her. Their solemn agreement was almost comical and Matson grabbed two beers from the cooler before they departed the boat and walked in the direction of the dive shop. The green towel had not caught their attention or maybe it didn't belong to either of them.

Jim and Farmer appeared on the dock within five minutes.

Bev grasped the side rail of the boat and easily made the short step down onto the damp planks.

Jim's slightly plump face was placid. Bev knew that meant he was either satisfied with what he'd been told or he was suspicious and had no intention of voicing his suspicions until he had a chance to talk to her alone.

"Detective Osborn told me about Greg," Farmer said quietly. "I didn't have much hope, but there was always the chance that I was too pessimistic."

He didn't seem to be overly distressed for someone who'd had his business partner die in front of him.

"I'd like to telephone Karen Silsby, Greg's girlfriend, if you don't mind. I'll offer to go to the hospital for whatever paperwork is needed to spare her that. Greg doesn't have any family here."

Bev raised her eyebrows to Jim, who shrugged and scratched his jaw.

"Sure," she said, surprised that Jim was evidently going to let her take the lead after all. She had answered the radio call, but she'd guessed wrong before about when Jim would exert his seniority. "We'll wait here while you call, but we'll need to speak with her at some point. You can either let her know or I'll talk with her after you've finished."

Farmer nodded and they waited until he was out of hearing distance. Jim waved his hand across the water and belched loudly.

"So far it looks pretty clean. Mr. Gregory Sherman Wiley, aged twenty-nine, was doing that free dive shit, the stuff without tanks, and something went wrong. Farmer got him onto the boat and worked on him until the Marine Patrol answered the call and they took over. Seems like the deceased had a reputation for edging around restricted areas, hot-dogging, and shit like that. Both the patrolmen said they figured Wiley was an accident waiting for a place to happen. What about the two tourists?"

Unlike Jim, Bev referred to her carefully written notes. "Nothing out of order except for a dead body. Everything points toward an accident, although Bibbins and Matson were on the boat the whole time, which means they were a good sixty, seventy feet away when the trouble started in the water," she said and stopped when Farmer walked up.

His mouth was turned downward and he handed Bev a pale yellow piece of paper inscribed with the Adventures Below name, e-mail address, and telephone and fax numbers. "Karen said she doesn't mind going to the hospital and she'll be glad to speak with you whenever, but it will take her about half an hour to get there. This is her address and telephone number if you want to talk to her before she leaves the condo."

"No, we'll catch her at the hospital," Bev said without consulting Jim. "Thanks for your help, but we'll need to check with you on some further details while we're completing the investigation."

Farmer extended his hand again. "Of course. I've been in this business long enough to know the drill. I'm here at the shop most of the time and you've got my home number as well. Just let me know what you need."

With that, he hopped back onto the boat and began to gather more gear. He scooped up the towel and slung it across one shoulder.

Bev looked around one more time. The marina had returned to normal with only a few boaters or deliverymen in sight. The spring break congestion had ended and it was another month until the summer tourists arrived to crowd the marinas in their desire to cram as many adventures as possible into the time they'd allotted from their regular routines. A quartet of sea gulls was perched on posts near the seafood market, either resting after gorging on fish parts or waiting for the next load of scraps to be hauled outside.

Bev radioed the station of their destination as Jim drove the five miles to the only hospital in town. A new wing was under construction and Bev had heard that it was supposed to include a dialysis center. She didn't know they needed one, but the number of permanent residents in Verde

Key was on the rise.

Bev and Jim parked near the emergency room entrance and Bev wrinkled her nose at the antiseptic smells when they stepped through the wide sliding doors. Despite the dozens of times she'd stood over dead bodies or interviewed bleeding victims, she disliked the institutional scents.

The nurse at the desk directed them toward the last curtained cubicle and when they approached it, Bev saw that the green fabric had been pulled aside. It was obvious that Mr. Wiley had no further use for privacy. The middle-aged, plump nurse who was filling out some kind of form offered to find the attending physician.

Jim and Bev began to check for any signs of trauma while they waited, but Mr. Wiley's nearly perfectly sculpted body showed nothing that would indicate foul play. There were a few patches of scraped skin that Bev assumed had occurred as he was being hauled into the boat and an old scar was squiggled across his muscular left biceps. No new or old needle marks were visible and Bev didn't see any nostril damage from cocaine use.

The nurse returned with an apologetic smile and said the doctor was making his rounds and would be available after that, but there was a young lady at the desk inquiring about the victim.

"His girlfriend, a Karen Silsby, was supposed to be on her way," Jim said with a tiny grunt. "That's probably her. We need to speak with her and you need some information don't you?"

The nurse nodded and motioned for the detectives to stay with the corpse. "Yes, there are several questions we need to ask her if you can wait. I'll see if she has the information and be right back."

Bev was making another annotation in her notebook when she heard Jim give a low whistle. Bev raised her head and saw the woman who she assumed was Karen Silsby walking toward them with the air of a woman who was accustomed to drawing attention. Her thick, wavy black hair tumbled

Shades of Murder

around an oval face and spilled across her shoulders. She was wearing a straight white skirt with a slit up the side and a pale pink and white striped silk top cut with a deep vee which in no way concealed her noticeable cleavage.

Well, maybe Mr. Farmer hadn't explained that Mr. Wiley was probably dead and Miss Silsby had planned to try and cheer him up, Bev thought. It was a good bet that her outfit would have gotten his pulse going if he'd had one left.

Jim took a step forward and momentarily screened her from the view. "Are you Miss Silsby?" he asked in the most solicitous tone Bev had ever heard him use. On the other hand, she couldn't recall them having ever interviewed a woman who looked like she belonged on a swimsuit calendar.

"Yes," the woman answered quietly and briefly shook hands. "You must be the detectives Tom told me about."

"Uh, yes ma'am. I'm Jim Osborn and this is Beverly Henderson," Jim said.

Miss Silsby moved sideways in order to see Wiley and Bev braced herself for the messy reaction.

Maybe she *had* known what to expect because she pressed a manicured hand to her mouth and breathed deeply, but displayed no overt emotion. She turned to face them and Bev noticed there was no trace of tears in the large jade colored eyes. Her full eyelashes were too soft to be artificial.

"Tom didn't really explain much," she said softly. "He just said there'd been an accident and he didn't think Greg was going to make it. Not that something wasn't bound to happen sooner or later, but can you give me any details?"

Bev mentally registered Miss Silsby's comment as Jim cleared his throat. Bev presumed he was trying to speak without drooling.

"Well ma'am," he said in a suitably official voice, "we don't have the whole story yet and we do need to ask you some questions. If you feel up to talking we could go to the cafeteria for a cup of coffee or something."

"Please call me Karen," the young woman said with a

smile. Her straight, white teeth matched the rest of her appearance. "That will be fine if you don't mind waiting a few minutes for me to give some information to the nurse."

"No problem," Bev interjected to take control of the situation again. Now she'd find out who was to be in charge. "We'll wait here."

Miss Silsby walked away with a sway of her hips that Jim obligingly ogled and Bev repressed a snort at his utterly predictable male behavior.

Jim caught her expression and held out his hands. "I know, but give me a break Bev, it's not my fault she looks like that," he said sheepishly.

"Yeah right," Bev replied without much sting. She'd been around Jim since she was a little girl and knew that he enjoyed looking, but didn't have enough nerve to cheat on his wife, Myrtle.

Jim gave Bev an open-handed, light pat on the arm. "Come on Kid, don't get your feathers ruffled. I'm serious about you having the lead on this and I'll even keep my eyes on her face this time."

Before Bev could retort, Miss Silsby moved away from the conversation with the nurse and looked ready to go. If Jim was going to let her run the case then she could indulge him a little. She gave him a tiny push to get him started toward the cafeteria. He fell into step with the incredibly attractive young woman and Bev walked behind them.

There was nothing intrinsically wrong with the fact that neither the girlfriend nor the business partner seemed terribly grief-stricken at Mr. Wiley's death, but she wanted to pursue why Miss Silsby had said what she did about something happening sooner or later. That kind of remark was worth a question or two.

Chapter Two

The cafeteria was almost empty when they entered and Jim announced that he would bring the coffee if the women would have a seat. Bev selected a table against the wall away from the few occupants in the spacious room and sat next to Silsby. Maybe it was unfair on her part, but she had the feeling that Silsby would cozy up to Jim in the way women who looked like her had a tendency to do.

Jim walked up with a tray and three diner-style, white mugs, handed the mugs around and scattered a small mound of sugar and artificial sweetener packets and tiny plastic containers of cream in the center of the table.

Bev took her coffee and spoke quietly. "Miss Silsby, we're sorry for your loss, but you indicated a few minutes ago that you weren't terribly surprised. Why would that be?"

"Please do call me Karen," she said with a half smile and a tiny shake of her head. "Look, if you've talked to anyone about Greg, you'll know he is, I mean, was one of those macho men who pushed the envelope in everything he did. Fast cars, the souped-up boat, hang gliding, whatever. He got a thrill out of it. I don't mean he had a death wish or anything — let's just say he had an exaggerated notion of his own prowess. The invincible kind, if you know what I mean." She paused to take a sip of coffee.

Silsby hardly appeared to be the delicate type, so Bev didn't try to soften her next question. "Did that include the use of recreational drugs?"

"As if something could have interfered with his judgement today or slowed his reflexes?" Silsby asked without seeming to take offense at the question. "No, Greg wasn't into drugs other than alcohol and he usually waited until after diving for that. Do you have some reason to think this was more than an accident; that he might have been high or out of control?"

Jim shifted his chair and the metal legs scrapped against the highly polished linoleum. "Not really Karen," he said. "We have to cover all the bases and if he was incapacitated in some way, we might as well find it out now. It will make things easier."

She swung her steady gaze between the detectives. "Of course I understand and I'll be glad to tell you what I can, but from what Tom explained to me, it sounds pretty uncomplicated. Like I said no drugs and no booze of any significance last night. We went out to eat and had a before dinner drink, split a bottle of wine, and had another drink when we got home, even though neither one of us was drunk. All I know for sure is that he was fine when he left this morning."

Bev wondered again at her composure, but there was no good reason to question that directly. She asked instead how long Tom Farmer and Greg had been partners and how many years of diving experience Greg had.

Silsby quickly responded to Bev's queries. Yes, Greg was an accomplished diver, but no, not in the same league as Tom. No, he'd never had trouble before as far as she knew, but no, they didn't spend a lot of time talking about it and no, she didn't dive and didn't have a whole lot of interest in it.

Jim didn't interrupt and Bev knew he was watching Silsby for any change of emotion or signs of distress at the questions that Bev posed. At least, that was what he was supposed to be watching for.

Bev ran through the checklist she'd made and within another fifteen minutes the session slowed to a stopping point. Silsby stood, shook their hands politely, provided her telephone number again and walked away without a backward glance.

Not unexpectedly, two young Hispanic men arranging

tables and chairs paused to stare and one of them licked his lips and said something Bev didn't hear. Not that it was difficult to make a guess.

The smell of roast beef floated into the room when a nondescript man in cook's whites carried a load of dirty dishes through the metal double doors into the kitchen. The noise level in the cafeteria had elevated as the evening shift began preparations for the dinner meal.

"She didn't seem overcome with grief," Bev said and slipped her pen into the slot in her notebook. "And in case you hadn't noticed, Farmer, the partner, wasn't too broken up, either."

Jim rubbed the back of his neck and flexed his shoulders. "Yeah, but between what the Marine Patrolmen told me and what the girlfriend said, it's looking like this guy was living on borrowed time. That could be why nobody's shocked. Let's go see if the doctor is available and then get back to the station. Claude is going to want to know what we've got so far."

They found the doctor at the nurses' station. He looked young enough to be newly out of internship and confirmed that death was from ordinary drowning, specifically caused by the onset of shallow water blackout. The toxicology tests would take a few days although he'd seen no sign of drug use or trauma and anticipated that the autopsy would verify his initial diagnosis.

"I prefer an overturned boat with some old goat who has a heart attack," Jim grumbled when they exited the hospital. "That's the simplest kind. At least he was one of our locals so the Chamber of Commerce doesn't have to bust a gut trying to smooth over a tourist buying it. That kind of publicity makes them uncomfortable."

"Nice sentiment," Bev said and slid into the passenger's side. There was no sense in asking to drive. Jim's silent, and sometimes not so silent, reactions to her abilities were more bothersome than taking the right hand seat. Bev didn't mind asserting herself, but she selected her battles carefully around both Jim and Chief Taylor.

It was after four o'clock when they made it back to the station and Sheila, the administrative assistant, told them the boss had been looking for them for the past hour. Jim flipped his hand in acknowledgement and they went into the rectangular shaped office they shared.

The entire station had been freshly painted during the winter and the new furniture that Bev had convinced Chief Taylor to authorize was color coordinated, albeit in standard blacks, blues and grays. It hardly looked as though they'd consulted an interior decorator, but it was a definite improvement over what had been a mismatched collection.

Bev barely had time to sit down when Chief Taylor came through the door and propped himself against Jim's desk. Fortunately the aged wooden desk was still sturdy enough to withstand the Chief's bulk. He looked like his ulcer was bothering him and he popped a couple of antacid tablets into his mouth. He crunched them more than actually chewed and frowned.

"So what's the deal?" he asked. "We're coming up on summer season and the Chamber will be having a fit if tourists start getting killed already."

Jim winked at Bev at the Chief's concern. "Not a public relations problem, boss; one of our own for the past few years. Name was Gregory Wiley and he was a partner in the Adventures Below dive operation. We'll need to wait for the autopsy, but first call is that he screwed up doing that free diving shit, suffered shallow water blackout and drowned."

Chief Taylor picked a piece of antacid from his lip and put it in his mouth. "Free diving? What the hell is that?"

"It's diving without air tanks," Bev explained and exhausted her knowledge of the sport. "Like the pearl divers you see on television."

His frown had disappeared with the idea that it was a careless accident. "Stupid son-of-a-bitch," he said. "You'd think those guys would figure out we don't have gills for a reason. Any chance the boat captain or anybody else made some kind of mistake and helped him along?"

Bev tapped her finger against her notebook. "We've got to check another couple of things, but like Jim said, it looks pretty clean. We should be able to wrap it within a day of when we get the autopsy report. I don't think they're too busy, although we can try and rush them if you want us to."

Chief Taylor rubbed his bald spot. The remaining fringe of gray flecked black hair was rapidly losing ground. "No need for that if there's no tourist angle. Anybody asks for a statement, tell them the investigation is on going, accidental death will probably be the ruling and so forth. Oh yeah, while you were on this call we got word about what may be a pair of psychos headed cross country. There were a couple of convenience stores hit in Alabama and a liquor store in Lutz early this morning. There's a pattern."

Jim wadded a sheet of notebook paper and nailed the trashcan from four feet away. "We got an identification?"

Chief Taylor shifted his weight and unconsciously scratched his crotch. "Shit no, they've been killing everybody they hit and they're smart enough to take the tapes out of the places that have a video camera. One clerk in each place for a body count of three. It may not even be two guys. There haven't been any prints, and there's only one gun being used, but with the amount of stuff taken, and in and out as fast as it seems to be, you figure there's got to be a second guy involved. Right now though it's somebody else's problem, so take care of this one quick as you can."

He slipped the knot on his tie down another inch, left the office and stopped to talk to one of the sergeants.

"Bad news with the killings," Bev said. "Three people just trying to make a living and some asshole comes in and blows them away. Even when you take abnormal psychology into account, it's a pisser."

Jim shoved some papers around, scattering folders and empty candy bar wrappers. "I quit trying to figure the really bad ones years ago, Kid," he said and extracted a clean notepad from the disorganized jumble on his desk.

"The shrinks and social workers can spend their time worrying about whether or not they grew up in deprived homes. If we're lucky, some state troopers will pop them and they'll be killed resisting arrest. It takes lawyers out of the equation, saves the taxpayers a lot of money and makes the outcome a lot cleaner."

He checked the clock on the wall, picked up a pencil and began to doodle. "It's almost quitting time, but let's go over the boat captain's statement again to see if we missed something. If there's negligence involved, it'll be his fault."

Bev nodded and the image of Wiley's nearly perfect and very dead body flashed through her mind. Would they would find an inconsistency in the witnesses' account of events or was it as the girlfriend indicated and Wiley had simply pushed the adventure envelope a little too far and discovered how mortal he really was?

Chapter Three

Willie Denton slumped in the shower after he shot his wad and wished he could have a woman instead of beating his meat. They had passed a couple of beer joints on the way to the motel and he was sure there would be some available action, but he was afraid to take the chance of going into a public place. He still couldn't believe they were on the loose with a trail of dead bodies behind them, but Hal's plan was working so far and he couldn't risk fucking it up just to get fucked.

He almost smiled at the joke he'd made, sighed instead and turned off the tepid stream of water. He reached for the cheap, thin towel that hung on the nail driven into the wall in place of a towel rack. The cracked mirror in the small bathroom was filmed with steam, but at least he'd had hot water for ten minutes and the cockroaches scuttling around the corners of the room were small. He hated the big ones.

Willie wiped an irregular circle on the mirror with his hand and stared at the unfamiliar beard. He turned his head slowly back and forth for a view from the right and left. Actually, he didn't look bad in a beard. He'd been expecting the gray he'd begun to find sprinkled in his hair to show, but the beard was all brown. As Hal had explained, he would be able to use peroxide later and go to a lighter shade or even a reddish color if he needed to.

Hal had shaved off not only his beard, but his hair as well and the transformation had been startling. It's not that either man was disguised exactly, but they didn't immediately match the description of the photographs on file with the state of Mississippi. In barely two weeks, Willie's whole damn life had changed and he sure as hell hadn't figured it would have turned out the way it did.

He picked up a pair of nail scissors and carefully trimmed a few stray hairs and thought about their options. Hal was smart and he wasn't, but for the hundredth time or more, he wished he'd never met him or at least that he hadn't agreed to help when Hal started talking about robbing the nigger drug pusher. Hal had made it all sound so easy and yeah, Willie was tired of the bullshit job, the bullshit town, his bitch of an ex-wife, and no real prospects for improvement. But goddamn, this wasn't what he'd had in mind! Everything had just moved too damned fast.

Hal had come to work at the warehouse right from the state penitentiary, but it didn't bother Willie that he was an ex-convict. He pulled his share of the load and even covered for Willie one morning when he was dog-sick hung over and had to crawl behind a stack of crates to sleep it off.

Willie had invited Hal to join him for a drink by way of thanks and then it became a daily routine to stop by The Full Keg. Willie had never paid much attention to most of the bar's regulars, but Hal had a knack for learning about people even though he didn't seem to have any friends. He's the one who told him that the loudmouth nigger who always dressed flashy and drove the red Caddy was a drug dealer.

One night, Hal started going on about how the nigger was too stupid to be a good drug dealer and how simple it would be to rip him off. Willie thought it was just trash talk, but Hal claimed he could present himself as a go-between for a buy and he laid out a plan for he and Willie to do the job.

Hal explained that they could grab the drugs and the wad of bills the nigger always carried and be out of the county within an hour. Out of the county, then the state and on to somewhere new. They'd get new Social Security cards and drivers' licenses with no problem from some contact Hal knew, take on different identities and have another try at life.

Willie had been in jail a couple of times on piss-ant

charges and had never thought about getting involved in anything that could result in hard time. The way Hal talked about everything though it didn't seem like a real crime. After all, drug dealing was a seriously bad thing so that meant stealing money from a pusher would be sort of like helping the law. And if that gave Hal and Willie a chance to start a better life, then what the hell was wrong with that? It wasn't like anybody was really gonna get hurt.

Hal hadn't given him many details, but he sounded so confident that after thinking about it for a while, Willie declared he was ready and followed Hal's instructions about tying up loose ends around town.

He had fed his ex-wife and boss a story about going to look for work in Texas. No one had been suspicious or particularly curious, but hell, he'd always figured nobody gave a shit about him anyway. He'd picked up his final paycheck, left the cramped apartment where he lived and spent the day in a town forty miles away. He caught a couple of movies and didn't run into anyone he knew.

He'd been nervous though and had driven to their meeting place at the abandoned quarry an hour early. Hal had arrived on schedule and taken a small suitcase from his truck and put it in Willie's car. He patiently explained twice that all Willie needed to do was to carry the briefcase, walk toward the nigger and let Hal take care of everything else. Willie had asked where Hal was going to be and he told him not to worry, that he'd be right next to him.

The rendezvous point was at a dilapidated farmhouse and Hal stopped several hundred feet behind the wood line. Willie wasn't expecting the stop and he almost rear-ended him. Hal got out of his old pickup and climbed into Willie's car with no explanation. They drove up to a weathered barn with the roof caving in and Willie took the briefcase. It felt empty and he didn't know what he was supposed to do with it. The head nigger was leaning against the trunk of the Caddy jaw-jacking with the two uppity assholes that hung with him. They'd been laughing about something and Willie had wondered if it was at him. Hal wasn't the kind of guy people laughed at.

As soon as Willie and Hal approached them, Hal had whipped out a pistol and shot all three in rapid succession without saying a word. The pusher had tried to duck behind his car, but Hal had caught him in between his shoulder blades and he'd fallen face down. Willie had been stunned, momentarily unable to understand what he was seeing.

Hal had walked forward, kicked the bodies to check for movement and grinned at Willie. "Don't look so surprised. I couldn't come up with enough cash to fool them and they'd have done the same to us as soon as they knew. Give me a hand and we'll trade our case for what's in the trunk."

Willie had felt like he was in a dream as Hal swapped out his scuffed case for a black, honest-to-God alligator one filled with cash, marijuana and cocaine packets. Willie had choked down the nausea rising in his throat as Hal had swung the object by its handle, gathered the weapons and ammunition from the corpses and tossed one of the pistols to Willie. It fell to the ground and Willie had jumped to the side at one more unexpected gesture. Then he'd bent down and picked the gun up in his right hand and stared at it. What was he supposed to do with it?

Hal had chuckled at what he seemed to think was a joke and jerked his head to Willie to come forward to open the trunk of his car. Willie's right hand was shaking as he did what he was told and Hal had pushed the briefcase case toward the back and tugged a piece of olive drab cloth tarpaulin over it. He'd stuck his own pistol in his belt, strolled to his truck and drove it up next to the car. Willie had stood there wordlessly with the gun held loosely in his hand and wondered what the hell he was going to do. He thought about dropping it and getting the hell out, but he'd been too confused.

Hal had a soiled blue blanket in his arms. He wrapped the extra gun in it and extracted a set of Louisiana license plates that he attached to Willie's car. He shoved the blanket into the trunk with the other items. When he finished, he winked at Willie and then walked back, grabbed one of the bodies underneath the arms and dragged him into the truck.

He propped the dead man up on the passenger's side and leaned his head against the window as if he was taking a nap. "Let's get some good use out of this dipshit," he'd said with a grin. "Get in your car and follow me."

Willie thought about taking off in the opposite direction, but didn't know where he'd go. Hal had the plan, not him. Hal led him several miles down a back road that ran between Hal's trailer and town and stopped about a mile from his place.

Willie sat in the car for a moment and watched in disbelief as Hal jumped out, opened the hood and tinkered underneath it for a few minutes. Then he stepped back and opened the passenger's door. He shoved the dead man over until he was behind the steering wheel, took a bottle of whiskey from under the seat, splashed the rest of the contents on the dashboard and dropped the empty bottle on the floorboard. When he finished, he reached across the body, and cranked the ignition.

Willie got out of his car and smelled gasoline burning before he saw the smoke curling out of the engine compartment. Hal grinned again, released the emergency brake, slammed the door shut and jumped back. The truck rolled down the slight incline into a stand of trees and even without gaining much speed, the sound of the impact echoed. Willie had thrown himself into his car at Hal's signal and by the time he was in reverse, the front of the truck had exploded into flames.

Hal told Willie to wait at a distance until the fire had spread to the cab and then he nodded for them to continue to drive.

"They'll only figure it out if they check closely," Hal had said much too calmly. "There's a good chance they won't bother, and even if they do, we'll be long gone. Nobody's liable to find the niggers until sometime tomorrow. Anybody looking for them won't go to the cops first. Head north and we'll cut across the state line."

Willie had done as he was told, more confused than

frightened and he wanted to ask Hal if he had planned the killings all along, but he didn't want to sound stupid. He had figured they would tie them up or something, but it would have been two against three and that might not have worked. And it wasn't like the dead men would be missed by anyone who counted and maybe Hal was right – maybe this was the best way.

Willie's confidence in Hal hit rock bottom though when they made the late night stop just across the state line. Hal had been smiling when he told Willie to gas up the car while he went in for cigarettes. The clerk had been reading a newspaper when Willie came in to tell Hal how much they owed on the gas. Hal had grinned as if he'd just heard something funny, stepped up to the counter, shot the clerk at point blank range, emptied the cash register drawer and then casually leaned the dead man face forward against the machine as his blood streamed onto the floor.

"Grab a couple of cases of cold beer," was all Hal said to Willie. "And make sure you wipe your prints off the door handle."

Willie couldn't hold back the nausea this time and puked his guts out onto the aisle as Hal had shaken his head and lifted two twelve packs of beer out of the cooler himself.

"Get your ass in gear, Willie, or I'll take the keys and leave you here with the stiff," Hal had said quietly.

Willie wiped his mouth on the sleeve of his shirt and hurried out of the store as fast as he could with his legs trembling. He gripped the steering wheel tightly to maintain control and Hal directed him onto another two-lane road at the second intersection. They drove without speaking and finally stopped at a rundown motel in the pre-dawn hours.

Willie waited anxiously in the car while Hal checked them in with little, if any, interest displayed by the slow-moving man on duty. After they had hauled the briefcase and guns into the room Willie watched Hal inventory the money and drugs and asked why the second robbery and why the murder. Hal had shrugged and popped the top off a can of beer.

Shades of Murder

"It made the most sense," he said with such calm that Willie was reminded of a scene in a movie. "Nobody knows you and I are together and right now, nobody that's seen us can talk about it. Besides Willie, he was some skinny old fart who probably had a nagging wife and a couple of snot-nosed kids. I might have done him a favor. Drink a beer and don't worry about it. And look what we've got; the nigger had more than I was expecting. We're rich and we're on our way to paradise. We do a few places like the one tonight for traveling money and that leaves the whole stash for later. You let me take care of the planning, do what I tell you, and everything is going to work out fine."

And so the pattern had been set. A criss-crossing trail to a destination Hal had not yet revealed. A few days of quiet as they checked in and out of small motels where no one questioned them or perhaps did not even notice them. Didn't notice despite the news reports of convenience store murders and robberies, but as Hal reminded him with a kind of creepy laugh, what was there to notice? Two men traveling together wasn't unusual, they didn't cause any trouble and they paid their bill in full. Nothing about the two of them seemed out of the ordinary, so why should anyone care?

The Alabama authorities correctly assumed the shootings were the work of the same man, or men, but they left no clues and the police admitted they had nothing to go on. The dead drug dealer in Mississippi didn't even make the Alabama newspapers, so why would anyone think there was a connection?

The money from the other robberies is what they'd been using to pay for food and motels in small bills, worn and crumpled from going hand to hand. Hal had explained that was the smart way to do things and that's part of why nobody could track them down. He said that flashing money around or buying a lot of stuff at one time was what got people in trouble.

The sound of the television came through the bathroom door and interrupted Willie's recollection of how he'd come to be where he was. It was probably one of the afternoon business or news shows that Hal liked and Willie slept through. He was getting awfully tired of it and he wished Hal would tell him where they were going and when they would get there.

The idea of having more than sixty thousand dollars in cash and drugs to sell for even more money was still hard for Willie to believe. What he did know was that once they arrived at their destination his plans included a bottle of expensive bourbon, a big steak dinner and the prettiest hooker in town. He'd pay her for the whole night and be done with Hal Grayson once and for all.

Chapter Four

Bev and Jim stopped work at five o'clock and Bev retrieved a bottle of Pinot Grigio from the old, battered refrigerator in the corner of the office. She was due at her Aunt Lorna's house for an early dinner and she'd known she wouldn't have time to stop for wine en route so she'd brought the bottle in.

Bev thought that eating dinner before the evening news was over was uncivilized, but Lorna had called that morning and asked if she could come at five-thirty and said she would explain later. They usually had dinner together every week and Bev had almost asked if they could re-schedule, but aside from the fact that she thoroughly enjoyed Lorna's company, she was a terrific cook. Her affection for her mother's older sister went far deeper than family obligation and a little inconvenience wasn't too much to ask.

Bev drove past the fitness center where she was a member and made a note to herself to pick up a new pair of running shoes. The heels on the ones she had were starting to wear down and she wanted to increase the level of cushioning she was using.

She turned into Aunt Lorna's quiet, well groomed neighborhood that was dominated by 1950s style houses and a shortage of swimming pools compared to the newer developments. Bev maneuvered her green Triumph Spitfire into Aunt Lorna's driveway next to the dark red 1957 Chevy pickup truck that was impeccably maintained by the combined efforts of Lorna, Bev's father, and the only mechanic in town that was allowed to touch the classic vehicle. Bev opened her door carefully to avoid bumping the side of the truck. It had its share of dings, but she made a habit of trying not to add to them.

She tucked the bottle of wine under her arm and stooped to pick up a plastic bag that was caught in a bed of daffodils. The yard was small, but well proportioned to the white frame bungalow and was landscaped into neatly balanced sections of greenery and flowering plants. Lorna owned a florist shop across town and Bev calculated that she and Bev's mother had spent thousands of hours swapping gardening ideas.

Bev bound up the three steps onto the porch. "It's me," she called out as she entered the short front hallway and sniffed the fragrant smell of rosemary chicken.

"In the kitchen," Lorna responded. Bev deposited the bag in the wastepaper basket in the hall, dropped her purse onto the couch in the den and passed through the archway into the kitchen. "It smells great in here," she said.

"Oh, nothing too elaborate," Aunt Lorna replied and stepped around the island to hug Bev. "Chicken, a new rice pilaf I found and some green beans almondine," she said and smiled at the bottle of wine that Bev held out for inspection.

"Well, isn't that lovely? Do you want to open it now? The chicken needs another ten or fifteen minutes."

"Sure," Bev said. "Are you going to have time for more than one glass?" she asked and set the bottle on the counter.

Lorna nodded her head and rolled her eyes. "I'll probably need the whole bottle, but I'll share," she said and peered through the window of the wall oven.

Bev raised her eyebrows and reached for the wineglasses displayed on a wooden tray decorated with an inlay of a trio of dolphins. It was a beautiful piece that Bev had found in a boutique in Key West and given to Lorna as a Christmas present.

"It's your Aunt Inez," the older woman continued, apparently satisfied with the progress of the dish. "She was supposed to come for one of her visits next month when your mother was here too, but in her typical fashion she suddenly decided to change all her plans and go off to

Aruba and then on to Buenos Aries and she's flying in this evening. She'll be in around seven o'clock and I couldn't see subjecting you to that. Of course you're welcome to hang around if you'd like."

Bev had already begun to shake her head at the mention of her other aunt's name. "I'm willing to provide moral support if you need it, but if you can do without me, I'll pass," she said and poured the wine.

Aunt Lorna grinned and held out her hand for the glass. "I've been handling Inez for fifty years, so I can manage. How about getting the salad out while I check the rolls?"

Bev set her glass down on the end of the island, slipped the bottle of wine into the refrigerator and took out the two bowls of salad. She passed through a second archway into the dining area and positioned the salads next to the place settings. The round table covered in a sunflower motif tablecloth was already set and she glanced across it to see if anything else was missing. She listened to Lorna's movements and thought about her mother and two aunts.

Bev was certain that she wasn't the only one who wondered how the three Mitchell girls could have belonged to the same family. Emma, the middle daughter, was very nearly an exact duplicate of Granny Mitchell, God rest her soul; a respectable homemaker who took pride in her house and family with no discernible interests beyond that and the social life of the church.

Lorna, the oldest, was the rebellious one who allegedly had sneaked cigarettes at an early age and been lectured regularly by Granny Mitchell for unladylike behavior. The story was that by the time she was thirteen she was accurately labeled as an old maid in the making by the neighborhood quilting circle. Bev had never quite understood why it mattered, but it seemed that when Lorna ran off and spent several years in the Peace Corps, that had been viewed as reckless rather than good citizenship. Apparently, it would have been different if she had gone on behalf of missionary work and Bev gathered it was something that Granny Mitchell had never completed accepted.

Bev was convinced that her own mother's deep-seated domesticity was due to Granny's fervent efforts to rectify whatever mistakes she thought she'd made with Lorna.

Inez was the baby of the family and had suffered from a weak respiratory system as an infant. She had immediately been identified as *delicate* and that sense of fragility had been reinforced when she, of all three girls, had inherited the pale blonde hair, blue eyes and petite figure of Great-grandmother Brown. From what Myrtle Osborn had told Bev, Inez had more or less floated through her teenage years and managed to meet and charm a well-to-do businessman from New York who had come to the Keys on a fishing trip. He had swept her away to the Bahamas for a quick marriage and she had accompanied him home where she promptly immersed herself in cultural lessons to remove any semblance of her small town upbringing.

Her visits were normally a non-stop recital of her husband's business successes; her tribulations in keeping up with their busy social obligations and whatever the latest crisis was with the noxious miniature poodle that substituted for a child.

Aunt Inez's complete personal makeover was somewhat fascinating, but only in small doses. Her saving grace was that she was oblivious to the family's opinion of her and therefore constantly provided generous gifts to her older sisters and their off-spring as a way of sharing her good fortune since her siblings would obviously never be able to afford the finer things in life. She had also spent thousands of dollars to make Granny Mitchell's last months as comfortable as possible. Her good intentions were tainted by the fact that she was an annoying, fluttery, overly jeweled snob, but she didn't know it and no one in the family thought it would do any good to tell her.

"I think we're ready to eat," Lorna said interrupting Bev's musings.

Bev stepped back into the kitchen and watched Lorna arrange the food on the plates. She carried them to the table while Bev brought the bottle of wine.

They sat down and spent the next hour enjoying the meal and exchanging news of recent events. Bev insisted on helping clean up and as she departed Aunt Lorna suggested they try again later in the week.

Bev said she would give her a call, but she knew that Lorna's schedule was probably busier than hers was. Bev didn't have much other than work and her regular workout regimen going on at the moment. She'd broken off with the man she'd been seeing and hadn't met anyone lately that stirred her interest.

It was still a few minutes before seven o'clock and Bev swung into Harry's Hideaway, her dad's neighborhood hangout, on the way to her parents' house. Bev lived at the opposite end of town, but there had been a fire in her apartment building and the renovations had extended from the original projected time. Aunt Lorna had offered the use of her sleeper sofa, and as much as Bev enjoyed her aunt, she didn't think that much closeness would be good for either of them.

Luckily, Bev's older brother and his wife had planned a second honeymoon for their tenth anniversary and Bev's parents had gone to Mobile to stay with the children, so the timing had worked out well for everyone. Bev had moved into the guest bedroom and Emma had left strict instructions for watering the plants.

Harry's Hideaway was at the edge of the marina where Bev's father and his partner had their charter fishing boat. It was the kind of bar where the boat crews and fishermen gathered, rather than the hotel guests who opted for polished Caribbean décor. The barrel of roasted peanuts in the corner by the pool tables and a jukebox dominated by Country and Western kept out the sort of customer who tended to order frozen concoctions.

"Where's the Happy Hour crowd?" Bev asked and motioned for a mug. "I'll have a red ale." Harry didn't believe in imported beer, but did keep the regional microbrewery's products on tap.

Harry tilted the iced mug at an angle guaranteed to produce the perfect layer of head and said, "Not too many today. Most folks are using the extra daylight to get ready for the summer business. Hey, I caught the news - you get involved in the thing with Greg Wiley?"

Bev nodded and took the mug from him. "Yeah, Jim and I picked that one up. You know him, I guess?"

Harry picked up a dishcloth in his massive, roughened hand and wiped a wet ring from the bar. "Anybody works around the boats knows him. Understand shallow water blackout got him. Ordinarily I'd say, tough break, but not a lot of loss there and at least Tom Farmer should be happy."

Bev reached for the rest of a bowl of peanuts someone had left. "The boat captain, his partner?"

"Yep, hated his guts," Harry said.

Bev cracked a peanut and threw the shell to the floor. *Well, what was that about?* Harry wasn't nosy, but he'd been around a long time and generally kept up with what was going on. She kept her voice neutral, but this was too interesting to let pass. "What do you mean? Seems like hating the guy would make it tough to be in business together."

Harry scratched idly at his sizeable paunch. "It was common knowledge. I don't know all the particulars since their shop is over at Tug Jackson's marina, but I've known Tom for several years and it was no secret that he was looking to get Wiley out of the picture."

Bev licked a streak of froth from the top of her mug. "So how much do you know about them?"

Harry held his hand up and walked to the other end of the bar to take care of a customer. He returned and drew Bev a fresh draft and scowled in concentration. It was the same look Bev's father had when he was trying to remember details.

"Let's see," Harry said. "Tom's been here almost as long as me; used to work with the dive shop down the street. He went independent about six, maybe seven years ago. He was doing well, then split up with his old lady, hit some problems, not really sure what, and took Wiley on as a partner not quite two years ago now. Guess they must have gotten along at the time and something happened. Who knows, maybe it was the girl. Wouldn't be the first time a woman caused a strain between two men."

Bev pushed her mug to one side and propped her elbows on the bar, but resisted the urge to reach in her purse for her notebook; that might offend Harry. "The brunette with the big chest? The one living with Wiley?"

Harry nodded and ran one hand over the top of his gray flat top. "A beauty, that one. Hell, women like that are always causing bad blood."

My, my, this was getting better and better, Bev thought. Maybe it wasn't important, but a flash of suspicion sparked across her mind when she thought about how calm Silsby had seemed during the interview. "Like what, Harry? You mean she was fooling around with Farmer?"

Harry laughed. "I doubt it since she had a good deal going with Wiley. There's money in his family I understand. Anyway, Wiley found her in some strip joint in Miami and moved her in last fall. She doesn't mind strutting her stuff and mind you, has every right to be proud of what the Good Lord gave her. But you got to figure she's around the dive shop much, Tom's going to be looking at least and I do recall one of the arguments Tom and Wiley had in here was something about how the girl's future wasn't any of Tom's business. I wasn't paying too much attention, but they were pretty loud that night. It was maybe a month ago." He paused. "Any chance this wasn't an accident? Tom didn't dunk him back under the water or anything like that did he? Tom's a good guy, but Wiley was a real pain, you know?"

Bev thought about that. Harry had never struck her as the type of man given to exaggeration, but that was a hell of a question. "On the face of it, it seems pretty straight up," she said. "You know anything about free diving?"

A group came in and Harry looked toward them, but they were milling around the dockside tables, not ready to order.

"No," he said, "not to speak of. I've always been more

of a fishing guy, same as your dad. You can talk to the folks over here at the Diving Belle where Tom used to work, or to Steve Dillworth who owns the Scarlet Macaw at Jackson's marina. Steve was a big time diver before he got shot up in the Gulf War and that's Farmer's regular place to hang out. I think he knows him pretty well. You want another beer?"

Bev was anxious to capture her notes before she forgot what Harry had told her. "No thanks, got to go. Keep your ears open for me, okay?"

Harry laughed. "Hey, anything to help the cops. Tell Dan we're keeping his bar stool warm for him and don't tell your mamma I said that."

Bev left with a quick wave and drove the six blocks to her parents' home. They had sold the frame house where Bev and her brother had grown up when Bev's father's, with her mother's blessing, decided to turn his lifelong fishing hobby into his second career. They moved into one of the neighborhoods that was laid out along a series of manmade canals and their pale blue, painted cinderblock, nearly hurricane proof house included a separate workshop for her father and one of the three bedrooms served as a crafts room for her mother. The fishing charter partnership appeared to be on solid financial footing and as far as Bev could tell, her parents were happy.

She took the mail out of the box and carried it inside still thinking about what Harry had said. Maybe there was a good reason for Farmer's lack of grief and the girlfriend's composure after all.

A stripper, huh? That was going to be a great way to start Jim's morning. Neither of them had inquired about Silsby's occupation and she hadn't volunteered the information, but Bev could see why. The few strip joints on the outskirts of town didn't draw what Bev would call an elite crowd and the women who worked there probably didn't make much. Whatever kind of woman Silsby was, she didn't look like she would be satisfied with dollar tips. And if Wiley had brought her to town as a live-in, the odds were he wouldn't have wanted her dancing in one of the local spots.

Bev took a can of diet Coke, sat in the dining nook of the country kitchen and wrote down the important parts of the conversation. Jim knew some guys in the Miami police department and he could touch base with them to see if they had a record of Wiley or Silsby. If Wiley was into some of the designer drugs, they wouldn't have noticed that just from looking at the body and he could have easily taken something on the boat without being seen. If either Wiley or Silsby had ever been arrested for drugs in Miami, the odds were they wouldn't have cleaned up their act. She'd call and ask the Medical Examiner to speed up the autopsy after all.

Scarlet Macaw, Steve Dillworth, she read from her notes. She'd see if she could talk with him and find out more about the situation between Wiley and Farmer.

If Wiley's death was linked to a substance, what if he hadn't taken something himself? Murder, less the occasional stabbing death from a brawl, wasn't at the top of their crime statistics and Bev didn't want to jump to conclusions. Then again, business partners who didn't get along and a sex-pot girlfriend thrown into the mix was something that deserved a second look.

Chapter Five

The next morning Bev couldn't keep from grinning when she told Jim about Silsby's alleged background. He took it philosophically and agreed to check Miami to see what he could find out. Bev assumed he was picturing Silsby in a G-string and pasties when she telephoned the Medical Examiner's office to request to have the report on Wiley expedited. The assistant who answered the phone told her she could come by after one o'clock.

She found the number for the Scarlet Macaw, reached Steve Dillworth, introduced herself and wasn't surprised to hear that Harry had already called him to say she might come by.

Jim was on the last bite of a second chocolate covered donut and pushed the box in her direction, but she declined the offer. Had the man ever in his life eaten a breakfast that didn't shoot to the top of the cholesterol scale?

She slapped a bright blue note with *1:30 - ME's office*, on her desk calendar and left for the Scarlet Macaw. It was at the top end of the marina and in line of sight of the Adventures Below dive shop, although Bev hadn't noticed it the day before.

The exterior of the building was gray stained wooden shingles and it was a bit larger than Harry's place. She didn't see a barrel of roasted peanuts in the corner, but Dillworth hadn't gone for frosted glass panels and brass fixtures either. Ceiling fans with rattan tipped wooden blades turned slowly on a low setting and the bar's namesake was a beautiful bird kept in a black wrought iron cage on a stand against the wall. He, or maybe it was a she, was asleep on the perch.

Diving was the dominate theme with old gear displayed

on the wall and huge posters of underwater shots from the local area, the Red Sea and other exotic destinations.

Steve Dillworth was in his early forties, a head taller than Bev and had the build of a man who worked out regularly. A faded, but easily noticeable series of scars along the left side of his neck extended down somewhere into his shirt. He poured Bev a mug of aromatic coffee and led her to a table where he could watch the front and kitchen doors at the same time.

"Harry told me that you had questions about shallow water blackout and free diving," Dillworth said.

Bev sipped the coffee – Jamaican Blue Mountain or another Caribbean flavor was her guess. "I'd like to get an idea of what might have gone wrong," she replied. Better to start with a neutral topic. "Harry said you were an avid diver and could fill me in on what it's all about."

He gestured to the posters and smiled. "Yeah, diving is something I know about. I'd logged over 1,000 dives and had been an instructor for six years. I was in the Army Reserves and got too close to a land mine during the Gulf War - a collapsed left lung was the worst part. Sort of put a stop to most of my diving, although I keep current with the literature, do some consulting and I can still handle shallow stuff."

"That's a tough break," she said. With the kind of scarring Bev could see, the wounds must have been grotesque when they were fresh.

He shrugged. "Giving up the kind of diving I used to do was hard, but hey, I got a chunk of disability, this is a great bar, and I came back alive. That puts me ahead of the game when you think about it."

Bev liked his attitude and hoped she could trust what he told her.

Dillworth turned the sleeves of his blue chambray shirt up to his forearms. "How much do you want to know about free diving? Details or just the basics?"

"Well, I'm not sure," Bev admitted. "Yesterday the doctor acted like this wasn't unusual, but I've never heard much about it. Do we have a lot of free diving here?"

Dillworth picked up his black mug decorated with tiny sea turtles. "It's not that popular in this area. Greg did that for the same reason he did everything else; just to push the envelope," he said.

No effort to hide his contempt; a lot like Harry had acted, Bev noted without writing it down.

"Anyway, let me explain about free diving," he continued and dropped to a smoother tone. "The idea is that you hyperventilate to fill your lungs as much as possible before you begin your descent. Then as you go down you slow your heart rate with focus techniques that are similar to meditation. This reduces the rate at which you use the oxygen you've built up and when you begin to surface, the remaining air in your lungs expands naturally. While going too deep can obviously get you into trouble, believe it or not, one of the greatest dangers comes when you hit fifteen to ten feet. Your body can go into hypoxia, which really means your hemoglobin is eating up the oxygen supply in your lungs too fast. That causes severe damage to the nerve tissue, you lose consciousness, and drown practically at the surface. You always have at least one, and preferably two, safety divers in the water watching so if that happens they get you to the surface and immediately start mouth-to-mouth and then give oxygen as soon as possible."

He paused to take a swallow of coffee while Bev used her own version of shorthand to keep up with him.

"How deep are you talking about?" she asked.

"The world champ did better than four hundred feet not long ago and he's planning to try deeper," he said casually.

Bev stared at him, not sure she'd heard correctly. "More than four hundred feet underwater with no air source?"

He smiled. "That's how you get to be the world champion. The guy's pretty remarkable, although I don't go in for it myself. At any rate, nobody around here tries much more than sixty or maybe seventy feet. You really have to go through some serious training to get much beyond that and I can promise you Greg wouldn't take the time to be properly trained."

What was it Harry had said? *Not a lot of loss* or something along those lines. It sounded like Dillworth might share the sentiment, but she'd get to that in a few minutes.

Bev glanced back through her notebook to the note about how Farmer had been functioning as the safety diver – the only one. "If the point of the safety diver is to pay attention specifically for something like shallow water blackout, then why wouldn't Farmer have reacted immediately and known what the problem was?"

"I may have oversimplified it," Dillworth said and got up to get the coffeepot. "For example, it's easy for a safety diver to be in the wrong spot. When a diver begins to surface it's not a straight line thing like climbing a rope. If you're twenty or thirty feet apart, it's not much, but there will be some delay in connecting. Plus, if there's some chop like there was yesterday, it slows your forward movement. Then if Tom started in-water resuscitation, as I'm sure he did, it would have slowed him down a bit more. That's why it's best to have two safety divers if possible – one does mouth-to-mouth and the other pulls the two divers back to the boat."

Dillworth refilled Bev's mug first and then drained the rest of the coffee into his.

"Wouldn't Farmer and Wiley have known that?"

Dillworth shook his head in disgust. "Sure, but from what I heard, the two divers they had out were green and there's no way you want some novice in the water with you – that's really asking for trouble. To be honest, I can't say that I'm going to lose a lot of sleep about Greg, but I hope the publicity won't be too bad for Tom."

Definitely no question about his feelings and it was a great lead-in statement. "What is the story with the dive shop?" she asked. "Harry couldn't remember exactly how Wiley and Farmer partnered up."

Dillworth grinned and showed a row of slightly crooked bottom teeth. "And I presume during your discussion he mentioned they didn't get along? And I presume you want to know about that as well as the buxom Karen?"

Bev smiled. It was so much easier when people went straight to the point. "Well, Harry did kind of bring that up."

Dillworth turned his head briefly as the macaw squawked loudly to alert him that he, or she, was awake. "How much time do you have?"

Bev flipped to a clean page in her notebook. "As much as we need," she replied.

He settled further back into his chair and started at the time he'd opened the Scarlet Macaw and met Farmer. Bev didn't want to rush him even though her real interest was in the partnership of the other two men.

"It was a real shame about Tom's divorce," Dillworth said after he'd run through the first part of his story. "Tom busted his ass to make the shop a success, knows his stuff and I always recommended him to divers. I always got the impression that Crystal, his ex, thought he was going to get rich in the business and when that didn't happen, she wanted to move on. She got herself a sleazebag divorce lawyer and Tom didn't want to fight it. He got taken to the cleaners in the settlement and it was right after he'd added on to the shop and then he had a slump in business – one of those cyclic things, but it couldn't have come at a worse time. His cash flow was tight and the bank wasn't exactly bending over backwards. He's got too much pride to dump his troubles on anyone, but I knew he was worried."

He tilted his chair and balanced it on the two back legs and then dropped forward again. "Greg had come down from Miami and done some diving with him so I guess they got to talking one day and I'm still not sure how it all came down, but next thing I knew, Greg had pumped in enough cash to bail Tom out. I didn't think it was a good match, but he didn't ask my opinion and it really wasn't my place to say anything."

The last sentence was wrapped in the tone of someone who felt they'd let a friend down and Dillworth half shrugged. "Don't get me wrong, I think a lot of Tom, but he tends to give people the benefit of the doubt – not naïve, just too willing to overlook faults, if you understand."

Bev nodded. This was what she was looking for. "And Mr. Wiley's faults would have been what?"

Dillworth showed his teeth, but it wasn't quite a grin. "I'm not sure you have that much time," he said. "In a nutshell, he was an arrogant asshole, though he could turn on the charm whenever he wanted to. I think that's why Tom was caught off-guard and why he wasn't paying attention."

Bev smiled encouragingly. "Not paying attention how? To the business you mean?"

Dillworth pointed out into the general direction of the marina. "Not exactly. There's a lot that goes into running a business – paperwork, inventory and all and you can't be out on the water with charters, running dive classes and keeping the store up all at the same time. Greg liked the fun part and Tom was getting less time on the boats. Then groups of Greg's friends started showing up to dive – loud-mouthed and obnoxious, but money to throw around." Dillworth spread his hands wide. "There are accepted protocols in boat diving and good divers know how to behave. It's a big turn-off for folks if they have to share space with a rowdy bunch of rude jerks. Word gets around."

"And that was a problem I assume?" Bev said cautiously. She didn't want to seem too eager for dirt.

Dillworth stared into the empty mug too long. What was he reluctant to tell her?

He sighed and looked at Bev again. "Yeah, that was a problem, but it was the least of them as it sits right now." He hesitated again. "You don't know anything about diving at all?"

Bev shook her head and leaned forward. "Look, Mr. Dillworth, I'm just trying to find out what happened and if you know something I would really appreciate you telling me," she said easily in her best *trust me* voice.

"It may not be directly related to the accident," Dillworth said, "but it has a lot to do with Greg's whole attitude. To make a long story short, diving is a safe sport, but it's not without risk. One of the biggest headaches in the industry is when people want to dive beyond their capability. What I mean is, for example, basic level divers aren't supposed to go below a moderate depth and if someone appears to be uncomfortable with their equipment or surroundings, it's better to abort a dive than put them in the water."

Bev wrinkled her brow trying to see where Dillworth was headed.

"Greg took chances with divers that he never should have and allowed some things on the charters that were risky at best," he said bluntly. "A couple of the independent boat captains told Tom they wouldn't go out with Greg anymore and Greg blew it off when Tom called him on it. Again, word gets around and it was starting to be difficult for some of us to recommend clients to Adventures Below. That's when Tom decided to try and buy Greg out, but he wasn't in a position to. Then about two or three months ago, an incident happened on board with a tourist and after she returned home she reported it to the Global Organization of Dive Professionals, GODP, for short. That's the outfit Tom's shop is linked to and they're real watchdogs when it comes to safety issues. The young lady in question wasn't hurt, but she could have been and a GODP investigator is due here next week."

Bev nodded – she didn't have to understand all the details to recognize what might be at stake. "How serious is this?"

Dillworth slowly rotated the empty coffee mug in his hands, but his voice was firm. "It's never good, but Tom should come out okay; he's top notch and Greg was the one at fault. That kind of crap, acting like you can pick and choose which safety rules to follow, is why you're not going to find many people surprised about Greg. I don't know exactly what happened, but I'd put money down that Greg screwed up the dive."

Another screech from the macaw and the chiming of an old ship's clock startled them. Dillworth looked at his watch and smiled apologetically. "I'm sorry, but I don't have much more time this morning."

Bev underlined *GODP investigation* and shifted subjects. "Thanks for the time you've given me and just one more quick thing – Miss Silsby."

"Quick might be the best way to describe Karen," he said with a grin. "I don't mean that in a bad way," he added when Bev raised her eyebrows. "I heard talk about Miami, but I don't know Karen all that well. She came in with Greg sometimes and every now and then she'd be in with Tom for a drink. I'm not trying to be sexist, but it's easy for guys to take a look at Karen and not realize that she's sharp, too. There's not much doubt that she's been around, if you know what I mean, but she's no dummy."

"No, she didn't come across that way when we spoke with her," Bev agreed. "I understand she came here because of Mr. Wiley.

Dillworth tapped the handle of his mug with his thumb. "Yeah, but I don't think it was any kind of great love affair. My impression was that it was convenient for both of them and Greg wasn't any less of an asshole around her than he was anyone else. He could be abusive, verbally I mean, not physically, but it always seemed like Karen could hold her own. I think it bothered Tom, but he knew it wasn't really his business."

"So Mr. Farmer and Miss Silsby are friends?" Bev asked and watched Dillworth's face.

He shrugged and didn't change his tone. "They're friendly. Karen flirts a lot, but I don't think she and Tom have spent any time together to speak of."

The telephone behind the bar rang twice and someone in the office or the kitchen must have answered it. Dillworth snapped his fingers. "I'm not sure what else I can tell you, but I do have an extra copy of a Recreational Diving encyclopedia on CD ROM if that will help."

He had started to fidget and Bev had picked up more than she'd expected. Dillworth's insistence that Farmer wouldn't have been at fault was sincere, but heartfelt opinions from family and friends was rarely worth taking into account.

"Yes, I'd appreciate that if it's no trouble," she said instead.

Dillworth stood and gathered both mugs in one hand. "Not at all. I'll be back in a minute and don't forget you can come back as a customer, too."

"I may take you up on that," Bev said with a smile.

Dillworth returned in less than five minutes with a square padded envelope. Bev thanked him for the CD ROM and his time.

She created different scenarios as she drove to the station and most of them weren't flattering to Farmer. She was eager to hear if Jim had found anything out from the Miami police, but as soon as she stepped into the station, Sheila waved her over. Her square face was set in a smile, but her gray eyes flashed *I need help*.

Two neatly groomed young men in dark suits and carrying the telltale briefcases of salesmen introduced themselves. Oh damn, the computer company that Bev had contacted about a package deal for the station! She'd forgotten the appointment. No wonder Sheila looked relieved that she'd arrived. Bev apologized for being late and hurried them into the room that doubled as a classroom or for conferences.

The station's collection of office automation was pitiful with only three computers, one off-brand fax machine and a copier that practically required an on-site maintenance technician. The previous administrative assistant, who had connections to the mayor in lieu of competence, had finally retired and left behind a backlog of paperwork and an almost incomprehensible filing system. The regular secretary had quit to spend more time at home and Kristie, the temp, tried hard, but she was young and inexperienced, but also the Fire Chief's niece so no one was willing to send her packing. The deputy chief of police was only half way through an extended training course in Tallahassee and while Chief Taylor's flattened organization that emphasized street work instead of paperwork normally made sense, the archaic administrative procedures were taking their toll.

Sheila had struggled with the workload from her first day on the job and only the most important items ever got completed. As stalwart as she was, she had practically sobbed her frustration to Bev one day in the privacy of the ladies room.

It had taken several discussions, but between Bev, Sheila and a phone call from the deputy chief, they had convinced Chief Taylor that the station shouldn't go into the twenty-first century with the cutting edge technology of electric typewriters. Bev had managed to line the computer deal up within a week of the Chief's reluctant agreement.

She and Sheila spent over an hour reviewing the details of the plan for delivery and training. The younger officers would need little more than an introduction to the new system, but the key was to make sure that the older officers who hadn't grown up playing computer games were given enough training to get them beyond their initial hesitation. Bev knew that Chief Taylor was skeptical despite her assurances and she didn't want a negative reaction when the machines were first installed.

Once everyone was satisfied with the deal as outlined, Sheila signed the paperwork and they took a few minutes to walk around the station area before the computer salesmen departed.

Chief Taylor stepped out of his office as they left. He turned sideways and pointed a tobacco stained forefinger at his desk. "Did you remember that I don't want one of those goddamn contraptions near this office?"

Sheila coughed and went toward the ladies room.

Bev stifled her urge to respond sarcastically about not subjecting a computer to his hands. "Yes Chief, I remembered," she said. "They'll start delivery in a couple of days and by late next week everything will be in place. It's not going to interrupt work and it really will make things easier for everyone."

Chief Taylor frowned, but the gesture was without hostility. "I hear you, but I'll believe it when I see it," he

Shades of Murder

said, turned abruptly and re-entered his office.

Bev sighed at his recalcitrance and hoped the office transition would go as she predicted. All the hell she was trying to do was bring the goddamn place out of the goddamn 1970s and there were times when she didn't know why she bothered. She walked into the office and saw Jim grinning at what he had probably overheard.

"Hey Kid, I was beginning to wonder if you were ever going to finish with the geeky boys there," he said unsympathetically.

Bev scrunched her face at him, dropped her notebook on her desk, grabbed a bottle of water from the refrigerator and then yanked the desk chair out. She flopped down and upgraded the scrunched face to a mild glare.

Jim seemed amused by her lack of humor and waved a sheet of white paper like a flag of truce.

"Okay Kid, but I couldn't resist, so lighten up with those baby blues and I'll give you the skinny on the delectable Karen."

Bev switched her glare to a curious look – the computers could wait. "My eyes are hazel, not blue," she reminded him. "Is it juicy?"

Jim laid the piece of paper in front of him, touched his finger to it and made a sizzling sound. "And not only that, but I had time to check up on our victim. There's some interesting stuff if you care to come down off your hover and listen."

Bev's aggravation with the Chief dissipated at the prospect of what Jim had to say and she swiveled the chair to rest one elbow on her desk.

"Just for the record, I'm not hovering, but yes I'm listening and then I'll tell you about my morning. If what you found out matches with what I was told, I bet the ME will have evidence of more than accidental drowning for us."

Chapter Six

Jim didn't read from the sheet of paper he'd laid down. "I know you'd probably rather start with Karen, but let me tell you about the deceased first. The bottom line is that he was not a nice person. His parents live in Jacksonville and his father, or step-father to be precise, makes big chunks of money as one of the land developers we're all so fond of. The younger Mr. Wiley seems to have been in and out of a number of career fields, most of which were bankrolled by Dad. He relocated here from Miami after a number of meetings with the police. Driver's license suspended once, known to frequent the high roller hotspots and to have a questionable circle of friends, but no evidence of being personally involved in drug dealings."

Jim paused and rubbed the tiny bump in the center of his red-veined nose. "The biggies are arrest for domestic violence for pounding his girlfriend - not the current one - and charges filed for a date rape."

Bev stopped in the middle of taking a drink and raised her eyebrows. "Let me guess. Charges dropped in both cases?"

Jim nodded. "I can see why Mr. Wiley left town. He's kept a lower profile here and switched from pissing off cops to mostly pissing off the Marine Patrol."

Bev leaned forward and drummed her pen against the top of her notebook. "The description of him tracks with what we've been hearing from other people. And the story on our Miss Silsby?"

"No police record of any kind, but according to my old buddy in Vice, Karen's stage name was Monique and the club she danced in was one of the classier ones," he said.

"Heavy spenders who tipped well and didn't expect too much in return. The talk was also that she expanded her talents into the adult, independent film-making area. She's certainly got the body for it."

Bev twisted a lock of hair that slipped loose. "Porn flicks?"

"Strictly regional stuff, but hey, if it's important to our case, I'll see if I can run that lead down and maybe pick up a video," Jim said sincerely.

Bev curled her upper lip without a comment. *What a sacrifice for him.*

Jim leaned back in his chair and made a cross with his fingers to ward off her look. "Okay I won't dash to the video store, but I figure we do need to talk to her again."

"Absolutely," Bev said sweetly. "And with the paperwork you've got to catch up on I'll take care of it for you."

"That kind of help I don't need," Jim said quickly. "But it's your turn and from the way you've been acting, you've found something that has your brain in high gear."

She might as well see how Jim reacted – he was usually at least as doubting as Chief Taylor. She glanced back and forth between reading her notes and watching his body language.

"The relationship with the boat captain and partner, Farmer, is what's particularly important. Farmer was a scuba instructor who went independent and opened the Adventures Below. He's well-liked within the marina and diving communities, but a little over two years ago he did some major improvements in the shop, then hit a slump in business and got into a serious cash flow problem. Apparently the settlement with his ex-wife had drained his financial reserves."

Jim had crossed his hands behind his head as he listened. "That sounds normal," he said.

Bev grinned, unable to resist a dig on behalf of her gender. "Only because men deserve it. At any rate, along comes Mr. Gregory Wiley, a studly sort of fellow with money to burn, so to speak. Farmer is running out of time, Wiley apparently thinks being part owner of a dive shop would be cool and that's how he becomes a partner. Steve Dillworth, the guy I was talking to, said Wiley was an arrogant bastard, but things were okay for the first few months. Then when the finances were sufficiently complicated, Wiley started making changes in the way they do business - changes Farmer didn't like."

Jim looked interested at last. "Aha, do we have conflict?"

Bev pursed her lips. "You bet," she said. "To cut to the chase, Wiley virtually ran the old clientele off and the shop started getting a reputation as one that was willing to cut safety corners in order to provide adventuresome dives for customers who had more money than time."

Jim released his hands and rubbed the bump. "And this isn't good?"

Bev finished the bottle of water before she answered. "The way Dillworth explained it to me, folks sometimes show up who want to dive and maybe it's been a while since they were trained and they don't want to waste vacation days with the boring stuff like extra instruction or staying within their certification limits."

"And Adventures Below would accommodate them?"

Bev leaned over and patted Jim's arm. "Wow, you catch on quick. Dillworth said Farmer was busting his ass to recoup the money to buy Wiley out. It seems that someone recently made a complaint to one of the watchdogs of the dive industry, the Global Organization of Dive Professionals. That's the outfit Adventures Below is aligned with and they notified Farmer that they were going to open an investigation into potential safety violations. I'm not sure of all the mechanics, but from the way Dillworth was acting, it will be bad for business."

Jim kicked back in his chair and propped his feet on his desk; a sign he was beginning to form his own scenarios. "And had the investigation commenced?"

Bev smiled and let loose the piece of information she'd been building up to. "Funny thing, that. The investigating official is due in next week. That makes the timing of

Wiley's accident questionable, wouldn't you say?"

Jim frowned and asked the obvious. "Well, won't they investigate the death, too? I mean, if they were concerned about safety, you'd think this would put them over the top."

Bev had worked through that question. "Sure, but accidents do happen and if we've already closed the book with no suspicions aroused, how much more do you think they're going to dig? And if Wiley was the one cutting corners, I'm sure Farmer would find a way to get that across. Besides, there's more about what went on between the two guys."

Jim strained across his substantial stomach and retied a shoe lace. "I'm listening."

"Ever since Silsby showed up on the scene, tensions between the partners increased. According to Dillworth, Farmer thought Wiley mistreated her and he had a hard time dealing with that. Dillworth's impression is that Silsby handled it better than Farmer did."

Jim closed one eye and stared at a spot on the wall as Bev waited quietly. She could almost hear him trying to mentally fit the pieces together. It didn't take him long.

"Money troubles and a woman. All right, it's looking like you've got motive," he said and swung his feet off the desk. "Now let's look at opportunity. There are four people around, two of whom are not seasoned divers. The only people in the water are Wiley and Farmer, and it's a good bet neither of the guys on the boat are paying close attention until things start to go wrong. Farmer looks like he's doing everything he can when he starts the rescue efforts, but that's what they're expecting to see. Could work. That leaves means - a little tricky. Wiley was in good shape, so if there had been some kind of struggle, it would have been easy to see and neither of the witnesses mentioned it. But if Farmer slipped Wiley something in between dives, which didn't start to take effect until around the time he re-entered the water, and that interfered with his responses...hmmm... it's possible. It would have to be the right stuff though, otherwise the timing would be off."

Bev smiled when Jim came to same conclusion she had. "The ME should be finished by now."

Jim shoved back his chair and snapped his fingers. "Then let's go talk to him."

They were on the way out the door when Sheila stopped them with a paper in her hand. "Jim, I checked Mr. Wiley's insurance like you asked. He had a small policy of $30,000, with his parents as beneficiaries, but a bigger one for $50,000 was for a Miss Karen Silsby, same address as the deceased."

Jim and Bev looked at each other.

"Thanks Sheila, leave that on my desk, please." Jim said and motioned Bev through the door. "Well, how about we pay Karen a call after we see the doc?"

"Sounds like a good idea," Bev agreed. "We are racking up some coincidences."

Chief Taylor would want more than coincidences, but maybe the discussion with the Medical Examiner could answer some of their questions.

Bev's anticipation of a dramatic finding was premature. Dr. Cooke supported the initial ruling of cause of death by accidental drowning with no unusual bruising or contusions. The basic toxicology screen was negative, but he agreed to run extra tests for some substances Bev couldn't pronounce.

He seemed intrigued by the thought of poisons or drugs and promised to push the samples through for a quick response. As almost an afterthought, Bev asked him how long it would have taken Wiley to reach the point when the chances of revival became minimal. He confirmed that in a warm water situation, four to six minutes could be critical.

"So," Bev said as they drove to the condo address Farmer had given them, "I suppose it could be that Wiley gets into trouble and Farmer just takes advantage of an opportunity handed to him. He doesn't go after Wiley immediately, gives him an extra few minutes in an unconscious state and then the odds are, he's toast."

Jim frowned and pointed out the obvious again. He had a long standing habit of doing that. "Could be, but failing to administer first aid soon enough might get you criminal negligence and not much else. Not to mention that it would be a bitch to prove."

Bev chewed her lower lip in thought as Jim drove through the white gates of the Gulf Breeze, one of the newest complexes in town. It was the kind of place with private boat slips, tennis courts, a fitness center and the other amenities a six figure income could buy.

"There had to be money from somewhere," Jim said as they approached B406, a bayside unit. "Dive operations in town don't fund places like this."

Silsby was home and answered the door clad in a pair of denim shorts and a red halter top; neither of which contained much cloth. She gave them a nod of hello before Bev had a chance to say anything and led them through the foyer that opened into a great room with a cathedral ceiling. Her bare feet left only faint impressions in the cream colored, thick carpet as she continued into the dining room. She sat down at the glass-topped dining room table and picked up a brush to finish the manicure they had interrupted.

She listened without comment and didn't act either surprised or disturbed when Bev mentioned they'd run a routine check on her.

She shrugged and dabbed a spot of polish onto a deep red fingernail. "Look, I would have told you about Miami if you'd asked. Sure, I worked the Chez Femme, did some skin flicks and made good money at it, but it was paying my way through college; a major in Business Management with a minor in Information Management, if that matters. Greg showed up in the club one night handing out tens instead of fives and we clicked together. He came back on a regular basis and after a while he asked me if I wanted to move down here and give him exclusive privileges. The university has remote classes that I'm finishing up by e-mail so it was a good deal for me."

Jim made notes with little more than a glance at the pad. It was a skill Bev envied.

"And you were planning to stay with Mr. Wiley for how

long?" he asked.

Silsby expertly dragged the brush across the last nail, inserted the applicator into the bottle and wiggled her fingers to get them to dry faster.

She waved one hand around the room filled with the sort of modern furnishings that Bev thought belonged on a display floor – lots of chrome and no comfortable looking seats. "Until I graduated, if it worked that long. This place may not be done in my preferred décor, but it's sure as hell nicer than anything I've ever had. I'm not going to waste time describing how poor I grew up – let's just say that a family wasn't something I could depend on. I was pulling down decent money, but I lived on a shoestring so I could put most of it toward school. Once I get my degree I intend to move up North or out West. Greg was an okay guy and the sex was hot. He wanted to move me in here, buy me clothes and take me out for lobster dinners, there's no reason for me to turn it down."

"I got the impression from some people that maybe he didn't treat you very well all the time," Bev said.

Silsby laughed without much humor. "I didn't say he was a goddamn saint. He considered me his exclusive property and he liked to flaunt me around. You know the deal; a lot of cleavage showing, short skirts and tight jeans. Then there were times when he got a little rough in the sack and left bruises every now and again, but it wasn't that bad."

"I see," Bev said. How could she care so little about her own body? Was a waterfront condo worth that to her? "What kind of relationship do you have with Tom Farmer?" she asked instead.

Silsby tilted her head and hesitated for a moment. "Poor Tom. Sure I flirted with him, had a beer or cup of coffee with him when Greg was out with his buddies. Look, he's a hell of a nice man, and as I guess you've found out, Greg did wrong by him with some of the business dealings, but Tom has a little of the missionary streak in him. I think he always wanted to save me and couldn't really grasp that I didn't need it. I think he said something to Greg a couple of times, but it was no big deal."

Jim took the lead and cleared his throat. "Well Karen, we'd like to know about the insurance policy."

The young woman grinned. "I wondered when you would get to that," she said with no hint of guilt. "Greg was a fast lane guy and with some of his habits, it was a good bet he'd do something stupid, although I admit, I thought he'd crash the car or crack the boat up. I took a term insurance policy out on him and paid the premiums. I didn't want to have given up my source of income and then be left dangling if he took a nose dive off the road or whatever. He used to laugh about it and as they say in finance class, nothing like getting a good payoff for limited investment - not that the insurance company is happy about it."

Bev tightened her mouth. *Cold, if ever she'd seen it.* She shortened the interview with a reminder that they wanted her to stay in town until they notified her that the investigation was completed.

Jim was silent as they left and then scratched his head before cranking the car.

"A pretty package, but some real ice in those veins," he said reflectively. "Bev, we've got to talk to Claude this afternoon and tell him what we're looking at."

Bev rolled the window down and propped her arm against the frame without adding her assessment of Silsby. Ice in her veins was being kind as far as she was concerned – one step from hooking seemed a more accurate description. "Yeah I know, but I don't want the Chief acting like I'm some kid who's seen a monster under the bed."

Jim honked the horn at a cyclist who was using the street instead of the bicycle lane. "You are a kid. Hell, you're the youngest one who's ever made detective and a degree in Criminal Science doesn't make you a day older. Claude thinks you do a good job, but that's not going to keep him from ragging your butt."

Like that was something she didn't know. Bev ran through the dialogue in her head to brace herself for Chief Taylor's skepticism and thought about letting Jim broach the subject of possible foul play. No, that wasn't worth thinking about – she was the one who got the first lead and developed the theory and she wasn't going to duck behind Jim's seniority.

The Chief was alone in his office when they returned to the station and he reacted exactly like Bev expected as she quietly explained why the case was going to be open for a few more days.

"What in the fuck are you talking about?" he grumbled. "You two got nothing better to do than think up this shit? A premeditated murder by planning to have a couple of witnesses on hand?"

"We have run across several coincidences," Jim said.

The Chief swung his gaze past Jim. "Bev, this is your idea, isn't it? That imagination running away with you?"

"The doctor is screening for suspicious substances," Bev said and felt her stubborn streak making its way to the front of her brain – the part that was too close to her tongue as her father often warned. "At a minimum, we need to wait for those test results." This wasn't the time to take the Chief on.

Chief Taylor shook his head impatiently. "Great, he finds something, we'll talk. In the meantime, get the hell out of my office and go catch a real criminal." He popped an antacid tablet into his mouth. "And by the way, give the DA a call and check elements of proof for criminal negligence and shit like that. If you start poking around a respectable business owner, make goddamn sure we're not getting into harassment."

The others in the central room clapped when they emerged –Chief Taylor hadn't kept his voice low.

Bev made a face at the crowd, but Jim held his laughter until they were in their own office. Bev sharply punched the speed dial button to the District Attorney's office. "Call the DA's office for Christ's sake – like I don't know what negligence is."

"Or it may be an accident," Jim reminded her.

"My ass," she said and held her hand up to Jim when someone answered the telephone. A harried sounding woman asked if she could please hold for a moment. Bev held her hand over the mouthpiece.

"My gut tells me it's Farmer or when you think about the policy, maybe Farmer and the girl," she said. "He does the deed and she gets him a chunk of the insurance. Even if she double-crosses him and lights out with all the cash, he gets his business back."

"It does have a nice ring," Jim said. "Poison or drugs would make for a tidy murder and we'd have some physical evidence to work with."

Bev nodded in agreement and spoke into the phone when the woman came on again and apologized for the delay. Bev explained that they needed to discuss a case and was assured that the new assistant District Attorney would be available later that day. The woman said he would probably stop by, or if not, she would call and set up an appointment for the office.

Bev relayed the information to Jim and decided to start some research into scuba diving accidents. She didn't have a single unsolved case and she wasn't about to have one with the death of Greg Wiley. There was something wrong with Farmer's story and she was going to find out what is was. She might have to put up with some shit from Chief Taylor, but it wouldn't be the first time and sure as hell wouldn't be the last.

Chapter Seven

Bev shook off the acerbic conversation with Chief Taylor, took the CD ROM disk that Dillworth had given her and worked her way through the index. The disk contained an encyclopedia of recreational diving and she was reading about shallow water blackout when she heard someone come into the office. Jim said hello, but her back was to the door and she couldn't see whom he was talking to. She hit the print button on a couple of pages before she turned around. "Hi, I'm Kyle Stewart from the DA's office," the man said and held out his right hand. His handshake was firm and he kept direct eye contact during the introduction. Bev had to lift her head to look him in the eye and judging by his build she assumed he was athletic, but not into weight lifting. Tennis or maybe racquetball. And golf of course since he was lawyer.

Not bad at all. She instinctively checked the left hand that held a saddle tan leather briefcase. No ring of any kind and no tell-tale mark of a man who wore a ring and slipped it off when he found it to be inconvenient.

Kyle sat in the extra chair Jim pulled up to the desk. It was adjusted too low for the length of his legs and he reached down to raise the seat. Bev filled him in on what they had found to date while Jim made a copy of their initial report.

Kyle listened attentively and didn't interrupt with bullshit, lawyerish questions. Bev resisted the urge to fidget when he took a few minutes to review his notes before he responded to their pitch.

"Okay," he said, "motive is looking pretty solid, but as you've already pointed out, there are several unanswered questions. It will be a lot easier if the ME finds something, although if he doesn't, that won't necessarily be definitive. There are substances that can wear off."

It was encouraging that he was taking them seriously, but it could be simply because he was relishing a possible murder case. As a new arrival, he might be finding the local crime environment too mild. Other than the periodic manslaughter charge, the last violent death in town had been when Rita Collins emptied a shotgun into her husband and her defense lawyer had successfully won an acquittal based on battered wife syndrome. The DA had fumed at the loss, but the collective opinion of the police force was that Rita Collins' real crime was that she hadn't killed her husband earlier.

They spent a while longer working through the checklist of the elements of proof needed to support a charge of first degree murder, or the lesser charges of second degree murder and negligent homicide.

In the midst of the discussion Bev repositioned her chair and breathed in the scent of Kyle's cologne. It was the light kind of musk that gently touched rather than assaulted her nose. She drifted momentarily in the memory of her face buried in a male chest and exhaled quickly as she caught herself. *Focus on the conversation!* Luckily Kyle had turned to say something to Jim and apparently hadn't noticed her lapse. Okay he was attractive, but she didn't want him to think she was the type who flustered easily.

Kyle ran out of questions, snapped his briefcase closed and pushed the chair back from the desk.

Jim suddenly changed the subject. "So counselor, I heard you're from Chicago. How are you fitting into our little town?"

"Pretty good so far," he said and swung his briefcase against his leg. "I've learned my way around even though I haven't found a place yet that cooks calamari quite right."

Jim shuddered. "Squid? I'm a steak man myself. Hey Bev, you've got some hole-in-the-wall place you go to that serves that stuff, don't you?"

Christ, could Jim have been any clumsier? Did he think

she needed his help in getting a date for crying out loud?

Kyle smiled before Bev had a chance to protest. It was an open smile, hard to resist and no come-on glint in his eyes. "Lightly breaded and fried crisp?" he asked. A polite, but inviting question.

Bev nodded. "Hardly a drop of grease and as crunchy as you'd want, but I've got to warn you, it's only a little seafood joint down in a marina. There's nothing fancy about it."

"I'd rather have good food than a waiter in a tux," he said and handed her his card. "If you don't mind sharing your secret, how about give me a call and maybe we could grab a quick bite tomorrow evening?"

Time for a little stall, Bev thought – he seemed nice enough, but there was no rush. "Uh sure," Bev said and was saved from further comment by the ringing of the telephone. She grabbed it and nodded to Kyle's good-bye wave. By the time she replaced the receiver, Jim was chuckling at her discomfort.

"What the hell was that about?" she asked in exasperation and jerked the middle desk drawer open. "I'm perfectly capable of asking a man to dinner if that's what I want to do."

"Come on Kid, you work too hard and take life too seriously sometimes," Jim replied and rubbed his jaw. "When's the last time you had a date? Been a couple of months now, hasn't it? And besides, you can't tell me this one didn't catch your eye. You're not the only one who can look at a left hand."

"You're starting to sound like my mother," Bev said as she felt for the stapler toward the back of the drawer.

Jim shook his head. "Nah, I'm not looking for you to get married and knocked up, I just think you should get laid," he said and turned when Kevin Waters came in with a sheet of paper in one hand and an angry look on his face.

"What's wrong?" Bev asked automatically. Must be something to cause an expression like that.

Kevin slapped the paper on Jim's desk. "Another report on those two dirtbags running loose. They got a convenience store up in Holopaw. That brings the body count to four."

"Are they sure it's the same ones?" Bev asked.

"Well, it's the same as the other places," Kevin said. "A shot straight to the chest on the clerk."

Jim picked the report up and read it rapidly. "The .357 is the same kind of gun as before, the quick in and out is the same pattern and no prints or useable tire tracks again," he said. He paused and then exhaled. "These guys are smart enough to be using common guns and they're paying attention to details like removing the security camera tapes. Whoever they are, we're not talking about hopped-up potheads."

"Well, they may have gotten out of Alabama, but if they hang around this state, we'll nail them," Kevin said and left muttering.

Bev ran her hand across her forehead. "Christ Jim, a killing spree across two states and nobody knows who to even look for? What's wrong with this picture?"

Jim shoved the report under the perpetual pile of folders on his desk. "No clues is what's wrong, Bev. A two-state alert, but what the hell does it really say? There are two men, we think? Kids? Older guys? For all anyone knows maybe it's two women or a man and woman team. It's a bitch, but they'll make a mistake or someone will get a license number that can be run down. I can't imagine they're headed this way though; there's not much maneuvering room in the Keys. They'll probably cut back north."

Bev sighed - what a waste of life. Well, there was no sense in dwelling on the thought of four dead people nowhere near her jurisdiction. With any luck at all, the killers would be identified and caught before they hit another place. The Wiley case wasn't as gruesome, but it was theirs to work.

Chapter Eight

Willie Denton held the gun across his stomach, looked out the window at the empty parking lot and tried to ignore the dead clerk that Hal had propped on the stool behind the counter. When Hal did that, it was even spookier than just knowing the guy was dead. There he was sitting like he was maybe taking a quick snooze and all the time his blood was pouring out and God Almighty, the way his eyes looked all wide open and shocked.

Nobody had ever come in while they were in a place and the man who pulled up in front of the door got out in such a hurry and rushed inside so fast that it took Willie by surprise – he'd only looked away for a minute – honest to God, that was all. Hal was at the other end of the store and Willie didn't know what to do.

The man's face went pale when he saw the pistol, but Willie figured he was too scared to remember what they looked like. He was only going to knock him in the head, but then Hal was yelling to shoot and the man was screaming at him not to shoot and he got confused. Somehow the gun fired even though Willie hadn't meant to pull the trigger and oh Jesus, the guy staggered into the rack of road maps, knocked it over and lay still.

Hal ran to the front and kicked the body as he grabbed Willie's arm. "Let's go!" he shouted and shoved him out the door.

Willie was already in the car with the engine cranked when Hal cursed, walked around to the second car and fired two rounds. The passenger's door was open and a little boy's body flopped to the pavement.

Willie started shaking, but Hal told him to get a move on

and he backed out slowly instead of gunning the engine just like Hal had taught him. No tire tracks to be left, no sudden burst of speed; nothing out of the ordinary and if no one showed up for thirty or forty seconds they would be out of sight. Why had the man and the boy come along? Why couldn't they have waited?

"That was one unlucky son-of-a-bitch," Hal said as they rounded a curve and there were no lights behind them. "Five more minutes and we'd been gone. Well, it was his last fucking mistake."

"God Almighty Hal," Willie said as he kept their speed just over the posted limit. "I shot that guy. I didn't mean to and then you shot that kid. What the hell are we gonna do?"

Hal looked at him and shook his head as if to emphasize the stupidity of his question. "Willie, we're going to do the same as we have been. We'll drive nice and easy for a few hours and find a little motel to rest for a couple of days. So you shot a guy. It's about fucking time you did. And besides, it was some Spic and he was probably some goddamn commie from Cuba."

Sweat rolled down Willie's back. "But a kid, man, why did you shoot the kid? He couldn't have really seen anything."

Hal lit a cigarette and blew a stream of smoke toward the windshield. "He didn't have to be able to describe us in detail, you idiot. Right now the cops don't have shit and if we keep our cool it will stay that way. I was checking the map earlier; there should be an intersection a couple of miles ahead. Take a left when we get there."

Willie shut up after that. He didn't like Hal calling him an idiot. He took the road Hal told him and crossed two county lines before they stopped at the Traveling Man's Motel not long before sunrise.

As always, Hal took care of checking them in and they hauled the original stash of money, drugs and guns in for safe keeping. Hal pushed the briefcase and the second bag with the night's take underneath his bed and transferred the pistol in his belt to the nightstand. Willie sat on the bed and watched – he didn't feel like talking.

After he was finished, Hal opened a bottle of premium bourbon and passed it to Willie. "Look Willie," he said. "I shouldn't have called you an idiot; you're a stand-up kind of guy. You and me are a team and you shooting the guy tonight is just one of those things – it's nothing to get upset about. I mean, come on; think about how it felt when you pulled that trigger. Think about the power you had right there in your hand. It felt good, didn't it? Nobody's going to mess with when you've got a gun like that."

Willie took a swallow straight from the bottle and felt the tension loosen. Hal's voice was as calm as ever.

"You gotta remember that we're on our way to a better life and there's nobody around that gives a shit about either one of us getting ahead. You deserve a break, Willie, just like I do and when people are in your way you have to do whatever it takes. It's not your fault that some guy shows up like that. It was bad luck for him is all and the boy, well, now who knows, maybe he was a retard or something and didn't have much of a life anyway."

Willie wanted to ask Hal where they were going, but his head started to spin and he laid back against the lumpy pillow to steady himself. Maybe Hal was right, maybe there wasn't any other way for them to be safe. He couldn't recall how it felt when he shot the man, but there was nothing that could be done about it now. He closed his eyes to shut out the image.

Willie woke up later to the sound of the television and reached for the bottle he'd set on the floor. It was one of those business shows again. He pulled himself up and half-listened to the man talking about that Dow thing. Hal, sitting on the other bed, nodded along and stroked the cover of a business magazine that he'd lifted during one of the robberies.

Willie was trying to remember how many there had been. It was four, he thought, but maybe it was three, or had tonight made five? He cradled the bottle in the crook of his arm -

maybe it would be easier for him to talk to Hal and to sleep if he kept drinking. What a fucking mess with the guy and the kid! A little more whiskey and maybe the whole thing would get out of his head.

"Hey man," Hal said and brought Willie away from his thoughts of what he'd done. "You know anything about investing money? You ever try it?"

Willie stared at Hal. "You mean like some damn banker or something? Where the hell would I get money for that?"

Hal pointed at the television. "You don't have to be a banker. All you need is a little capital and pay attention to what the market's doing. And that's what we've got now, Willie, capital. Five or six thousand in the right place and you can double your money in no time at all. Then you re-invest the proceeds and you're on your way." Hal waved his cigarette as he spoke and a smoke trail encircled his face.

Willie was fully awake now and squinted his eyes. "Don't you have to have some kind of college degree or something like that?"

Hal lifted the magazine from his lap and shook it. "Hell, no. There's all kinds of guys who wear fancy suits and go to fucking business schools who don't know a damn more about this stuff than I do," he said. "I just needed to get my hands on enough cash to get started."

Willie raised the bottle again. "So where did you learn about money? It's not like you ever had any, either."

Hal coughed and took a deep drag on the cigarette. "That's what I'm telling you, man. I never had nothing because nobody ever gave me a break. A guy who was in the cell next to me when I was at State was into this and taught me how it all worked. He'd made a bundle in the market."

"If he was so smart, why was he in jail?" Willie asked doubtfully. He didn't want to piss Hal off, but it was a fair question.

Hal didn't seem to mind. "He worked for the mob taking their money and putting it into legitimate businesses and got caught when someone snitched," he said. "All he had to do was keep his mouth shut, let his investments build up while he was in the joint and then he was all set. When he got out, he was going to be a fucking millionaire. And that's the same way we're going to be. Well, not millionaires right away, but in a whole lot better shape than we were before. You'll see."

Was what Hal said true, or was it all bullshit? Could he really take the money they had and make more? Hal was smart and he read a lot, so he might know about this stuff too.

The man on television stopped talking and a commercial for the new Lincoln came on. Jesus, it was sure a nice car. Willie had never had a car like that, but it was kinda snooty and a good truck was probably better for him. He'd never had any kind of dreams about being a rich man – he just wanted a decent place to live, good whiskey to drink, some pretty girls and yeah, a new truck would be good. If Hal wanted to try and make a bunch more money, that was his business.

Willie didn't know exactly what all he would do with his share of the money – all he knew for sure was that he wanted to stop thinking about how that kid had looked with his skull shattered.

Chapter Nine

The strident squawking of gulls wheeling over the canal awakened Bev before her alarm clock went off. Bury her head in the pillow or get up and do an early morning jog? There was something on her calendar for the afternoon that she couldn't recall the details of, but she might not be able to make it to the gym and there was the new pair of jeans she'd bought.... She rolled out of bed and did a quick set of stretches before she tugged on a pair of black running tights and a T-shirt from the last ten-kilometer race she ran.

The neighborhood was quiet and Bev waved casually to the few residents who had wandered out for their morning paper. She reached her turn around point and started back to her parents' house as enticing smells of frying bacon and coffee seeped onto the sidewalk. Stop for a sausage egg and biscuit sandwich on the way in to work or stick with a low-fat apple cinnamon muffin that would sit easier in her stomach?

She looked at her watch when she reached the front yard and realized that she was five minutes behind schedule. Breakfast would have to be a double orange juice – she could drink that while she drove. The light wasn't on in the office when she arrived and Sheila told her that Jim had called and said he would be in later. She turned the computer on, pulled up the calendar and groaned at the annotation of a mandatory equal opportunity training session. No wonder she'd put it out of her mind. She wouldn't mind so much if they would as least get someone upbeat to conduct the training.

She put the coffee on to brew and eyed the drawer with the Wiley file in it. She'd let some paperwork pile up and if she could get it cleared out by the time the class started, then she'd be able to concentrate exclusively on the Wiley drowning afterwards.

The pot gurgled the end of the brew cycle. Bev filled her mug and took a sip. God, she loved the lift of that first cup in the morning. *Now* she could deal with the stack of uninteresting minutia. She made good progress and then flipped open her notebook and saw Kyle's business card. She took it out and propped it against the telephone. Should she take him at his word and call? She pushed her chair back, crossed her ankles and rested her feet on the edge of the open bottom desk drawer.

She didn't want to admit it to Jim, but she was about ready to try dating again and Kyle *was* attractive - good-looking rather than gorgeous, but that was fine since men that were too handsome tended to have unmanageable egos. Kyle had been pleasant and able to carry on a conversation which was certainly something to consider.

And it wasn't necessarily a real date - she was being neighborly and sharing a bit of local color with a newcomer. Besides, she would need something positive to end the day with. The worst that could happen is she'd find out Kyle wasn't such great company and she'd still have a good meal.

Oh hell, quit over-analyzing and call!, she thought. Kyle answered his own phone and didn't hesitate when she suggested they meet at The Fish Hut at six-thirty.

"Hey Kid, sorry I'm so late," Jim said when he wandered in and went straight to the coffee pot. Bev was startled to see that it was almost noon.

"Anything hot?" he asked and sank into his chair as if he was in pain.

Bev raised her eyebrows. "Nothing new," she said. "No offense Jim, but you don't look so good. Are you okay?"

He pushed aside enough paper to make room for his mug and held up his arm. "Myrtle's been on my ass about getting a check-up and the doc must have been watching vampire movies last night," he said. "Three vials of blood and too much poking and prodding." He shook his head, moved a folder off the calendar and squeezed one eye shut. Sheila had probably penned in the class as a reminder.

"Yeah, I know," Bev said when he groaned. "It's a pain in the ass, but it's only once a year."

Jim grinned and scratched through the entry. "The day Claude busts my balls for missing a bullshit class like this is the day it's time for me to call it quits. I feel the urgent need to go over to County and check on a couple of things. You can take notes if you think there's something I should know about."

One of the men from the computer company called and Jim disappeared while Bev was on the telephone. He hadn't returned by the time the class started.

Bev struggled to stay awake in the stuffy classroom while listening to an uninspiring lecture about the importance of harmonious diversity in the workplace. The three hour session thankfully ended – a waste of an afternoon, but some pencil pushing bureaucrat somewhere could take credit for their participation. Bev was a bit surprised that Jim still wasn't around, but she signed off on the last of what she had wanted to accomplish with an hour to spare for a quick shower and a change of clothes.

She drove home, grabbed the mail from the box and turned the sprinkler on in the front yard to run while she got ready. She slipped into her new stone washed jeans and a short sleeve, lavender cotton sweater that showed off her perpetual tan. She finished the outfit with a brown braided leather belt, a silver turtle pendant and loosely clasped her hair in a clamp decorated with silver seahorses. Her friend, Helen, had finally quit nagging her to chop it off and go from auburn to red. Bev dotted perfume in the hollow of her throat and was satisfied with the effect.

The Fish Hut was a short distance away and when she pulled into the parking lot she saw Kyle in her rearview mirror. He climbed out of his black Explorer and walked quickly around Bev's Triumph. She was glad to see he had swapped his suit for a pair of khakis and a red and navy rugby shirt.

"British racing green," he said with the right touch of admiration. "That's one of the only colors you should ever have for one of these and it's in great shape. How do you keep it running?"

She waved her hand down the length of the car. "This and my Aunt Lorna's '57 pickup are my dad's hobbies. He bought this for my twenty-first birthday, fixed it up and babies it instead of me."

Kyle stepped aside to let Bev walk ahead. "It sounds like you made a good deal."

The Fish Hut was strictly a local place with a dozen wooden picnic tables on the dockside and not many more inside. It sat less than a hundred feet from McNeal's Seafood Market and while that guaranteed a fresh meal, the odor on a hot day could be overwhelmingly pungent.

The temperature was moderate enough not to worry about that and only a slight breeze was coming off the water so Bev suggested they sit outside. The wide serving window was open onto the deck and Bev breathed in the scent of hot oil that came from the row of deep fat fryers in the kitchen. It was a good thing she'd had a salad at lunch – she wasn't in the mood to skimp on dinner.

Tina, the owner's oldest daughter, brought two cold drafts without asking, handed Kyle a plastic coated, single sheet menu and said she'd be back with an order of conch fritters.

"Yeah, I'm what you'd call a regular," Bev said when Kyle looked at her questioningly.

He set the menu down and took a drink. "Then what should I have along with the calamari?"

"If you get the basket, it comes with some of the best coleslaw you'll find, hushpuppies and George's seasoned fries," Bev said and peeled away the napkin that clung to the mug.

Kyle nodded. One of the popular double-decked sunset cruise boats motored slowly down the canal and passed the restaurant. Kyle raised his hand in response to the group of people leaning across the upper rail waving to everyone on shore.

"So you were born and raised here?" Kyle asked and turned his blue eyes on Bev. They reminded her of the cornflowers in Lorna's garden. "And your Dad is retired from the police department?"

Who he had asked about her? One of the women in the DA's office or had he been listening to general talk?

"Yeah, I'm an actual native - fourth generation believe it or not. Dad put thirty years in and finally decided it was time to fish for a living instead of just on weekends. He and one of the other cops that retired about the same time teamed up right before I came on the force and started a charter business. It's one of the small outfits, but they do okay, have a lot of fun, and it keeps him out from under Mamma's feet. And you? Didn't Jim say you were from Chicago?"

Tina brought the fritters and Kyle waited until they ordered to sample his first bite of George's cooking.

"If this is what everything else is like, I may become a regular myself," he said. "And yes, I was in Chicago, but I'm originally from Michigan and went to school right in Ann Arbor, my father's alma mater. He's an environmental lawyer, but I decided criminal law was more interesting. After I graduated I was recruited to work among the many in the Chicago District Attorney's office and spent the past three years with a respectable win to loss ratio against an assortment of bad guys. Nothing that made the national papers."

He paused to finish his beer and shrugged. "Then one very cold winter day I was sitting at a luncheon with your district attorney when he was in town for a convention. We had a lengthy conversation and unknown to me, my predecessor had given notice that he was quitting and your DA was on the lookout for a replacement. The weather was lousy, I was at loggerheads with my office on how to prosecute a case, and my girlfriend had announced she needed to re-think our relationship. The Keys sounded awfully good and I'd be only one of two assistant DA's instead of part of a stable."

Bev noted the comment about the girlfriend, but he went by that without a pause and she saw no reason to ask more about it. "So now that you're here, do you regret the impulsive choice?"

Kyle grinned confidently. "It wasn't all that impulsive, plus I packed away my wool overcoat, rented a condo at Emerald Shores and so far I like the job. It doesn't have the variety of Chicago crime, but we're keeping busy. Now tell me what you do around here for fun."

The evening passed quickly and they spent longer than Bev intended talking about a range of topics. It wasn't a particularly busy night, although the other regular patrons stopped by the table and Bev lost count of the times she introduced Kyle. Somewhere in the conversation about the area's attractions she agreed to join him on Saturday for a bike ride along one of the scenic ocean paths and lunch at a popular beachside tavern.

Bev realized it was almost ten o'clock when the cruise boat returned up the waterway with the dance music blaring from the speakers. She motioned to Tina for the bill and then lost the argument with Kyle for it.

He walked her to her car and held the door open.

"Hey thanks for the tip, this is a great place," he said. "I'll call and we'll set up a time for Saturday."

Bev slid behind the wheel. "Sure, around ten-thirty is probably good, but take a look and see if that works for you. It's about fifteen miles from here. Talk to you later."

She was pretty sure that Kyle watched her as she backed out and drove away. It had certainly been enjoyable, although the lack of awkwardness may have been because it wasn't like a real date.

Bev thought about the people who'd been in the restaurant and knew that if her mother was in town, she would want a full report and would have chided Bev for not having learned more of Kyle's background. No, if her mother had been in town, she would have simply gone to the beauty parlor and within an hour known everything she wanted to about Kyle Stewart. The accuracy of the beauty parlor information network still mystified her.

Maybe she'd be able to see how Saturday turned out before she was asked to give a report to either her parents or Aunt Lorna for that matter. Her mother's concern for her single status was understandable and sometimes tiresome. It didn't take too much brain power to know that one of her mother's unstated issues was that she didn't want to acknowledge her daughter was far more like Lorna than she was her. Not that it was the kind of thing Bev planned to say out loud – at least not anytime soon.

Bev felt no personal urgency in choosing between the lifestyles of her parents' marriage and Lorna's unshakable unmarried state. Too many women she knew set some arbitrary timeline for finding the right man and then allowed their standards to slip rather than wait. Maybe she would settle down in her twenties and maybe not. It wasn't a big deal. Well, it *shouldn't* be a big deal.

On the other hand, she wasn't like her one friend who, to the best of her knowledge, was continuing to embrace a life of celibacy. Moderation in sex, like in so many other matters, was a good rule of thumb.

Bev parked underneath the carport and strolled across the dew damp patch of lawn to double check that she'd turned the sprinkler all the way off. Failing to follow her mother's instructions on yard care was likely to get her into more trouble than not having a future husband picked out.

Chapter Ten

The next morning Bev met Jim at the pistol range for their periodic qualification. He accepted her abbreviated description of dinner and the planned Saturday outing with an *I told you so kind of smile*. She didn't want to encourage him so she centered herself to shut out everything except the pop-up targets that would start through the automated cycle whether she was prepared or not.

Bev's first trip to a pistol range had been at age ten when she tagged along with her father and brother. She'd always prided herself on good marksmanship, but the one time she'd been forced to shoot on the job, the shot that should have wounded the man had ripped through his neck instead. It had been declared a clean shoot, but Bev had sworn she'd never leave a range again without scoring close to a hundred percent.

When they finished and returned to the station Sheila handed Jim a smudged white envelope with his name misspelled. Jim ripped it open as they walked into the office, took out a single type written sheet and started to laugh after he read it.

Bev dropped into her chair and waited for an explanation.

"You have the folder on the Swenson Electronics boost handy?" Jim asked and picked up the telephone.

Bev located the file within seconds while Jim carried on a brief conversation. Swenson's had received a truckload of top brand merchandise in preparation for their annual spring sale and the entire shipment had disappeared by the time Mr. Swenson opened his doors the next morning.

Bev held the folder to her chest. "Okay, what am I looking for?"

Jim waved the paper. "The home address of the nervous guy that we thought was on the inside. It seems as though he quit his job last week with no notice."

Bev grinned. "The one whose girlfriend provided his alibi?"

Jim held the note at arm's length in Bev's direction. "The very same girlfriend, or should I say *ex-girlfriend*, who has kindly let us know she's leaving town and won't be around to testify in case we want to re-question the, and I quote, 'skinny little shit who wasn't with me the night of the job like I said he was'."

Bev laughed. Neither she nor Jim had doubted Sam Haughton's guilt, but he'd been smart enough to bring in a lawyer right away and their evidence was circumstantial. The girlfriend had been surly and insistent in support of his alibi.

They had decided to back off and wait for the kid to try and move the goods since an operation of this size required access to a fence. Bev had taken the precaution of discussing the police department's concerns with the two known individuals who could handle the volume. She explained that if, just theoretically speaking, they were approached about a deal that it would be in their best interest to decline Haughton's business. Although their cooperation wasn't to be taken for granted, it did increase the odds that Haughton or an accomplice would be forced to seek outside assistance. The more people who became involved, the greater the likelihood that someone would make a mistake. On the other hand, a spiteful ex-girlfriend was just as good.

"Let's take a run out and see if our man Sam is at home. If we bring him in, he'll want his lawyer," Jim said and slipped the note into the envelope. And I'll call for a warrant and we'll take it with us just in case."

"I'll see who's available," Bev said and Jim chuckled.

"Sam's a squirrelly little guy," he said. "No sense tying up a patrol – we can call if we find anything and need extra hands."

Bev frowned, but Jim was only a stickler for procedure when he wanted to be and he was already on the phone to the judge's secretary. They briefed Chief Taylor about the new information and were on their way within an hour.

Haughton's junker car was in the driveway and Bev looked around the property of the small ranch house as they sidestepped the cracks in the walk. Missing shutters and a sagging screen door didn't speak much for Haughton's handyman ability and from the looks of thriving weeds in the yard, gardening wasn't among his talents either. Interesting though - the peeling paint didn't match the new padlock on the garage. Maybe she would go ahead and call for that patrol car.

Jim rang the doorbell and when no sound echoed, he knocked sharply. There was no peephole, but Haughton could have easily seen them drive up.

Bev was standing behind Jim when Haughton partially opened the door and blocked their entry with his unimpressive, slender body. Bev's first reaction when she'd met him was that his prominent nose had no doubt been the source of jokes all his life. His eyes were a washed out green that had no strength and the corner of his lower lip twitched when he became agitated. It had twitched a lot during the interview at the station.

"Well Sam, how nice to find you home," Jim said pleasantly and pushed his hand against the door. "I'm sure you won't mind if Detective Henderson and I come in for a moment to ask you a couple of follow-up questions."

The pressure of Jim's hand must have emphasized the difference between the bulk of the two men. Haughton stepped backwards and spoke hesitantly. "Uh look, I already told you what I know and anyway, I'm not saying anything without a lawyer."

Bev followed Jim into the cluttered living room as her partner shook his head in bewilderment.

"Now Sam, what kind of attitude is that? This is not a big deal. It won't take us five minutes and you don't want to pay a lawyer a hundred bucks for some five minute conversation, do you?"

Bev stood toward the middle of the dimly lit room and

scanned the inside of the house as she had the yard. Sam had told them he lived alone and it was hard to tell if the pile of dirty glasses, empty beer bottles and paper plates strewn around the coffee table was accumulated from just him or if others had been there recently. She could see most of the kitchen and heard the muted sound of a radio or television coming from that direction. The door to a bathroom was slightly ajar, but two other doors to what she presumed were bedrooms were closed.

Bev watched Sam's eyes flick back and forth to one of closed rooms as his voice pitched higher in contrast to Jim's nearly jovial tone.

She unsnapped the holster of her pistol and took a step toward the first bedroom when she heard a noise outside the back entrance. She darted into the kitchen, pressed her back against the wall and yanked her gun out. She thumbed the safety off as she hollered, "Police, stay where you are!" She opened the door to the outside and the black mongrel dog rummaging in the metal garbage can dropped to all fours. He tucked his tail and scurried away.

Okay, it was just a mutt, but *something* was making Haughton nervous. She was halfway through the kitchen when Jim cursed and Sam Haughton cried out. Shit! What was Jim doing? She strode into the room expecting to see Haughton on his ass and stopped abruptly at the sight of a man holding a pistol aimed at Jim. She gripped her weapon against her leg.

"Hold it, bitch," the man said.

Jim stood quietly and Sam Haughton nervously rocked his weight from one foot to the other. "Jesus Nick, what are you doing?" he asked.

"Don't fucking start whining," the man called Nick said. "Get the old guy's gun."

Bev assessed him rapidly. He was taller than Haughton and looked to be four or five years older. His narrow face was pinched and he was gripping the revolver tensely in the way of someone unaccustomed to holding a handgun. Bev knew that Jim could tell they were dealing with an amateur, but he was an amateur with a loaded pistol.

"You over there," Nick snapped. "You drop your gun out in front."

Bev held her pistol loosely and positioned it to where she could lift and fire within a fraction of a second. She shifted her eyes without moving her head. Sam was still in her line of sight, but appeared to be immobilized despite the other man's instructions to take Jim's gun.

She spoke calmly. "Nick, it is Nick, right? Look, I'm not sure what's going on, but you need to think through this for a minute. All you have to do is put your gun on the table and we can work out a solution. There's no need to do something dumb."

He shook his head before she finished talking and Bev saw the beads of sweat that clung to his brow. Was it nervousness or was he high on something? She took a deep breath, expelled it slowly and took one step forward.

"Stop where you are, bitch!" Nick screamed. "Put your gun down, goddamn it, just like I said! Sam, I told you to take the old guy's gun!"

Bev was focused on Nick, but she was certain that Jim was poised so he could dive to the floor and roll behind the large stuffed chair if given the slightest opportunity.

Sam moaned, turned pale and looked like he might throw up. Nick momentarily swiveled his head and Bev lifted her arm in a quick, smooth motion.

"You think I won't shoot," Nick said with a mixture of confusion and desperation when he saw what had happened. "I will, goddamn it, I will if you don't drop it right now!"

Bev's voice was as calm as before and she locked her eyes to the young man. "Nick, you're holding a .25 caliber gun and Jim is kind of a big guy so unless your aim is really good, you're not going to hurt him too badly. I've got a 9mm and less than three hours ago I fired perfectly at the range. You can shoot, but I promise you you'll be dead as soon as you pull that trigger because if I see your finger move I will blow a hole in your head. Now if you hand Detective Osborn the gun, we'll tell the DA how cooperative you were. A couple of hot stereos aren't worth dying for."

Bev breathed slowly and shallowly in order to maintain an unwavering stance. "I'm not going to hurt you unless I have to," she continued. She saw the tremor in his hand increase and then Haughton unexpectedly emitted a gurgling sound and keeled forward.

Nick swore at the dead weight of the falling body against his arm, but Jim moved quickly and rammed him in the stomach with his shoulder. He tumbled back and the gun dropped from his hand and clunked against the edge of the table. Jim had him face down on the floor by the time Bev crossed the room.

"Stay still, you worthless shithead," Jim said and rested his knee on the man's back as he fastened the handcuffs. Bev retrieved the weapon, lifted Haughton to his feet and dumped him onto the couch.

"It was Nick. Everything was his idea," Sam said groggily and shook his head slowly. "I never wanted to do it."

"Shut up, you fucking little weasel," Nick said in a choked voice.

"Take your own advice, asshole," Jim said and dragged him to a kneeling position. "I don't want you interrupting me while I read you your rights."

Bev handcuffed Haughton and dialed the station for the backup she had wanted in the first place. She politely refrained from mentioning to Jim that they had goddamn procedures for a goddamn reason. Christ, he knew better and she shouldn't have let him off the hook.

The team arrived in minutes and began to sort through the stolen goods that were stacked in the garage. Sam had willingly given them the keys and talked so fast that Bev could barely keep up with his confession as Nick railed at him for his stupidity.

Earl, one of the senior sergeants on the force, came in and frowned at the cowering Haughton. "Hey Jim, you ready for me to take these guys out?"

Jim rubbed his hand across his face and looked at Bev. She nodded and closed her notebook.

"Yeah, we can finish them up at the station," he said.

At six foot three and well over two hundred pounds, Earl easily shepherded both men outside.

Jim and Bev looked around to make sure they hadn't left anything and Jim patted his shirt pocket with the search warrant they'd never shown Haughton. "We'll put this in the folder; wouldn't want the defense guys to think we'd cut any corners. You ready to go, Kid?"

Bev repositioned the strap of her shoulder holster and smiled at him. "Yes, but I'm not feeling much like a kid right now," she said.

He stepped aside for her to pass through the door. "Come on, we just got through playing cops and robbers; how much more like

being a kid could you ask for?"

"Good point," Bev said and watched the patrol car pull away with Nick and Haughton.

"And speaking of good points," Jim said from behind her, "if we're ever in this situation again just shoot the bastard instead of telling him that a .25 caliber slug probably won't hurt me much. You were right, but I'd rather not find out."

Bev laughed and opened the passenger's side. "Don't worry, I was watching and I've got terrific reflexes - he'd never have gotten a shot off."

Jim walked to the driver's side and shook his head. "Bev, I know you're good, but I'm getting too old to be cutting the margins very close," he said. "And don't forget that not all of them would hesitate as long as Nick did. A drawn gun pointed at a cop equals a clean shoot any day of the week in this town. No one would fault you."

"Yes Jim, I've got it," Bev said and rolled the window down. Save your partner's life and get a lecture about how to handle a basic take down maneuver. Maybe when she turned thirty, he and the Chief would treat her more like an experienced detective than the little girl they'd seen grow up. Yeah, right. Not much sense in holding her breath until that day came.

Chapter Eleven

Bev was helping Jim with the Swenson robbery paperwork when her mother called.

It took a moment to understand that someone had telephoned with the news of the stand-off and Bev spent more time than she wanted reassuring her mother that the danger reported had been exaggerated. She thought she had the situation under control until her father insisted on hearing Jim's version. She sighed in exasperation and transferred the call to Jim. As satisfying as it was to be the second generation of Hendersons to serve on the police force, Bev wished her father didn't have such easy access to the station's internal workings.

She left the room to talk to Sheila about the computer delivery schedule - *that* was something neither her father nor Jim knew anything about. When she returned to the office Jim's grin was much too close to a smirk and she held up a warning finger for him to keep his mouth shut.

She snatched the phone when it rang again and relaxed when Kyle said, "Hi, is this the fearless, steely-eyed, Detective Henderson who holds criminals at bay?"

"I don't think I'd put it quite like that," she laughed. "We weren't dealing with pros."

Jim looked at her questioningly and she made a brushing motion with her free hand. He took the hint and left.

"Maybe not, but it should make for a slam dunk prosecution," Kyle said. "And now that business is out of the way, are we still on for Saturday?"

Bev wrapped the phone cord loosely around her index finger. "Sure and ten o'clock looks good on my end," she said. They spent a few minutes working out the logistics and Bev was glad Jim stayed out of the room. She was beginning to get excited about the prospect of the weekend and she didn't want Jim to know that yet.

It was close to quitting time when Steve Dillworth telephoned and invited her to the Scarlet Macaw to meet a friend of his whom was a dive physiologist. Bev hadn't touched the Wiley folder all day and the toxicology report wouldn't be ready until Monday. This would give her a chance to gather some more background about free diving and highlight specific questions she should be asking.

The bar wasn't crowded when Bev arrived and Dillworth took her to a back table. A stocky man who looked to be in his mid-thirties stood and shook hands with a grip that was gentle considering his thick forearms. His skin was a deep brown and his hair was cropped close to his bullet shaped head.

"Bev, this is Dr. Mike Cleary, a member of the staff of the Diver's Alert Network," Dillworth said and motioned for her to have a seat. "DAN, as it's referred to, is associated with the Medical Center at Duke University and Tom reported Greg's accident for entry into their files. It's standard practice in the dive business," he explained.

"We maintain the largest data repository in the world on diving," Dr. Cleary said proudly in lieu of a standard *hello, nice to meet you*. "We publish annual reports, conduct research into all aspects of diving, have a first class medical team, run a hot line, and of course, have an extensive web site. We have data back to 1970 and we pay particular attention to fatal accidents in order to track causes and provide whatever information we can to the public."

Bev sat next to him and opened her notebook. "Then it sounds like you're who I need to talk to, Dr. Cleary."

Dillworth excused himself and said he'd send drinks over. Dr. Cleary's cold draft looked tempting, but she'd stick with diet Coke until she finished the interview. The smell of popcorn from the large capacity machine behind the bar tickled her nostrils. Maybe when she had the beer.

"I'll only talk if you promise to call me Mike," he said and smiled. "You live here and don't dive?"

Bev shook her head. "My dad's always been a fisherman and he emphasized staying on the surface. I may get around to it one of these days."

Mike's dark eyes reminded Bev of charcoal chunks. "It's a fantastic sport and if you ever get started I can almost promise you'll be hooked from the beginning. I guess hearing about that isn't on your agenda right now though, so what can I tell you about free diving? Do you want procedures or statistics?"

Bev lifted her hands. "Both, I suppose, since I don't know anything about it. My first question is, did anything about Mr. Wiley's death strike you as unusual?"

He took a sip of beer and spoke from memory. "No. I accessed the report and checked it when Steve told me you might want to come by. The two dives Mr. Wiley did prior to his free dive were within acceptable limits. During the free dive he reached a depth of eighty feet within an appropriate time and started his ascent. He ascended with no difficulty until approximately twenty feet. Tom Farmer reported that he was hovering just below the surface as he should have been and noticed the problem, but Mr. Wiley was unconscious as he approached the actual ascent point. He immediately descended, hauled Wiley to the surface, began in-water artificial respiration and then administered oxygen once he got him to the boat. That was the correct treatment, but it was too late. That's not unexpected though, because when a diver is unconscious you only have a few minutes in which to react."

Bev jotted a note to see if Farmer would give her a copy of the report he'd submitted. She could get it through other channels, but she wanted to see how he would respond to her request.

"When I talked to Steve last time he mentioned having more than one safety diver during a free dive. That wasn't the case here. Wouldn't Farmer and Wiley have known better?" She wondered if Mike's answer would match with Dillworth's assessment.

"I'm not sure that's the right question," Mike said and

then paused to finish his beer. "It's always a good idea to have extra safety divers, not an absolute requirement. For a person who has free diving experience, the depth we're talking wasn't extreme. There would have been no compelling reason to take extra precautions."

A memory of something Bev had been told earlier nagged at her. She tugged at her ear, squinted at her scribbling and couldn't place the thought. "Okay, let's back up and explain to me why someone free dives anyway. I mean, isn't it dangerous?"

Mike caught Dillworth's attention to send another round and waved his hand to encompass the diving paraphernalia displayed on the walls.

"When you think about it, free diving has been with us since we became land-based creatures and it's far more common than scuba in many parts of the world. The dangers of diving are really quite small, although I won't get on my soapbox and spout statistics," he said. "Scuba is an incredible sport, but you always have a group of participants who want to take it to another level. Free divers fall into that category, but true aficionados are careful and go through the proper training. I've done limited free diving at around thirty to fifty feet. You're more at one with the ocean, unencumbered by the tanks and other gear. Underwater photographers and a number of divers who spear fish like it because they can move without the sound of bubbles. There are different reasons, but a lot of people swear by it and wouldn't think of going back to scuba."

Dillworth heard Mike's last sentence and set the full mug on the table. His sleeves were rolled up past his elbows and Bev saw part of an intricate tattoo of a red parrot. It would be interesting to know if the bird in the corner or the tattoo came first, sort of a variation on the "chicken and egg question".

"I prefer having the time to hang around underwater and even the best free divers can't stay long," Dillworth said. "Besides, Greg didn't give a rat's ass about the Zen-like quality of anything, much less diving. I don't know how much free diving he really did, but it would have been to win a bet, show off, or because some woman he was attracted to was a free diver and he used that as a come on."

Bev eyed the amber tones of Mike's draft. "So I take that to mean that he and Miss Silsby didn't have a monogamous relationship?"

Dillowrth snorted and waved to a couple that entered the bar. "Monogamous was not a word in Greg's vocabulary and it's not like Karen lets a lot of grass grow under her feet either. I don't mean to rush you Bev, but I want to introduce Mike to the couple that just came in."

It was time for a cold beer after the kind of day she'd had and she could easily follow-up by telephone or e-mail. She read through what she'd written and closed her notebook.

"Hey, I appreciate you guys taking this time and it was a pleasure to meet you, Mike. You don't mind if I call later for more information, do you?"

Mike slid a business card across the table. "Take this, and even if I'm not around, tell anyone at the DAN headquarters who you are and what you're looking for and they'll take care of you."

Bev took the card and stood. "Thanks again and I'll call or come up on the net if I figure out some more questions."

She shook hands in parting and walked to the ladies' room. When she came out she noticed Silsby sitting at the bar. The strapless floral dress she wore didn't convey a sense of mourning although it did provide an unimpeded view of the tops of her breasts. It appeared that she was alone, at least temporarily. It was a pretty good bet that wouldn't last long with her wearing a dress she was practically falling out of.

Silsby turned, saw her and raised her hand. "Well, Detective Henderson. It's Beverly, I mean Bev, isn't it?" she asked and patted the stool next to her. "How about a drink?"

It might be useful to talk to Silsby with a little booze in her. Bev laid a twenty on the bar. "Sure, as long as it's on me," she said and settled against the vinyl padded backrest.

"How are things going?"

Silsby removed the cherry from her drink and ate it before answering. "All right, I suppose. Greg's stepfather put the condo on the market, but has agreed to allow me to stay until it sells. And since almost all my course work is done, I plan on leaving town pretty soon after the insurance check comes through," she said neutrally. "Of course, the insurance company won't do anything until they have a death certificate, and that won't be available until the Medical Examiner finishes whatever it is he's doing. I'm not sure which of us is more anxious for his report." She smiled as though she had no worries.

"We did ask for additional tests," Bev said and watched for any reaction. "We needed to rule out a couple of possibilities."

Silsby gave no indication that she was concerned. She swung her stool to face Bev and her luxurious hair fell across her bare shoulder. "You don't particularly like coincidences, do you?"

Bev wanted to draw her out and tempered her response. "We heard about the pending investigation of Adventures Below and we added that to what we heard about the problems between Mr. Wiley and Mr. Farmer. That's enough to make us ask questions," she said quietly. She lifted the mug and took a tiny sip.

Silsby looked puzzled. "I know Greg and Tom argued about the business and once in a while Greg would say something about how easy it was to get Tom in a lather. I'm pretty sure that Tom was anxious to buy Greg out, but I don't know what you mean about an investigation. Neither of them ever mentioned anything to me."

"Speaking of Mr. Farmer, I'm still not quite clear on your relationship," Bev said.

Silsby smiled and started on her second drink. "He's never come right out and said that he has feelings for me, if that's what you're asking, but of course he does. He's a middle-aged divorced man and he thought Greg was bad for me. Bless his heart though; he can't figure out if he wants to screw me or treat me like his niece."

"And do you try to help him figure it out?" Bev asked and noticed that two men at a nearby table were checking them out. They were cute enough, but hardly what Bev had planned for the evening.

Silsby laughed. "Look, I told you before, Tom is a nice guy and a bit of a goody two shoes. He's the kind that I could tumble in a heartbeat and he'd fall in love in less time than that. Quite frankly, I don't need that in my life. I'm not going to say I've never flirted with him, but I kept the charm at half speed, so to speak."

Bev mentally rolled her eyes at the woman's ego. *Christ, no wonder she and Wiley had been attracted to each other.* She inwardly groaned when Silsby leaned against the bar and swept a slow smile past Bev and across to the two men. She calculated that she had time for one or two more questions before one of them would make a move.

"So do you think the business problems were bad enough that Mr. Farmer would want to get rid of Mr. Wiley?"

Silsby hiked her skirt up to expose a long line of perfect thigh and paid attention to Bev again. "I'm not going to say it isn't possible even though Tom hardly seems the type. And let's get real, how he would do something in broad daylight in front of two people?"

The taller of the men was approaching the bar and his intent was easy to read. Bev emptied her mug in three gulps and slipped off the barstool. "I've got to head out," she said instead of answering the question. "We may want to talk with you again soon."

"No problem," Silsby said and threw her shoulders back to emphasis the cut of her dress. "But I don't plan on being around much longer. I'm out of here after the insurance check clears and my last paper gets graded."

Bev walked away with a polite nod to the man who had now aligned himself on the other side of Silsby, who didn't look as if she was planning to keep her charm at anything other than full throttle.

Bev took the convertible top off her car. Silsby's

question about broad daylight and two witnesses was the same as everyone else. That would have been the whole point, the very thing Farmer would have relied on to deflect suspicion and something he might or might not have explained to Silsby if she was involved. But involved as a motive for Farmer or as the instigator? If Silsby was being truthful about Farmer, then he might have decided on his own that killing Wiley would be in her best interest without her knowing about it.

On the other hand, it was obvious that at least in Silsby's mind she could manipulate Farmer and if she was lying about everything, then she could have either openly enlisted his help or planted the idea with a few carefully crafted sentences. Bev had no difficulty in seeing her in that role, no difficulty at all. Figuring out the details was the tricky part.

Chapter Twelve

On Saturday, Bev bicycled to Kyle's condominium. A made to order day, she thought - a little breeze and a few clouds with no danger of building into an overcast layer.

Kyle was ready to go when she arrived and they negotiated the short distance to connect to the scenic path that had been carved out along the ocean.

"It's a nice trail," Bev said. "The end is about thirty miles down, but the Pirate's Den is at the mid-point. They've been open for a while and I've been meaning to try them out."

Kyle smiled. "I'm in your hands," he said.

Was there a double meaning to that statement? Maybe it was just an expression he used.

They rode side by side and wound in and out of native vegetation. Bev watched Kyle as they came to the first stretch that swung close to the distinctive green water. The sandy area was too narrow for most beach goers, but two sailboats were rounding the point ahead. It was a postcard shot complete with sun glints on the waves. The only thing missing was a pod of cavorting dolphins.

Kyle slowed and nodded. "Now this is what I call a view," he said. "No wonder people come for vacation and decide not to go home."

Bev laughed and kept the pace slow along the water's edge. "Yeah, it's easy to fall in love with it when the weather's mild and we do get a lot of transplants. One or two summers of the heat, humidity and swarms of bugs can be a little disenchanting for them though. Some move out entirely and others split the difference and just spend winters."

Kyle swung his gaze from the shore and grinned at her. "Do you natives take bets on which of us will last?"

Bev wrinkled her nose. "Not always."

The path curved and Kyle moved a few inches in front of her. "That sounds almost like a challenge," he said over his shoulder. "I think I can tough it out though."

A good reaction, Bev thought and hung behind him for a few minutes. His broad shoulders were fully defined in the T-shirt he was wearing and the muscles in his thighs flexed as he biked with practiced ease.

Her last relationship had now been over with for almost as long as it had lasted. He'd been a business teacher at the community college and while they enjoyed each other, it was never a coming together of exhilarating passion. Bev had broken off with him when she found out he was sleeping with his ex-girlfriend again and he acknowledged he had some issues to resolve. Bev hadn't been looking for a commitment, but having two different affairs at the same time seemed greedy and she sure as hell didn't a man with *issues*.

Kyle lifted slightly off the bicycle seat and Bev's eyes lingered on the shape of his butt longer than she intended. What was she thinking – this was only their first date! *Get a grip and pay attention to the path!*

Three other cyclists sped past from the opposite direction and Bev returned their greeting, then moved alongside Kyle again and made small talk about local sights until they wheeled into the tavern parking lot and slid their bikes into one of several racks. The smiling hostess seated them on the outside not far from a boisterous crowd, but it was friendly chatter that crossed the open-air deck in noisy bursts.

Vibrantly colored market umbrellas shaded the tables and more importantly, kept the direct sun off the pitcher of beer resting in a bucket of ice. It was a nice place, but Bev was withholding judgement until she tried the food.

"A little more upscale than the Fish Hut," she said and took the mug Kyle filled for her. "As you may have noticed, the nautical theme comes in a lot of packages around here."

"Works for me," Kyle replied. "I like casual and I'm a low maintenance guy. I do own a tux and I've got nothing against a night at the symphony, but I can do without it, too. And speaking of nautical, tell me some more about your dad's business."

Bev smiled. A guy that didn't keep the conversation on himself – another point in his favor. She had just finished explaining the transition from career cop to Florida Keys fisherman when their waitress appeared with a loaded tray.

Bev bit into her blackened grouper sandwich. The multigrain roll was soft and the complex blend of spices struck the right peppery hot balance. Oh yes, the Pirate's Den deserved its reputation. Kyle pointed to his seared tuna sandwich and mumbled approval.

After the remnants of lunch were taken away, Bev mentioned her conversation with Dr. Cleary and the encounter with Silsby.

"If we can find anything on Farmer, then the girlfriend's involvement could make sense," Kyle said and reached for Bev's mug to pour her another draft. "A girlfriend/wife offering a piece of the insurance money isn't what you'd call new, but there's nothing wrong with classic motive and we seem to have an interesting method. Or at least it's one I haven't run across before. I mean we had bodies wind up in the lake, but they usually had a couple of bullet holes in them first."

Bev leaned across the table. "The ME's report should be ready Monday. There's got to be something - either poison, drugs or maybe even a contusion we missed."

Kyle drummed his fingers on the tabletop in a thoughtful way. "That's what I'd like for him to find," he said. "It would make just make things a lot easier."

Laughter rolled from the nearby group and Kyle looked at his watch. "Would you like something else or are you ready to start back?" he asked and caught the attention of their waitress.

Bev shook her head and stood. "No I'm fine, but if you'll

excuse me for a minute, I'll be right out," she said and felt Kyle's gaze as she walked away.

She re-braided her hair once inside the ladies room and debated about extending the day by offering to make dinner. Not that she was an accomplished cook, but her three or four specialties were foolproof. That would mean entertaining him at her parents' house though and that seemed odd just thinking of it. No, better to hold off until she could be on her own turf.

Kyle was waiting at the entrance to the deck and handed her a bottle of sunscreen. She reapplied some across her face and checked the sky. The scattered clouds were little more than white smears and the breeze had lessened so that on the ride back Bev felt the sweat trickle down her back and between her breasts. Kyle's shirt was soaked and his musky scent set off a mental picture of what he might look like bared to the waist. Nothing like a good whiff of pheromones to push the imagination up a notch.

They arrived at Kyle's condominium and he turned his bicycle to face hers.

"If you're not in a hurry, I've got beer mugs in the freezer or a fresh pitcher of ice tea in the refrigerator if you'd rather. Why don't you come in for a bit?" he asked and smiled.

Was it seduction in those blue eyes or just a simple, polite invitation? *God, he had a great smile!*

"Sure, that sounds good," she replied and followed him into the garage. He apparently kept his Explorer in the driveway, since the space inside was taken with a tool cabinet, boxes, and a variety of sporting equipment.

He nodded to a kayak that rested against a wall. "I haven't been out much since I moved here, but it's on my list. Is kayaking one of your hobbies by any chance?"

He opened a door on the far side and held it for Bev to go through.

"I haven't tried it," she said and looked around. "But I'm always open to new experiences."

Kyle grinned. "I'll keep that in mind," he said and swept

his arm to encompass the room. "And this is my humble abode."

Bev stood in the center of what was the den while Kyle stepped into the kitchen area that was separated by an island. The downstairs was configured as spaciously as possible with no dividing walls and included a dining alcove to the side as well as a large sliding glass door that led to a small flagstone patio.

The airiness was enhanced with Kyle's minimalist approach to decorating. It might be deliberate, or if he was like her, he hadn't spent much effort in accumulating furniture. A large screen television and sound system occupied one wall. A tan leather sofa and matching recliner completed the setting. A couple of books, some CDs and magazines were cluttered around although the sloppy signs of discarded socks and dirty dishes were not to be seen.

"A glass of tea or water and then a beer?" Kyle asked as Bev stepped forward.

The kitchen island included a breakfast bar extension. Bev pulled out one of the oak stools pushed beneath the overhang, sat down and propped her forearms on the counter.

"Water first is a good idea," she said and consumed the contents of the glass he gave her while he poured two beers into cold, dark green ceramic mugs embossed with the University of Michigan seal.

"Let's go out on the patio," he suggested and led the way to the round redwood table with four short benches. A blue striped umbrella was folded shut and there was no need for its shade at this hour.

A row of red hibiscus had been planted around the perimeter to provide a natural type fence. A chaise lounge with a navy blue cushion and a shiny black charcoal grill in the corner were the only other items on the patio.

When Kyle sat on the short bench next to her Bev was intensely aware of his presence and she turned the discussion to the safe subject of the Marlins' new shortstop. The conversation was light, but as they talked, Kyle edged closer until his thigh was touching hers and Bev was startled at the electricity in the contact. She breathed deeply and fleetingly thought of the scientists' claim of the aphrodisiac nature of smell.

Somewhere at the bottom of her beer and in the middle of a sentence Bev was having trouble completing, Kyle leaned forward, put his forefinger to her chin and his lips to her mouth. The tip of his tongue barely touched her, but she opened her lips instinctively – it was that kind of kiss.

She simultaneously felt Kyle's hand stroke the side of her neck and her stomach flutter. He prolonged the kiss and his fingers began to trace along her collarbone to the hollow of her throat. The heel of his hand was at the swell of her breast – oh Christ!, what was she doing? She pulled back slightly and caught her breath, but she couldn't speak in a normal voice. She held one hand to his chest and braced the other one on the table.

"Kyle," she said hoarsely. "I don't know about this."

The physical desire she hadn't seen in his eyes earlier was there now and in his voice. He didn't move her hand, but pressed into it at the same time he gently ran his fingers along her arm.

"You probably won't believe I don't ordinarily move this fast either," he said softly. "And I'll stop if you want me to."

Kyle's face was only inches away and Bev reached out to touch his cheek. Even as she hesitated, she flushed with an undeniable heat. Her usual set of rules seemed unimportant and Kyle took her silence as permission.

He swung his legs to straddle the bench and pulled her to him. His tongue probed harder this time and she opened her mouth again with a suppressed moan. She felt lightheaded and was confused with the sensation. She thought momentarily of the fact that they were on the patio and nodded wordlessly when Kyle whispered that they should go upstairs.

His bedroom was dusky from the drawn curtains, but there was enough light to see as he helped her strip away her clothes and pulled her into another embrace. He'd dropped his shirt to the floor and Bev held her head into his chest as he ran his hands the length of her spine. She could feel how hard he was and quickly found the zipper to his shorts. He slowly guided her down onto the bed and worked his tongue in a sinuous, curving path all the way down to between her legs.

A spark of mental chastisement for giving in so easily was smothered when she arched in an orgasm. Kyle slowly moved up beside her again, kissed her deeply and then languidly ran his hands along her body in a way that left her gasping. She finally tugged at his arm to bring him on top of her, turned her head and bit into the pillow when he penetrated her. He held back until she shuddered into another orgasm and then groaned her name as he climaxed.

He slowly lifted his weight off her and they both laid on their backs for a few minutes. Loosened strands of hair clung to Bev's damp forehead.

"Wow," Kyle finally said and rolled up on his side. He reached to brush the hair away and kissed her. "Stay right there and I'll get a warm washcloth for you."

Bev closed her eyes to try and put together what had happened and heard the water running in the bathroom. What in the hell had come over her? She had an almost irresistible urge to giggle, but was afraid that could be too easily misinterpreted.

She sighed with pleasure when Kyle sat on the bed again and gently cleansed the inside of her thighs. Now *that* was really considerate. She smiled at him.

"Well counselor, I've had good days of bike riding in my life, but I must say, this one is at the top of the list."

He dropped the washcloth onto the floor. "I'd say it was pretty terrific," he agreed. "I don't know about you, but I could use something else cold to drink. Would you like another beer?"

Another beer and she'd fall asleep. Bev shook her head. "A glass of water is fine for me," she said and hesitated when he left.

This was the awkward time for her and maybe for him too for that matter. What to say? How long to stay? Should she get dressed? Kyle had slipped his shorts on and Bev wasn't sure if that was because the curtains were open downstairs or because he was expecting her to get dressed, too. If she didn't put her clothes on that was like asking for more and she was beginning to feel unsettled with how quickly she'd given in.

She put her clothes on within seconds and met Kyle at the head of the stairs. He held a glass of water in one hand and a glass of tea in the other.

"Ah," he said and stood at the next step down. "You didn't want to take a shower?"

Bev took her glass and pointed to the main floor. "Thanks for the offer, but I'll clean up when I get home. It's been a great day, but I need to go."

"Oh sure," he said over his shoulder. He didn't act like he was disappointed. Was that significant? "I'd be glad to drive you home. The bike will fit in the Explorer with no problem."

"No, that's okay," Bev said when they returned to the kitchen island. She perched on the edge of the stool instead of sitting. Kyle walked to the couch and retrieved the fanny pack that she'd dropped there when they came in. The awkwardness that she hadn't experienced up until now was edging its way into her voice and she wanted to leave before they reached the pregnant pause phase.

Kyle laid the pack on the counter and leaned forward to give her a gentle kiss on the mouth. "It was a great day. Any chance we can do dinner this week or catch a movie if you'd like?"

An up front invitation instead of a vague promise of a phone call. If he meant it.

Bev cleared her throat. "Yeah sure, I'll check my calendar and give you a call." Her calendar was almost empty, but that wasn't the point.

Kyle walked her outside, gave her another quick kiss and waved good-bye as she pedaled around the corner. As soon

Shades of Murder

as she arrived home she went immediately into the bathroom, turned the water on in the shower and stepped in once a cloud of steam rose from the enclosure. She leaned her head back to let the water stream down her stomach and then had to brace against the ceramic tile wall as she remembered the feel of Kyle's athletic body.

She switched the water to a cooler temperature and then blasted herself with all cold. That got her attention.

She toweled off quickly, wiped a clear spot in the mirror and stared at her reflection. What had gotten into her? She wasn't the kind of woman who took a tumble just because a man had a cute butt and a nice pair of shoulders. She pulled a comb through her wet hair and reviewed both the day and the evening they'd spent together at the Fish Hut.

She mentally ticked off the qualities she liked about Kyle and was mildly puzzled to find that she couldn't identify anything negative. That couldn't be right. She ran through the list a second time and came to the same conclusion.

She changed into her favorite pair of worn blue sweats, wandered into the kitchen and grabbed a diet Coke. She went out onto the deck and watched the neighborhood lights flick on as the sun began its downward track. A late returning fishing charter boat slowly moved up the canal and after it disappeared into the marina, she smiled ruefully in the twilight. What was the big deal anyway? What happened had happened and it wasn't like she jumped into bed with every man she dated. She'd enjoyed it and he would either call her again or he wouldn't. If, unlike what he'd claimed, this was his typical approach to women, and he was a wham-bam-thank you-ma'am type, then she might as well learn that early on.

And that was that. Bev went inside to see what was on the television schedule. A nice quiet evening with maybe a pizza for nourishment was what she needed.

Kyle called on Sunday to tell her that he had to go to Tallahassee for a few days on business, but wanted to have dinner Friday. Bev asked him to make it Saturday instead and when he immediately agreed, she wondered if she should have played hard to get. Then she wondered if it mattered. Then she wondered why she was spending so much time thinking about it and went for a five-mile jog -she had other things to do than think about Kyle Stewart.

Chapter Thirteen

On Monday, Jim didn't ask Bev much about her date, except to say how having someone in the department cozy with the District Attorney's staff would be handy.

Chief Taylor thrust his head and upper part of his body into the office and interrupted her comeback.

"I've got a meeting in an hour at the Chamber of Commerce and they're going to want to know the deal on the guy who drowned to make sure it won't cause any unfavorable publicity," he grouched with his usual Monday morning scowl. "You ready to close the case?"

Bev stopped herself before she rolled her eyes. "I'll call and see if the report is ready," she said instead. "I'm telling you Chief, this was no accident and it's got nothing to do with the tourist trade."

He grunted noncommittally. "Then get something we can take to the prosecutors. Suspicions aren't enough," he said and withdrew.

Bev sighed and reached for the telephone. Thank God they were given a ten o'clock appointment with the Medical Examiner. They could finally get to the bottom of this. They arrived on schedule and were shown in to the paneled, windowless office without a wait. Bev thought that if she spent her time in a chilled room slicing up bodies, she would want to at least retreat to a cheery workspace, but maybe the absence of corpses was all the break the ME needed.

Dr. Cooke looked across the desk, nodded rather than spoke and fanned out the sheets of paper he'd been consulting when they sat down. "Sorry folks, there was nothing to find," he said.

Bev opened her eyes wide. "What? Nothing, nothing at all?" She wanted to look at the report. Maybe Dr. Cooke couldn't read his own damn handwriting and he missed a note.

The doctor shook his head and readjusted his glasses that had slipped to the middle of his stubby nose. "I screened for the most likely substances; anything that could be injected or ingested and work in the specified timeframes to cause death or interference with physical responses such as temporary paralysis," he said in his nasal voice. "It was all negative."

Bev tried again. "Well, maybe there's some really strange stuff you didn't think to check."

He looked to Jim as if for support. "For crying out loud, Beverly," he said. "I've been doing autopsies since you wore diapers. You guessed wrong on this one. The cause of death stands as accidental. Plain and simple drowning."

Bev tensed at both his tone and his finding and tightened her fingers around the arms of the chair. Damn it, he had to be wrong!

"What about the chance for negligence?" Jim asked. "Any way to tell if Farmer started revival efforts when he should have?"

The doctor shrugged. "You're talking five or six minutes between living and dying and we can't be that exact. Maybe your witnesses can sequence events a little closer. Otherwise I'm sorry, but the medical evidence shows what it shows. I'll have the report completed this afternoon or tomorrow at the latest."

"Yeah well, thanks for getting the tests done, Doc," Jim said and motioned Bev out of the room before she could ask another question. She said good-bye through a clenched jaw and strode angrily outside to the car.

She yanked the car door open and banged her palm against the frame. "Shit, shit, shit! Can you believe that shit? Nothing! How in the hell could there be nothing?"

Jim let her curse until she was forced to stop to take a breath. He slid behind the wheel and spoke calmly. "You know, I'm in desperate need of a piece of apple pie and coffee from Annabelle's. My treat."

Bev threw herself into the car and snapped the seatbelt in place. "Transparent Jim, you're transparent as hell," she said in a sullen tone that she resented as unprofessional. But goddamn it, how could the tests have been clean?

"When you get to be my age, you'll understand the true therapeutic value of apple pie."

Bev seethed silently as he drove and ran through a list of options for her next move. It was a very short list. Anabelle's was between the breakfast and lunch periods so Bev and Jim took a booth by the window. She asked for coffee and protested when Jim ordered two servings of apple pie a la mode. He told the waitress to bring them anyway and Bev relented when the smell of buttery crust and cinnamon reached her nostrils.

He waited until her mouth was full when he spoke philosophically.

"Look Beverly, you're a terrific kid and a damn fine detective, but this is one you aren't going to win."

Bev swallowed hard – she damn well didn't need him to use her full name. "First I'm not a kid, Jim and second, you know I'm right. There are too many coincidences. Okay I admit, no drugs or poison makes it tough to buy premeditated, although the ME may not be as up to date as he thinks he is. I don't have a problem with asking for the report and sending it somewhere else for a second opinion. But for the sake of argument, let's say it wasn't planned, although I don't believe that for a minute. Let's say Wiley really did black out and Farmer was deliberately slow to react. I've just got to find a way to prove it."

Jim drank half his coffee.

"Bev, the District Attorney won't touch it. You've got four people on the scene; one is unconscious, if not already dead, one is Farmer, Bibbins is holding the helm and watching seagulls for all we know, and Matson was drinking beer. A defense attorney would love to cross-examine a line-up like that. He'd rip them apart in record time."

"So we give up, we let Farmer literally get away with murder? You do think he's guilty, don't you?" Bev strained to keep her voice under control.

Jim shrugged. "With what the doc told us, I'm more inclined to buy negligence. But you know, other than possibly his parents, you haven't found anyone yet that's mourning Mr. Wiley and it doesn't look like the world has lost a valuable individual."

Bev choked back her reply until the waitress gave them a refill and moved out of hearing range.

"Christ Jim, I don't believe this!" she said when they were alone again. "All right, Wiley got away with shit because he had connections and hell, maybe Farmer did do the world a favor. But it's not my place, or yours, or Farmer's to make those kinds of decisions. No one is supposed to cause someone else's death and walk away with no penalty."

Jim took his last bite of pie and swirled it around in the melted ice cream. "Part of the problem Bev is that you don't have any old, open cases. One of the things about this business is that you eventually get one you either can't solve or can't prove. This had to happen to you sooner or later."

"Oh for Christ's sake Jim, that's got nothing to do with it," she said abruptly.

Jim squinted one eye. "What was your standing when you graduated from high school?"

Bev was startled by the question. "Valedictorian."

"And college?"

"A 3.94 and yes Phi Beta Kappa, and I do not believe you're doing this," she said and shoved her plate to one side. "It's not about grading myself or keeping score. It's about what's right and wrong."

Jim scraped his plate for the miniscule crumbs he'd missed. "Bev, you're probably the most competitive individual that I know; you've been that way since you were in the first grade. You've never failed at anything you've tried and I say that with a great deal of respect, but if you'll stop being pissed at the doc for a few minutes, you might

Shades of Murder

think about that. As much as anything, you don't want to have made a mistake about this."

They sat in silence as Bev breathed deeply through her nostrils. Jim was wrong. Jim was mostly wrong. Jim wasn't entirely correct. At least he had the courtesy not to press his point.

"I just want to look at all the statements again," she said finally. "I know we missed something. I won't ask you to spend anymore of your time on it if you won't insist I give it up yet."

Jim picked up the check and batted her hand away.

"Sure Bev, that's fair. You want me to tell Claude about it?"

She stood up and tried to smile. "No, even in my competitive state of mind, I can admit that I'm stumped for the moment. And by the way, you were right about the pie."

His chuckle was the same as her father's. "I was right about more than the pie. Anyway, let's get back and talk to Claude. I'll give you my notes and who knows, maybe something will jump out at you."

A flash of pain crossed his face and disappeared when he belched.

Bev cocked her head to one side. "You okay, Jim?"

He dropped a dollar on the table and lightly patted his chest. "Just getting old, Bev. The heartburn comes on quicker and stays longer. One of these days I'm going to have to quit this job and ask your dad if they need another hand on the boat."

The earlier tension disappeared and they both laughed at the idea. Jim's dislike of water-related sports was no secret and he'd never learned to swim despite a lifetime of living near the ocean.

Chief Taylor was less caustic than Bev expected when they met in his office and gave him an update. "I'll let you go for another few days on this, but that's it," he said. "And speaking of real crimes, did you two see the paper this morning on the Devil's Duo?"

Bev shook her head and Jim nodded and curled his upper

lip in disgust.

"Yeah," he said. "What a load of media bullshit – the *Devil's Duo*. That makes them sound like a damn circus act instead of a couple of wackos."

Bev didn't remind him that the title had originated from the sheriff in a town where they'd killed the store clerk, a customer who had presumably walked in during the robbery and his eight year old son who had been found dangling from the passenger seat of a car.

"They hit another place, Chief?" Bev asked. No more kids, she hoped – that report had been hard to read.

The Chief flipped open the newspaper lying on the desk and pointed to a short article on the second page. "Another liquor store, right out of Coral Gables. It was one of those places known for not checking I.D.'s too carefully, so the guy had done a brisk business during the evening," Chief Taylor said and pulled a cigarette from a pack in his front shirt pocket. "He must have been short help though or something because he was alone at closing."

He lit up and inhaled deeply as Bev wrinkled her nose. Discussions about second hand smoke did no good with the Chief.

"The good news is that there may finally be a break. It seems as if a local drug pusher in Mississippi was killed right before this crap started. A Willie Denton, who was employed at a warehouse in the same town where the drug guy was whacked, had left his job a couple of days before. To add to it, a Hal Grayson who worked with Denton, was found dead in what was assumed to be a drunk driving accident at around the same time as the murders. It turns out that the burned body in the vehicle was not Grayson, but was instead one of the drug pusher's guys."

"Sounds like there's a reasonable connection," Bev said.

The Chief exhaled toward the floor. "Or at least enough to raise questions. Grayson, if he's still alive, is an ex-con who served fifteen years for second degree murder and that was because the prosecutor couldn't make a first degree charge stick. The second guy, Denton, hasn't done hard time, but has been in and out of trouble for years. Photographs are being sent out now, although technically they're just wanted for questioning in connection with, etc.," he said. "For all anyone knows, the faked death may be unrelated."

"You know Chief, Jim was right the other day when he said it makes no sense for these two to head south. I mean, you run out of hiding places real fast and there's only one main road north to south," Bev said.

Chief Taylor took a final drag from his cigarette and dropped it into the ashtray. "Yeah and I'm glad it's not our problem. Now let's get back to this deal with Wiley. I want it closed by the middle of next week unless you can find something resembling facts to support that it wasn't an accident."

Bev didn't like being given a deadline, but it was better than an edict to accept Dr. Cooke's ruling as final. She'd take Jim's notes like he suggested and re-read every word in the file until she found whatever lead they'd overlooked. Once she found it and proved she was right, she'd see what Jim had to say about competitiveness.

Chapter Fourteen

Sheila beckoned to Bev as soon as they emerged from Chief Taylor's office. She told her that the computers were in and delivery was scheduled for that afternoon with hookup and training the following day.

Bev frowned at the timing, but with all the work they'd put into the project, she knew she'd have to help get everything in place or else it would get off track. Sheila couldn't do it alone and even though she knew everyone in the station, she didn't have a firm grasp of who needed what training. There was no way Bev was going to take a chance on the first days being anything less than perfect; that would give Chief Taylor an excuse to veto some of the other ideas that she hadn't presented to him yet.

Jim listened to the first part of the conversation, reminded Bev that he didn't want a computer either and left to attend the monthly Lions Club luncheon.

Bev spent the rest of the day and most of the following one directing the movement of office furniture and soothingly translating basic computer terms into plain English for the ones who didn't know that RAM wasn't just a type of pickup truck. By the time the hardware was properly installed, the outer bay looked like a police station that actually belonged in modern times. Some of the younger officers had already given her a thumbs up and even the novice users seemed to be comfortable with their progress.

She and Sheila had discussed how long it might take to get everyone proficient with the new software and decided it made sense to leave a trio of electric typewriters in a communal area as both a backup and a security blanket.

It was close to three o'clock as the last of the systems

technicians departed. Bev glanced at the clock on the wall and smacked her forehead with the heel of her hand – the ceramic vases that her mother had made for the annual church bazaar! It had become a tradition for the sisters to team up with Emma making the vases and Lorna using some of them to create dried flower arrangements. Bev felt mildly guilty since she'd forgotten about the task and had faked her way through righteous indignation when her mother had called to ask if she'd delivered them or was waiting until the last minute. Fortunately Lorna had taken pity on her and was coming by at four to pick up the box.

As much as Bev wanted to get back to the Wiley file she wanted to go through it from start to finish without interruption and it wasn't practical with Lorna coming by, plus she was feeling tight from the two days of work with the computers. It would make more sense to go to the gym after Lorna's visit and review the notes later at home. She had time to go through the day's accumulated e-mail before she heard Lorna's voice in the outer bay.

Bev took her keys out of her purse and went out to Sheila's desk where she and Lorna were discussing the health of Sheila's African violets.

"Ah, my savior for the afternoon," Bev said with a smile as Sheila excused herself when the telephone rang. "Do you have time for a cup of coffee?"

Lorna shook her head. "I'd like to, but I need to get back to the house and get the last of the arrangements finished. What colors did Emma do this time?"

"Some blue and green swirled, a couple of yellow striped ones, and the rest with tropical fish on a blue background," Bev said and waited while Lorna scrawled something on a piece of paper and handed it to Sheila.

"Good, those should go over well," Lorna said and waved good-bye to Sheila who was still on the phone.

Lorna had parked next to the Spitfire and Bev lifted the box out of her car, tilted it into her chest and gently laid it in the floorboard of the Chevy.

"I really appreciate this," Bev said. "It's been pretty

hectic the last few days."

Lorna rummaged in her shapeless crocheted bag for her keys and grinned at Bev. "Speaking of being busy, are you going to tell me about this Kyle or am I going to have to rely on things I'm hearing?"

Bev felt herself flush slightly and she leaned against the passenger's side of her car. She'd try a dodge. "We've only had one actual date."

"And dinner at the Fish Hut," Lorna said. "I'm assuming you wouldn't have gone on the date if that hadn't been fun and I was told by a reliable source that he's a stud."

Bev shifted her feet. She didn't mind telling Lorna about Kyle, but she was still embarrassed that she'd responded to him as quickly as she had. Lorna would understand, but it was too early in the relationship to be passing along such intimate details.

"Well yes, and it doesn't hurt that he can carry on a decent conversation too," she said. "He's a pretty cool guy and we'll see how it goes."

Lorna tugged her keys loose, but a comb popped out of her purse and dropped to the ground. "Okay, I won't press and if your mamma doesn't think I wheedled enough information, I'll make up whatever I need to. And it sounds like work has been kind of tough lately."

Bev stooped to retrieve the comb and handed it to Lorna. "Getting the new computers in has kept us busy," she said and then realized Lorna was watching her quizzically. She knew that expression. "That's not what you meant is it?"

Lorna opened the door of the truck, tossed her purse onto the seat and turned back to Bev. "Oh, Myrtle was in yesterday and she mentioned that she thought you and Jim were having a disagreement with Claude about a case. Has something to do with that Wiley boy and Tom Farmer I gathered."

Bev sighed and impatiently brushed away a strand of hair that had blown across her mouth. Christ, what had Jim been saying? "Jesus Aunt Lorna, what did Myrtle tell you?"

Lorna smiled gently. "Oh, I don't think Jim said very

much, but there have been rumors floating around about the two of you asking questions."

Bev tucked the wayward strand of hair behind her ear. "Well, it's an ongoing investigation," she said, "and we're really not supposed to be discussing it."

Lorna flipped her hand to dismiss the statement. "Bev, those kinds of things don't stay quiet in this town. Besides, I've known Tom since he opened that dive shop and I can't imagine he didn't do everything he could to save that young man."

Bev overrode her resentment of Jim's indiscretion. "How well do know him?"

Lorna stood with the door of the truck open. "He's active in the community and does a lot of work with the Boy Scouts and the beach clean-ups – that sort of thing. He's very generous of his time and every dealing I've had with him has been pleasant. I don't know of anyone who doesn't like him."

"Then you knew Greg Wiley, too?" So some of the townspeople were gossiping, were they? Had Farmer also heard the rumors?

Lorna shook her head. "Not really. The one or two times I spoke to him were just in passing. And even though you feel like you shouldn't be talking about this, Tom is a good man and I can't imagine that he was at fault. He's quite an expert in the water from what I've heard and one of the things he teaches the Scouts is rescue techniques. People drown all the time; it's not terribly unusual."

Bev wanted to ask if Lorna had heard about the fights between the partners, but she doubted much was known about that outside the marina.

"I know that, but we have a few other things to check before we close the case," Bev said and exhaled in relief when Lorna looked down at her watch.

"Oops, I'd better get myself in gear. Give me a call and we'll do dinner soon," Lorna said and climbed into the truck with a quick wave.

Bev watched her drive away and then returned to the

office where she closed up, grabbed her gym bag and held her irritation with Jim in check as she politely said good night to Sheila. It was bad enough that the Chief didn't believe her suspicions were valid, but couldn't Jim have the common decency not to say anything to his wife?

Christ, there were times when she wished she hadn't decided to stay in her hometown. Jacksonville or Atlanta would have been about the right distance and she sure as hell wouldn't have half the population knowing who she was dating or asking questions about how she was handling a case.

She drove past the city park with the swimming pool where she'd learned to swim. It hadn't changed much since then and the town was making a conscious effort to incorporate new growth in a way that didn't noticeably alter the well-known landmarks. There was a sense of continuity and sameness that other towns had lost in their quest for big land developments.

Oh well, the truth was that she didn't like big city traffic, the crowds or that so many of the police calls involved chalk outlines of dead bodies. She didn't need huge shopping malls and she enjoyed being able to take a stroll alone late at night if she was restless. She knew she wasn't cut out for metropolitan bustle and having friends and relatives occasionally meddle in her business wasn't an intolerable price to pay.

Bev pulled into a parking slot at the health club. A hard run and maybe a short session in the sauna would sweat out her disgruntled feelings. Then she'd review the Wiley file again and figure out what they had missed. Hopefully Aunt Lorna wouldn't be too disappointed when she discovered that Farmer wasn't the great guy she thought him to be.

Chapter Fifteen

Bev worked until after eleven o'clock to find what could be the key piece, but gave up in frustration when she'd been through her notes three times. The words started to run together when she read them and nothing new came to her. She rubbed her eyes and flexed her shoulders. She'd try sleep and see if whatever was rattling around in the recesses of her brain would crystallize into the active area.

Her sleep was unsettled and she drifted in a restless limbo between blackness and consciousness; a heavy sensation of being unable to open her eyes, yet aware that she wasn't dreaming. She reluctantly awoke to the insistent sound of the alarm and blasted her body with cold water at the end of her shower. It was uncomfortably effective.

There was a message waiting for her when she arrived at the office and she was on the telephone when Jim came in with his usual large cup of coffee and pastries. She finished her conversation and yawned.

"You look tired," Jim said, his words partially smothered by a mouthful of cinnamon roll.

Bev thumped her finger on the receiver. "I didn't sleep very well. That was the insurance claims guy about the policy on Wiley. He was wondering about the medical report."

"They going to settle the claim since the doc signed off on accidental death?" he asked and caught a little glob of frosting as it landed on his chin.

Bev took a sip of coffee. "I told him we were checking a few more leads. They're not anxious to pay out $50,000 and will stall if they can."

Jim popped the last bit of roll into his mouth and chewed slowly. "You hoping the delay will rattle Karen enough to see if she'll slip up?"

How nice that Jim was so astute as this hour. "It could happen."

Jim pitched the lid of his coffee cup into the trash. "Trust me, that one won't budge. You might consider swinging by the Scarlet Macaw, though. Farmer is probably starting to relax and there's always a chance he's said something he shouldn't," Jim pointed out. "He wouldn't be the first guy to start mouthing off if he's had one too many and thinks he pulled one over on us."

Bev touched her fingertips lightly to her temples and massaged in tiny circles. Jim might be right, although she wanted to think that Dillworth wouldn't withhold that kind of information. Well hell, she was at a dead end, so it couldn't hurt and if nothing else, she'd get a good cup of coffee. She called and Dillworth said he'd be glad to talk with her.

The meeting was pleasant and Dillworth served her a robust Costa Rican coffee. The only useful piece of information was when told her that the diving investigator had been in town. That gave her a perfect excuse to meet with Farmer again. After all it was reasonable for her to ask about their report. Well, maybe it wasn't the precise conclusion that a lawyer would come to, but maybe Farmer wouldn't think to ask one.

Bev stopped by the Adventures Below dive shop and waited until the young man behind the counter finished writing in a ledger and looked up at her.

"Sorry," he said with a smile, "but I needed to get that reservation logged. Can I help you with something?" He was about her age and had the straight dark hair and almost black eyes that looked like a mix of Hispanic and Seminole. He was wearing a navy blue Adventures Below T-shirt, but Bev couldn't remember having seen him before.

"No problem, I'm Beverly Henderson, with the police department," she said. "Is Mr. Farmer here?"

Shades of Murder

"Hey cool – you're one of the detectives aren't you?" the young man asked and shook her hand enthusiastically. "I wasn't working that day, but it was really something about Greg, huh? Are you guys still checking it out?"

"Well, there are a few details left," Bev said politely. "And is Mr. Farmer here, by any chance?"

"Oh, I'm Danny and I work the shop part time," he said with a grin. "And no, Tom is out on a charter, but he'll be back around four o'clock. I'm trying to help him get caught up," Danny volunteered. "He's been trying to get out of the shop more and this afternoon's group was the one they had to reschedule from the other day. You know, the day with Greg." He dropped his voice slightly and shrugged. "Business has been down some and Tom needed to make this dive up – some regular clients and you want to keep them happy."

Bev remembered Dillworth's comment about how Farmer had lost some of his regular customers and Danny seemed eager to talk. It shouldn't be difficult to get him to talk about the business partners.

"I don't remember there being other divers that day," Bev said.

Danny shook his head and tapped the ledger he'd been writing in. "Oh, I don't mean they got bumped because of the accident. Tom had me cancel them the day before because he was having a little trouble with the boat and didn't want to take it out twice that day. He didn't want to cancel the tourists in case they couldn't reschedule," he said. "Bummer, huh? I mean if they'd had to get back for an afternoon dive, maybe Greg wouldn't have had time for the free dive that day. Or if he'd gone on the afternoon dive and done the free dive then, more experienced guys would have been on board and maybe could have helped. I guess you never know, do you?"

"No, I guess not," Bev said. Something about his statement didn't sound right, but before she could ask another question, a middle-aged couple entered the shop, smiled in greeting and walked over to one of the mannequins. The woman lifted some kind of instrument for a closer look and the man spoke over his shoulder.

"Hey Danny, no rush, but when you're finished, let's talk about this regulator – we're going to replace ours," he said and leaned forward when the woman made a comment to him.

"I'll be there in just a minute," Danny said with a grin and then whispered to Bev, "This could be a big sale – they always buy more than they start out to."

If he hadn't been at work the day of the drowning, Bev knew she didn't have a good reason to delay him. She handed him her card and tried to keep from smiling as he nearly raced around the counter to the couple. She didn't know how good a salesman he was, but at least he was enthusiastic.

She was trying to place what had seemed odd about the cancelled dive when she stepped out of the door and saw Silsby drive into the small parking lot.

She got out of her car, leaned against the front fender and waited for Bev to approach.

"Ah, Miss Silsby," Bev said. "Fancy seeing you here. Mr. Farmer isn't in if that's who you're looking for."

The young woman lit a cigarette with a silver lighter. "I was, but you being here saves me a call," she said. "I had an interesting conversation with an insurance investigator a little while ago and I think it's time we have a talk."

Bev looked her up and down. Silsby wasn't displaying her cleavage for a change, although the pair of jeans she wore were tight enough that they might have been painted on.

"I'm not sure you want to hear what I'm thinking," Bev said.

Karen blew a thin stream of smoke out her nostrils. "Bev, if you don't mind me calling you Bev, what you're thinking is pretty goddamn obvious. I'd just as soon take a walk along the dock if that's okay with you and keep this private. Oh, and do drop the *Miss Silsby* piece – it reminds me too much of a bitchy, old-maid English teacher I once had."

Bev assumed that was intended as a barb, but she'd be

damned if she'd take the bait. She gestured forward and fell into step as they strolled to the end of the walkway and came to a halt at an empty slip. Silsby, or *Karen* rather, ground her cigarette out on the heel of her sandal, turned sideways to face Bev and braced one hand on the railing. Her hair was held back by a red paisley scarf that matched her shirt.

"Let's not waste each other's time," she began. "I assume you've given me a role in whatever scenario you've developed because of the insurance money."

Bev slipped her sunglasses into her purse so she could have eye contact with Karen. There was no need to evade the issue. "The money is part of it. The other is the relationship between you and Mr. Farmer."

Karen's voice became reflective and for a moment she stared past Bev in the direction of the dive shop. "The relationship with Tom is easy to explain. I've told you already that I like Tom, but there's nothing else to it; at least not on my part. He's a decent man and quite frankly, Greg didn't do right by him, but that was between them. To be honest, all I know about their disagreements is that Greg was cutting some corners that Tom told him could get them in trouble, but I don't know the details. The only thing Greg ever said was that he would probably let Tom buy him out, but at a premium price."

Karen waved her hand in the air as though to dismiss the thought and lit another cigarette. "So, just for the hell of it, let's say you accept my version of the friendship. That still leaves the money, which I understand is a traditional motive for murder, so to speak. And since you absolutely exude disapproval of everything you think you know about me, I can see how me being involved makes for an attractive get-rich sort of situation," Karen said and flicked ash into the bay. "The truth, however, is that rather than me cooking up whatever scheme you've designed, I just happened to get lucky for once in my life."

Bev held back a snort. "Are you going to tell how unfair I'm being to you?"

Karen appraised Bev and blew a perfect smoke ring before she answered. "Look, I grew up in Miami in what we'll call one of the less desirable districts; hardly the section that the tourist bureau shows off. You know the kind I mean."

Bev nodded and wondered what that had to do with her comment. Every big city laid claim to vice-ridden pockets if that's what she was alluding to.

"I'm not going to get into a lot of detail here, but I don't have a clue who my father was and my mother died of a heroin overdose when I was fifteen," Karen said quietly. "By the time she died I knew my way around the streets and it wasn't what you'd define as sharing in the American dream. I'd seen what happened to some of the kids who'd been in the care of Social Services and I wanted no part of it. I could pass for eighteen and sure, I started dancing and I knocked out some skin flicks because that was what I had to work with. I made money and damn near every penny went to get me through school."

"Oh yeah, another aspiring co-ed," Bev said impatiently. "How fortunate that Mr. Wiley came along to save you."

Karen matched Bev's impatience. "Give me a fucking break. Greg was a son-of-a-bitch, albeit it a good-looking one, and he was a means to an end just like the dancing and the movies. We had a mutual understanding of what we both wanted. Just like I told you before, I'm on the verge of finishing my degree and I have a job interview lined up in Denver and one in Seattle pending receipt of my final grades. I got what I needed from Greg and I would be on my way even if he was still alive."

"A spare fifty thousand makes for a nice start," Bev said.

"That's right," Karen replied with no sign of embarrassment. "It sure does. Look, I really don't give a flying fuck about your opinion of me. What I do care about is you dragging this business out because, whether you like it or not, I had nothing to do with Greg's death. I mean, let's get real here; $50,000 sounds like a lot of money, but I picked a very marketable field and any respectable job offer will start me out in good shape. The fact that I shook my tits in front of a bunch of guys to get extra tips doesn't make me stupid or criminal. The money I made means I don't start out in debt and you can get on some moral high horse if you like, but I sure as hell wouldn't have paid my bills in full if I'd been a goddamn waitress in some coffee shop. Fifty grand is nice, but I was set up okay without it."

She did sound convincing.

"And Mr. Farmer? He was a long way from being okay in his business wasn't he?" Bev countered.

Karen's eyes clouded briefly and she softened her tone. "Tom may have had good reasons for wanting Greg out of the way, but even if he had become that desperate, I still don't see how he could have possibly pulled it off. There were two people in plain sight for God's sake. Why can't you accept that?"

She caught her lower lip between her teeth and frowned. "Unless what you're figuring is that Greg started having problems and Tom didn't react as quickly as he could have. I guess he sure as hell would have been tempted."

Was Karen being perceptive or manipulative? Suppose the prime reason for this conversation was for Karen to innocently come to this conclusion and lead away from a premeditated act?

"Do you think that's likely?" Bev asked matter-of-factly.

Karen looked in the direction of the dive shop again and then stared into Bev's eyes. "I'd rather that not be the case."

"An interesting phrasing," Bev said as Karen stubbed out the second cigarette.

"And even if he did do that, I think you'd have a hell of a hard time proving it," she said. "And if that's what he did, then it means he merely took advantage of an opportunity which occurred and since I was nowhere around, I could hardly be a part of it, now could I?" She turned to leave and stopped. "Look, maybe you are on to something, but hurry this up, will you? I don't want to hang around a day longer than necessary and risk losing one of these interviews."

"I'll be done with it as soon as I find out what really happened," Bev said evenly. "So if Mr. Farmer tells you anything that might be useful, how about give us a call?"

Karen almost smiled. "Sure Detective, as soon as Tom confesses his sins, I'll pick the phone up. In the meantime, I think I'll go finish the last paper that's due."

Bev stood on the dock and watched her walk away. She'd spent one summer working with the Jacksonville police department in the tough section of that city and it had been a disturbing nine weeks. She was neither particularly squeamish nor naïve, but she'd seen the people who plied those streets with their hardness and acceptance of defeat. If that had been Karen's upbringing, then using her body to get ahead would have been something she learned early on. That would explain her attitude and her attraction to Greg as a quicker way out.

Bev bounced her keys in the palm of her hand as she walked back to her car. She didn't like Karen and hadn't from almost the moment she'd met her. It was possible that she'd been too fast to draw her into the formula, but she was reluctant to back away from an idea that fit so well.

Karen's question about Farmer not helping Greg the way he'd claimed to tracked with the rumor Aunt Lorna had passed along and with what the coroner could support. The problem with buying into that idea was the timing.

Could Farmer really have been so fortunate as to have a chance like that handed to him right before an investigation commenced that could have put him out of business? It didn't make sense; it just didn't make sense. If Karen wasn't involved, then she was very lucky with the insurance money and if Wiley coincidentally presented Farmer with an easy way out of his problems, then he too was incredibly lucky. What were the odds of both of them being that lucky at the same time?

Chapter Sixteen

When Bev returned to the office, there was a note for her to call Kyle. He said his trip had been productive, double checked about their date and asked if she was free for a late lunch. She bypassed another chance to play hard to get and agreed to meet him at one o'clock.

Jim was rummaging in the filing cabinet and acted as if he hadn't heard the conversation.

"You find out anything that you liked?" he asked and sat heavily in his chair.

Bev rubbed her hand across her forehead. "A couple of things and it so happens that I ran into Karen Silsby. She thinks we're being unfair to her."

Jim lifted his hands. "She may be right about that," he said.

Bev puffed her cheeks out and exhaled. "I'm not ready to concede that yet and besides, you know that something's not right about this whole business."

Jim popped the top off a bottle of pills Bev didn't recognize and shook one onto the desk. "I'm with you about that, but the chances of proving anything are fading and the fact that Karen gets under your skin doesn't mean she's involved. The fifty grand is suspicious and could turn out to be exactly as she claimed. People win the damn lottery with odds of millions to one and this isn't so much different. Or if Farmer did pull this off and he knew about the insurance, maybe he did it to help Karen without her knowledge. If he's got the hots for her or even if he figures that's icing on the cake for getting rid of Wiley, that plays okay, too."

Bev ignored the last comment and looked at the note on her desk. "I'll tell Kyle about the test results and see what he has to say. By the way, what's that you're taking?"

Jim grimaced and swallowed the pill. "Some shit the doc gave me and if the assistant DA wants to spend any time on this, his interest is probably more in how cute your ass is instead of what happened to Wiley."

"You have a one track mind," Bev said and injected as much indignation as she could considering how their date had turned out. Jim didn't pick up on her comment and she looked closely at him. He wasn't in the prime of health on the best of days and he was looking more florid than usual. Bev was going to ask what the pills were for, but Kevin came in and handed two papers to Jim.

"Talk about not being much help," Jim said and thrust the papers in Bev's direction after a quick scan. "These are the photos from Mississippi of the guys wanted for questioning that may, or may not, also be the ones knocking off the stores. These two bozos are about as ordinary as you can ask for."

Bev took the papers and examined them thoroughly. It was the notice for William Thomas (Willie) Denton and Harold Robert (Hal) Grayson; wanted for questioning in a triple murder and as potential suspects as the Devil's Duo. Both men were average height, weight and build. Denton had short brown hair and brown eyes; Grayson had short black hair and brown eyes. Neither man had known scars, birthmarks, or tattoos. They were the kind of men that you could pass on a street and never notice; the kind that were indistinguishable in a crowd.

They could check quietly into off-road motels and be virtually anonymous. Even if every such motel in the three-state area was canvassed, it wasn't unusual for travelers to pay the low rates in cash and rarely did a desk clerk actually check a car tag or other form of identification. If the men were careful, and so far they had been, they would raise no alarm. The car listed as Denton's was a five year old green Cavalier and if these two were the Devil's Duo, Bev was certain that the registered tags would not still be on it. Maybe the two would slip up soon or they'd get stopped for something like a broken taillight – that sort of thing had happened before.

She deposited the papers in a desk drawer, opened the file on the Wiley case as a twinge of self-doubt flashed across her mind. Junior detective or not, she trusted her instincts. There was a chance she was wrong about Karen, but there was no way in hell she was wrong about Farmer. She snapped her fingers – *Danny and the cancelled dive*. Jim looked up in question.

"Hey Jim, I met this guy at Adventures Below – Danny, a part timer, and he mentioned that Farmer had been having trouble with the boat and they had cancelled a group dive scheduled for that afternoon. Did Farmer bring it up when you interviewed him?"

Jim shrugged and shuffled some file folders. "Doesn't ring a bell and I don't remember anyone else at the shop that day. Besides, what's that got to do with anything?" He found his notebook and turned the pages.

"Danny said he wasn't at work that day," Bev replied. "And I don't know, but it just sounded odd. From what Dillworth told me, I would think Farmer wouldn't want to be turning away customers if he could help it."

Jim checked his notes and shook his head. "Nothing here."

Bev tugged her ear. "Didn't the Marine Patrol say the *Dare Devil* followed them in? They must have been moving pretty fast and to be honest, the boat looked fairly new when I was on it."

Jim flipped another page, read through it and tossed the notebook back onto the pile. "Maybe Farmer decided there wasn't a problem or maybe he got it fixed quicker than he expected. I don't see that it matters."

That's because you've about made up your mind to believe Farmer, she thought and glanced at her watch to keep from blurting the sentence out. She did a quick calculation and spun her chair toward the corner of the office.

"Hey Jim, I'm going for a jog and then a late lunch. Want to come do a few laps with me?"

Jim moved his arm back and forth in a drinking motion. "Unless the laps are around a bar I'm not interested, Kid."

"I'm going to talk you into one of these days," Bev said out of habit, grabbed her black gym bag and left for the health club. It was a spacious, plain red brick building with adequate, if not state-of-the-art, equipment and was located on the edge of a park close to the police station. Bev had a regular five mile route mapped out, although she'd have to keep it at a three miler if she was going to be on time with Kyle.

Bev changed, went outside and worked her way through her stretches. Her first track coach had lectured her repeatedly about the value of stretching until it was an ingrained action even though she no longer ran competitively. Her mother had insisted that the boxes of trophies be moved out of the house and Bev thought they were somewhere in the back of her father's workshop. She'd considered retrieving them for her own place and then decided those glory days were gone. She'd switched to charity races, but didn't spend time training for one of the top slots. Not that she didn't still take an occasional medal and she knew there were only one or two guys at work who could match her in a footrace. Better yet, they knew it too.

Bev had the park almost to herself and enjoyed the rhythm of her movement as she breathed in the smell of newly mown grass. The outdoor scent triggered the thought of the previous Saturday and lunch with Kyle. She wondered if it would be awkward to see each other for the first time since their afternoon of what had been genuinely great sex. She felt a fluttery sensation in the pit of her stomach at the memory, but was she really comfortable with the spontaneous way she'd reacted to him?

He was probably expecting the same kind of response again and she wasn't sure if she wanted him to have those expectations. If she decided to say no, how was she going to explain it? On the other hand, she shouldn't have to explain, at least not if Kyle was the kind of guy she thought he was. Christ, there were moments when the whole business of dating, sex and figuring out relationships seemed like more trouble than it was worth. She turned into the final quarter mile of her run and increased her speed - she'd just have to see how she felt on Saturday.

The locker room was empty and after she dressed she did a quick check in front of the full length mirror. She was glad she'd worn the burgundy twill pants suit – it was a great color on her and she twisted for a view of her butt. Good, the line of her slacks was smooth – no sign of strain against her hips.

She arrived at the Corner Café before Kyle and took a table where she could see the door. The Corner, as it was commonly called, had been serving breakfast and lunch since the original municipal offices had been constructed and changes in the downtown area were captured in black and white photographs that hung on the walls. A counter with red vinyl padded stools fronted the kitchen area and the large room was filled with Formica topped tables. Squares of deep red and white tiles alternated on the floor and the Corner still served thick, creamy milkshakes created from an old fashioned machine.

Kyle was only a few minutes behind her and he smiled as he approached the table. His charcoal gray, double-breasted suit was a nice fit – not every guy could wear a cut like that. The white shirt was a little conservative, but a green print tie added a splash of color.

"Hi, how are you?" he asked with a quick kiss to her cheek.

"Oh, pretty good," she replied and handed him a menu. "You had a stack of work waiting when you got back?"

"More than I expected," he said and nodded to the waitress who appeared immediately. "And unfortunately, I have to do a couple of things I hadn't planned on this afternoon, so I'm afraid this will be a quick lunch. Are you ready to order or do you need more time?"

Bev shook her head. "A club sandwich is fine for me."

"Make that two," Kyle said and smiled again at Bev when the waitress left. "Oh, before I forget, is there any place special that you want to go on Saturday?"

A straight forward question with no innuendo. That was a good start. "Well, we don't have unlimited choices around here," she said. "The Paradisio does some good veal and pasta if you want a change from seafood."

"Yeah, I was there a while ago and liked it," Kyle said. "Is seven o'clock too early? And where should I pick you up? It occurred to me that I don't know your address."

Bev laughed. "Seven is fine and to be honest, I'm not sure where I'll be. My parents' house probably, although the apartment may be ready. I'll call and let you know."

The waitress brought their sandwiches and refilled the tea glasses. They ate quickly and made small talk between bites. Bev hesitated to mention the Wiley case since Kyle was in a hurry.

"Oh, I almost forgot to ask," he said and ate the last potato chip on his plate. "Any luck on the medical report from your dead guy?"

Bev tugged her left ear. "It came up clean, I'm afraid, but I'm going back through all the notes again. We were so sure evidence would show up in the tests that we stopped looking for other clues. I have to find whatever we missed and go from that angle."

"That's too bad," Kyle said and took the slip that the waitress left on the table. "I thought you might really be on to something."

Bev pursed her lips slightly and stood up. "All I said was that the medical report didn't show anything. If I recall an earlier discussion you and I had, you agreed a negative medical report wouldn't mean we had to give up."

Kyle turned his head as they walked to the register at the front of the café and he paid the cashier. "I didn't say you should give up, but I was hoping for physical evidence," he said and held the door open. "Otherwise, it points a lot more to negligence, if that."

Bev stepped into the parking lot and narrowed her eyes. "It's not like I've kept it a secret that there's more to this than negligence, for Christ's sake. Don't tell me you're going to roll over along with everybody else." Bev remembered Jim's crack about Kyle's real interest in the case. The thought rankled even though she didn't think it was true.

Kyle stopped at her car and held up his hands. "Whoa, I'm not looking to get on your bad side."

Bev brushed past him and opened the car. She sat down with the door ajar and looked up at him. "I'd sure hate to think you've just been humoring me," she said flatly. "Especially if the reason was to get into my pants."

Kyle sighed and leaned his hand on the top of her car. "Cut me some slack, will you? First of all, I wouldn't do that and second, I'm more than willing to go after whatever charge we can make stick, but Bev, I've got to have something more than your gut feelings," he said with a hint of exasperation. "You're too smart not to know that."

Bev bit her lower lip and slammed the door shut. There's was no sense in taking her frustration out on Kyle – he wasn't being any more negative than Jim. "Look, I know I can't back this up yet, but I've got some more things to check out," she said more sharply than she intended. "I'll figure it out though, so be ready when I do."

Kyle either didn't notice her tone or chose to ignore it. He raised his hands and gave her a lop-sided grin. "Yes ma'am, whatever you say – I am at your service."

And exactly what kind of service would that be? Bev made a half-hearted gestured and drove away without asking. Physical evidence was what he had been hoping for – well hell, what did he think she had wanted?

The uselessness of the medical report buzzed in her head like a mosquito in her ear and as she passed Chief Taylor's office she saw Jim inside with the door closed. They looked at her through the glass and she could tell by the expression on their faces that they must have been talking about her.

And just what was that about – something else Jim could pass on to Myrtle?

She punched in her voice mail code and retrieved the message that Farmer could talk to her if she could come by around four o'clock.

"Hey Kid," Jim said quietly and lowered himself onto his chair. The metallic creak she usually ignored caused her to flinch. "Claude and I were having a little talk."

Oh, like she wouldn't have noticed? "Yeah, I saw and I bet I know what it was about," she snapped. "You were no doubt discussing how to tell me to lay off this case and be willing to accept Farmer's bullshit story."

Jim looked at her strangely. "What put you in such a bitchy mood? Lunch with the counselor not go well?"

"There's not a damn thing wrong with my mood," Bev shot back and picked her notebook up off the desk. "And I'm getting tired of everyone treating me like I don't know what I'm doing." She shoved her chair back and grabbed her purse. "I have a couple of errands to run and then I'm going to see Farmer, so if you don't mind I'll pass on any condescending little lecture you may have prepared," she said pointedly.

Jim sighed and looked puzzled at what she knew he was chalking up as an over-reaction. "Okay, tomorrow might be a better time. I'll see you in the morning."

Bev walked away briskly and pretended not to see the head wags of the uniformed cops who would presume her hormones were out of control. She was already at her car when she took a deep breath. *What in the hell was wrong with her and why had she flared up like that?* She almost returned to apologize, but there wasn't a graceful way to do it. Besides, Jim had a tough hide and she could always bring him a bag of donuts in the morning to make amends.

Chapter Seventeen

Bev hissed impatiently when the third traffic light in a row turned red as she approached. She lurched forward when it was finally green and nearly popped the clutch. She whipped into a parking spot in front of the automated teller machine closest to the station and blinked her eyes when she saw a *Sorry for the Inconvenience* repair sign tapped over the screen. Christ, what a pisser!

She drove to the bank behind a dump truck spewing black diesel smoke and ground her teeth when she saw that the drive-through window at the bank was blocked for re-paving. She thought about leaving, but she was almost out of cash and there were only a few cars in the parking lot. She went inside and smiled weakly as the rotund lady in front of her chirped, "Oh hi, it's a lovely day today, isn't it?"

She stepped forward and by the time she retrieved an envelope from her enormous handbag, it became apparent that she was oblivious of the fact that she could have completed her deposit slip before walking up to the clerk's window. Bev fumed at the woman's incessant chatter and forced a neutral expression on her face when she finished and said, "Now you have a nice day, honey," in parting.

Bev arrived in the Adventures Below parking lot fifteen minutes later than she'd intended and sat in the car to try and squelch her irritation. Christ, this was the first time she would really talk to Farmer and being on edge would interfere with her ability to control the conversation. She had to calm down and focus.

She wanted to project a friendly, inquisitive manner and see if Farmer would volunteer something she could use without him perceiving her suspicions. Not yet, not until she had something more substantial. *Damn the lack of physical evidence! All she needed was one little piece to use as leverage!* Of course if he were aware of the rumors being whispered about, he would have had plenty of time to polish his story. Well, there was only one good way to find out.

Bev took several deep breaths and watched two men at the far door carry air tanks from a white van into the building.

Bev gave herself one more mental shake. When she'd regained her composure, she entered the dive shop and removed her sunglasses, although her eyes needed little time to adjust. The glass windows across the front added to the light from the overhead florescent fixtures.

Farmer was behind the counter working at the computer terminal and he signaled that he would be through in a minute. Bev hadn't looked around much when she'd been talking with Danny so she took the time to examine the area. There were two free standing display cases and the room seemed to be well stocked. The mannequin nearest the door was the one the couple had been interested in. It was attired in a colorful dive ensemble like the others arranged throughout the store and the wall had shelving filled with more equipment. Poster-sized photographs of marine life were interspersed among the shelves. A small round table with chairs was positioned near a credenza that held a two burner stand; one pot filled with coffee and the other hot water. Bev couldn't tell, but she assumed the small basket sitting alongside held tea bags and condiments. A number of magazines were fanned across the open space of the credenza and a large commercial size water bottle stood between the piece of furniture and a door that led toward the back.

The adjacent wall contained a collection of plaques from the city, photographs of Farmer with a Boy Scout Troop and one with a younger Farmer in a naval uniform at what appeared to be a ceremony. Bev was looking at the underwater cameras when Farmer walked over.

"Sorry to keep you waiting," he said politely. "We can

talk here or in the office, but there's a classroom in back that might be better. Would you care for something to drink?"

"The classroom sounds fine and I don't need anything, thanks," she said. "I guess you'll be looking for a new partner," she continued as Farmer led her out of the main room. The double doors to the left were open and Bev saw the two men who'd been hauling the air tanks. She cocked her head at an unfamiliar sound.

"That's the air compressor," Farmer explained. "They're refilling the tanks. As to your question, a new partner won't be necessary. I've managed to re-establish enough capital to stay independent." He stepped aside and motioned Bev into the classroom.

Six tables divided into two rows of three faced a large white board at the front of the room and a series of training aids lined the walls. Bev sat in one of the armless wooden chairs and Farmer grabbed a chair across the table from her.

"Mr. Wiley's heirs aren't interested in the shop?"

Farmer shook his head. "No. Greg's father has no desire to maintain a part of the business and we've worked out an equitable arrangement. Danny, the boy you met earlier, will probably come on full time and there are independent instructors around who can help teach classes on a part time basis."

"It must be a big relief for you," Bev said. "I understand there had been some difficulties with combining management styles." It was a probing question, but if Farmer thought he was in the clear, he might not rise to it.

He sighed very slightly. "Detective Henderson, I see no reason for us to play games. I presume that what you're leading up to is that you no longer, if you ever did, consider Greg's death to be an accident."

Well, that took care of that. Might as well go for the blunt approach. "There are too many coincidences, Mr. Farmer. You stood to gain too much from his death."

She was skirting the edge of when she should advise

Farmer of his right to an attorney, but if he brought it up, she'd back off.

He hesitated, although it seemed to be a thoughtful pause rather than one of reluctance. When he spoke his voice was steady. "Detective, I can see why you would be suspicious. I didn't mention the ill feelings between Greg and me during the first interview because I didn't think it was the appropriate time. There was no intent of deception and I apologize if I conveyed that to you or Detective Osborn."

An interesting position to take. Bev adjusted her tone to match his sincerity and switched to first names. That might throw him off guard. "Look Tom, and please call me Bev, there are a few points that I need to clarify. You've already mentioned buying the shop back and I heard about the investigation. I don't know anything about the dive business, but from what I understand that must have been disturbing for you."

Farmer's eyes clouded for a fraction of a second. "Of course it was disturbing; profoundly so. I'm certain Steve must have explained to you the gravity of being investigated for safety violations. And as you probably also know, those violations and others that weren't reported were committed by Greg. But you probably don't know that Greg had agreed to be out of town during the investigation so I could do as much damage control as possible. Since the particular incident in question had not resulted in actual harm to an individual, we were let off with a probationary period. I don't like that either, but at least I don't have to interrupt operations."

Bev arched her eyebrows. "Particularly not now that you're sole proprietor again?"

Farmer lifted his hands and dropped them to the table with no sound. "I see your point. Tell me Bev, do you have any idea what it's like to build up your own business? To take the chance to go out on your own, start from scratch and watch something grow?"

Bev leaned her forearms on the table and shook her head.

She'd listened to her father discuss it of course, but she wanted to keep Farmer talking.

He gestured around the room. "I know you don't dive, although you should try it sometime. Underwater is a fascinating world and I won't bore you with a description, but it's something I love. Running a dive business is hard, time-consuming work and a fourteen to sixteen hour day is standard. A shop like this doesn't operate with a big cash margin as my wife found out. Quite frankly between that and the hours I was putting in, it pretty well sealed the outcome of our marriage, and even that was something I could deal with. Losing the marriage was easier to take than having the business go under and I ran into some financial problems during the divorce."

He formed his fingertips into a steeple shape and was silently tapping them together. He didn't appear nervous, but paused and cleared his throat.

"It's embarrassing for me to acknowledge that I so poorly judged Greg's true character, although at the time I accepted his help, I was convinced it was my only choice and Greg could be quite charming and affable when he chose to be. As soon as it became obvious that I'd made a mistake, I began taking steps to put myself in a position to buy him out and dissolve the partnership as quickly as possible."

Bev watched him during the lengthy explanation and he kept his voice steady. It all sounded reasonable, just like it was supposed to.

"Look, I've talked to Steve and others," Bev said sympathetically. "I understand how you got jammed up with Wiley. In fact, he sounds like a real horse's ass and as far as we can tell, he wasn't any better with Karen. That had to have been tough to watch."

Farmer shifted his eyes rapidly at that. "I'd rather not bring Karen into this," he said softly.

Bev sounded as perplexed as she could. "Well Tom, you see, that's one of the other things I'm having trouble with. Karen is an attractive woman and as her friend she probably confided in you. It would be easy to see how you would develop feelings for her and Greg would have seen it too. I mean, it would be only natural for the two of you to argue about that. It just adds to the whole question of how bad things were between you and Greg."

Farmer's mouth compressed into a line. "I'm not the sort of man Karen would be interested in romantically, although yes, I have tried to be a friend to her. She deserves better than someone like Greg, yet in spite of that, she chose to stay with him. And as I'm sure you know, she'll be leaving town soon and I hope the best for her."

He didn't say anything about the insurance money and before Bev could bring the subject up, he caught her by surprise.

"Since we're speaking candidly, I assume that despite what the witnesses said, you believe I was somehow negligent and contributed to Greg's death?"

It was tempting to go for the shock effect and accuse him of murder, but she wanted to see where he might go with the negligence angle. After all, he was the one who put it into words first.

She leaned forward with her hands spread out, palms flat on the table. "Look, I know it was going to take time to buy Greg out and every day you spent as partners must have been stressful for you. Suddenly, the two of you are in the water and he starts having problems. A perfect opportunity presents itself and hey, who's to know if you're a little slower going to the rescue than you would have been if it was someone else? Is that how it happened, Tom – just a chance you couldn't pass up?"

"You do this quite well," he said with no hesitation, no waver in his voice, no fear of her question. He wasn't going to bite.

"You say you've talked to people about Greg. Then you must know that he was careless with others' lives and uncaring of them. His welfare and his alone mattered to him. He lived his life with the view that he could buy his way out of any damage he caused. He had neither a sense of personal responsibility nor remorse for any of his actions. Am I sorry he's dead? No. Am I better off now that he is? Yes. However Bev, that's not against the law. My statements are on record and I'm sorry that I can't tie up what you obviously consider to be untidy, loose ends."

Bev was sure that if she pressed him further, it would only make him more cautious and she couldn't risk that. She wanted to keep him thinking that she was a step behind him. Well she was a step behind him, but she sure as hell didn't plan to stay there.

She stood and shrugged. "Okay Tom, I don't want to be unfair here, but it would be sloppy police work if I didn't run down these details before we closed the books."

Farmer inclined his head. "I can see you're a dedicated person and even though it's easy for me to say that it should be an open and shut case, I understand your concerns. I'll cooperate however I can, but naturally I'd like to put this to rest as soon as possible."

As if that was unexpected. "Yes of course," Bev replied. "I appreciate your time this afternoon and I would like to have a copy of the report you filed with the Diver's Alert Network. Steve told me that was routine in situations like this."

"I'll get it from the office," Farmer said and stood up.

They walked silently back toward the main part of the shop and Tom entered the office. Bev waited for him by the front door and quickly ran through what he'd told her. Open about the problems with Greg, but had emphasized Wiley's shortcomings, too. *Misjudged him, careless of others* – it sounded like Dillworth and Harry.

Farmer was walking across the room with an envelope in his hand when Bev remembered the cancelled dive. She couldn't put her finger on it, but it still bothered her. "Oh by the way," she said, "Danny said something about problems with the boat and that you had to postpone a group scheduled to dive the other day. I guess the problem has been solved though."

He handed her the envelope. "The boat?" he asked and widen his eyes. "Oh yes. It turned out to be a minor problem, but Danny had rescheduled the group and it didn't seem practical to try and contact them on such short notice. Why do you ask?"

He had recovered almost instantaneously and Bev knew she would have missed the quiver in Farmer's voice if she hadn't been listening for it. *What had startled him about the question? Why was it important?*

"Oh, it's just that the *Dare Devil* seemed like a fairly new boat – not like one you would have problems with," Bev said.

"You are observant," he replied. "Greg ordered the *Dare Devil* about six months ago, but like I said, it was a minor problem that took less time than I expected to repair." He took a step toward the door and paused. "Is there anything else I can do for you?" he asked and pushed the door open a crack.

Bev smiled as though she'd gotten what she wanted. "No and I'm glad we were able to talk so openly. I know you're anxious to get this behind you."

He nodded without further comment and stood in the doorway as she returned to her car.

She checked her rearview mirror as she exited the parking lot and saw that he hadn't moved. Chief Taylor could scoff all he wanted and even if both Jim and Kyle were now doubting her theory, Farmer had openly admitted he was better off with Wiley dead. Okay, that wasn't a crime, but had he been rehearsing that line for the time this conversation would take place? He'd been at ease for most of the conversation, but she'd shaken him just a bit. Was it the cancelled dive or something else? Maybe there would be some kind of discrepancy in what he'd told them and what he'd reported. After all, Dillworth wasn't directly connected with the event and had she not heard about Dillworth from Harry, she would never have met him. And if she hadn't met Dillworth, she wouldn't have known about a separate report.

It would be best if she read the report, then began from the first page of her notes and reviewed things in a methodical fashion, but she was tired from her lack of sleep and the discordant afternoon. She'd be more productive in the morning if she gave herself some breathing room and got a little rest. Well, a cold draft or two at Harry's wouldn't hurt either.

Chapter Eighteen

Bev postponed the thought of Happy Hour at Harry's and drove back to the office to write up her notes. She typed a nearly verbatim account and entered the new points that she wanted to pursue. She decided not to bounce any more ideas off Jim until she'd read the report and their combined notes again. He and Chief Taylor were gone and she worked undisturbed for almost an hour.

It was after six o'clock when she logged off the computer and the effort had drained away most of the negative feelings that had built up during the day.

Bev rolled her neck clockwise, then counterclockwise and thought about calling Kyle's office to see if he was in. Probably not and she remembered that he had once mentioned that Bojangles was his regular after work stop. It wasn't out of the way and a cold beer there was as good as at Harry's. If she happened to run into Kyle, that would give her an opportunity to see if he had taken offense at her lunchtime moment of pique.

She stopped on her way out to speak with the duty officer and arrived at Bojangles in time to slide into a parking space a row behind Kyle's Explorer. She entered the restaurant and blinked her eyes at the kaleidoscopic impact of the colored lights against the dimmed interior.

Bojangles was the town's claim to a slice of New Orleans and they decorated with large brand name beer signs, bright neon outlines of jazz instruments along the walls and a glass tile ceiling that enhanced the effect.

Bev stepped to the edge of the lounge area, scanned the length of the bar and spotted Kyle near the far end. Good, the stool to the right of him was empty and his back was to her. She was stopped for a few minutes by two acquaintances from the health club. They exchanged greetings and when she took a rain check on their invitation to join them in the dining room, she walked quickly in Kyle's direction.

Bev was about to say hello when he shifted his position as a woman to his left swiveled her stool and in doing so, leaned forward and pressed her breast against his arm. She ran her hand up his thigh and practically into his crotch and he smilingly shook his head. Jesus Christ, it was Karen Silsby! Bev nearly gasped in reflex and she opened her eyes wider in case she'd made a mistake. No, not hardly.

She didn't know if she'd actually made a sound, but both Kyle and Karen turned and saw her at the same time. Kyle jerked himself upright while Karen grinned in wicked amusement.

"Bev, what a surprise," Kyle stood and said. "I called earlier, but Jim said you were out." He glanced nervously at Karen as Bev tried to think of what to say.

What in the hell was he doing?

Karen calmly lit a cigarette and blew a thin stream of smoke. "Yes indeed, Bev, what a surprise," she said smoothly. "Won't you join us for a drink?"

Us? Join us? What us? Bev clenched her jaw tightly and stared into Karen's glittering eyes. The smirk on her face telegraphed that she had read Kyle's body language and she understood why Bev was at Bojangles. She cast her eyes sideways at Kyle and gave a little shrug.

Bev vaguely heard Kyle cough and say, "Oh, you already know each other. Well, that saves an introduction. Uh, what can I get for you, Bev?"

How could he pretend this was normal? "Not a damn thing," she said harshly and spun around. She felt Kyle's hand on her elbow and couldn't pull free without drawing attention to them. She whipped her head around and glared at him instead.

"Hey Bev, this isn't what it looks like," he said in a hushed voice. "In fact, I was going to try and catch you at home to

Shades of Murder

see if you were still pissed at me."

"Well if I wasn't, I sure as hell am now," Bev hissed. "And what in the name of Christ are you doing with her anyway? Never mind, I don't want to know," she said.

Her face was hot and she heard Kyle say something, but couldn't make the words out and didn't wait for him to repeat whatever it was. She shook loose from him and hurried outside.

She was almost at her car when Kyle called her name loudly enough to carry across the parking lot. He loped toward her with his jacket unbuttoned and his tie loosened.

He covered the distance in long strides, stopped in front of her and held his hands open. "Bev, stop for a second, will you? For crying out loud, I know what you're probably thinking, but it isn't like that and I didn't know she was a friend of yours. I mean, I assume that's part of why you're upset."

Bev couldn't believe what she was hearing. "A friend of mine? Are you trying to tell me you don't know who she is? You didn't exactly seem to be strangers."

Kyle ran his hand across his jaw. "Okay, then I'm not sure what's going on. Look, I met Monique not long after I moved here. I don't want to get into a lot of detail, but I was sitting at the bar, she came in and we started talking. I admit she gets kind of physical pretty quickly, but like I said, I didn't know you were going to show up. Not that it would have mattered if you hadn't," he added in a rush. "I really was planning to give you a call in about an hour."

"Monique? You think her name is Monique?" Bev snapped and then realized what he *wasn't* saying. She groaned. "You don't know her last name, do you?"

Kyle looked uncomfortable, opened his mouth and closed it without answering.

"You don't, do you?" Bev demanded.

"Uh no, I don't," he said reluctantly. "Do you want to please tell me what this is all about?"

Bev exhaled sharply. "Well Kyle, for starters, Monique is not her real name - it's a stage name she used to use and her last name is Silsby. That makes her Karen Silsby, the girlfriend of the very dead Greg Wiley. That's who the hell she is."

Kyle dropped his head and then looked at Bev as though he was hoping this was a bad joke. "Shit, are you serious?"

"Well, it sure as hell isn't something I would make up," Bev said and bit her bottom lip as she remembered the sensuous way Karen had leaned into him. "I'm not blind, Kyle – that grope I saw was pretty obvious. You're having an affair with her, aren't you?"

His answer was much too slow. "Well, I don't think you could call it an affair," he started hesitantly. "And it's not really still..."

Bev stopped him with a warning look. "Then what does that make it, Kyle? She's some kind of convenient sex partner? A cozy little arrangement so you don't even need to know her last name? Christ, I don't want to hear this," she said angrily.

"Bev, I can explain," Kyle said and reached out to her.

She turned to open her car and he pressed the palm of his hand against the door frame.

"Don't do this," he said urgently. "I swear I had no idea about the name and it's got nothing to do with us. I..."

Bev shoved his hand off her car and opened the door partway. "Christ Kyle, don't give me some bullshit line," she said and stopped as a car parked two slots down and laughter rolled from the open windows. *Oh great, a scene in the middle of the parking lot – that's what she needed.*

Kyle lowered his voice. "Look, let's go somewhere quiet to talk this out."

She bit her bottom lip until the trio in the car moved toward the building. Kyle started to say something else, but Bev's ears were pounding with anger and the thought of the two of them together naked merely added to the mental cacophony.

She shook her head and yanked the car door fully open. "Kyle, I can't think straight right now. Just give me some breathing room."

He ran his hand through his hair and stepped back, his face hard to read. "Yeah, right," he said as another car turned in with the music cranked to a loud volume and the bass pulsating from the speakers.

Bev jumped into the seat and clutched the steering wheel. Kyle stretched his hand out again, dropped it and turned away. Bev backed rapidly out of the parking lot and concentrated on breathing in and out calmly, although she could feel the pressure still rising in her chest. Even in her anger, she could tell that Kyle had genuinely not known who Karen was, but in a way, that was worse. If he was in the habit of having sex with a woman and didn't bother to find out what her last name was, what did that say for the heated afternoon they had spent together? That she was, after all, nothing more than the easy lay of the moment? Another notch on a bedpost?

Goddamn it, this was the very reason she never should have gone to bed with him the way that she did - she knew better than to rush into any kind of relationship. Not that she and Kyle had a relationship, but it had looked as if there was a real possibility. What an idiot she'd been not to have waited!

Bev slammed to a stop at a traffic light and ground her teeth again at what the scene must have been like – Kyle new in town, alone at the bar, either actively seeking companionship or just looking deliciously available. And Karen out on the prowl, no doubt wearing something low-cut and clinging. Two or maybe three drinks, a first, casual contact of her body against his and a purred, *"Hi, I'm Monique and I don't think we've met."*, or some such greeting. As the evening progressed had she laughed away the question of a last name or had there been enough booze flowing to have obscured little details like that? Bev thought back to the afternoon she'd seen Karen flaunting herself at the Scarlet Macaw and how eagerly the man had reacted to her come-on. Shit!

She turned into Harry's place, switched off the ignition, sat in the dark and fought the urge to shriek her anger. She could go home, but she needed distraction, not an empty house. No, what she needed was a cold beer and a kick in the ass for caring about Kyle Stewart in the first damn place.

Chapter Nineteen

The tables at Harry's were almost full and Bev slid onto one of the stools at the bar. *Good, no need for small talk right away.* She listened to the sounds of the crowd and the music and nodded when Harry eased behind the bar and pointed to the tap. He didn't ask how she was, but brought her a fresh mug when she guzzled the first one.

"I don't know what kind of day you've had, but you look like you need a hot roast beef with grilled onions and hot peppers," he said, patted his paunch and disappeared into the swinging door that led to a miniscule kitchen.

Bev started to protest and then realized he was right. Chicken soup might be good for a cold, but there was nothing like a spicy sandwich and icy beer for any problem involving a man.

She stayed for an hour and after two more beers and the hefty sandwich, her anger submerged beneath an overwhelming desire to shower and fall into bed. Home, a hot shower and no dreams – that was what she wanted. Everything would look better in the morning – it had to.

Sleep came quickly and when she heard a ringing she automatically reached for the alarm clock. She depressed the snooze button, saw it was a quarter after five, located the true source of the noise and fumbled for the telephone.

Chief Taylor's rumbling voice cut through her grogginess and she came fully awake when he told her that Jim had been taken to the emergency room with a heart attack. She was dressed and on her way to the hospital in less than twenty minutes. The traffic on the streets was limited to a couple of police cruisers, delivery trucks and the town's early risers having breakfast.

The donut shop where Jim was a regular wasn't opened yet although lights were on in the kitchen area and Bev thought of how often she'd warned Jim to switch to bran muffins. Maybe she should have nagged more.

She wheeled into the emergency room parking lot and dashed inside. Chief Taylor was at the nurses' station and looked calm even though that didn't necessarily mean he should be. "Morning Bev," he said with a smile. "Sorry to wake you, but I thought you'd want to know right away."

Bev hoped the smile was a good sign. "Thanks, I'm glad you did. How is he and where's Myrtle?" she asked.

Chief Taylor pointed to the Intensive Care unit down the hall. "He's stable and Myrtle is with him. He woke up with what he thought was heartburn and when the pain spread he had enough sense to dial 911. They got to him pretty quickly; otherwise it would have been a lot worse."

Bev yawned in spite of herself. "That's good to hear. Is he talking?"

The Chief nodded and poked into his pocket for a cigarette. He extracted one and rolled it between his thumb and forefinger. "A little, but before you go in I'll warn you that he looks like shit. I'm going outside for a smoke before I go into nicotine withdrawal. Come get me if Myrtle needs anything."

Bev refrained from saying that he could find himself in the same spot as Jim if he didn't quit smoking. Why were they all so stubborn about things like smoking and high cholesterol?

Bev walked slowly toward the glassed-in Intensive Care area and tried to prepare herself for the sight of Jim hooked to various monitors and other medical paraphernalia. The young nurse at the desk raised her head with what Bev knew would be the standard announcement that only family members and hospital personnel were permitted to enter.

"I know the rules," Bev said with a smile and held out her badge. "I'm his partner and I just wanted to get some idea of how he's doing." She could see the back of Myrtle's head as she sat next to Jim's bed and no doubt clasped his hand.

The nurse hesitated since her first sentence had been taken before she had a chance to give the spiel about no visitors. A tiny frown of concentration appeared across her broad forehead.

"Mr. Osborn has stabilized and the doctor will be back in another two to three hours," she said and evidently decided to be helpful rather than bureaucratic. "The children were here and left a bit ago, but Mrs. Osborn told them she would stay until one of them returned."

Myrtle may have sensed their discussion because she shifted around in the chair and nodded to Bev in greeting. She leaned over, said something to Jim and came out of the room. When she stood up, Bev's view was unobstructed and she could see how pallid his face was.

"Bev, what on earth are you doing here at this time of morning?" Myrtle asked and stepped into Bev's opened arms.

"The Chief called me," Bev said and felt the tension in Myrtle's body. "He figured I wouldn't want to find out from someone else. How are you doing?"

Like Bev's mother, Myrtle Osborn was shorter than Bev and had a round face that showed deep wrinkles around her eyes. Right now the strain emphasized the lines at the corners of her mouth as well. She was wearing a pair of slacks, one of Jim's shirts and bedroom slippers on her feet. She must have snatched up whatever clothing was close at hand.

She rested her head for a moment on Bev's shoulder and then gave a weak smile. "It was quite a scare for us, but the ambulance came in minutes and those boys did a wonderful job. Thank God it turned out to be a fairly mild attack as these things go." She glanced quickly toward the room and then looked at Bev with a bleak expression. "The doctor said he's out of immediate danger, but it looks like they'll have to go in for a bypass as soon as they can. There's a good bit of damage."

Bev inhaled silently and draped her arm around Myrtle's

taut shoulders. "Can I get you a cup of coffee or anything?"

She shook her head and glanced down the hallway. "I'm okay. The kids left a few minutes ago to clean up and they're going to bring me a change of clothes and some make-up, so at least I don't look like I don't know how to dress myself. I wouldn't mind a quick trip to the ladies' room though, if you could sit with Jim while I'm gone. I don't want him to be alone."

Bev looked at the nurse who nodded silent permission.

Bev slipped quietly into the room and shuddered at the multitude of tubes that linked Jim to the machines that kept track of whatever they kept track of.

Jim's eyes fluttered open and Bev saw the suppressed pain.

"Hey Kid," he said in an unfamiliar raspy voice. "How's Myrtle holding up?"

Bev sat on the edge of the single chair and leaned forward. "She's taking a little break. She's a bit ragged, but you know how tough she is."

"Don't I though," he said and unsuccessfully tried to shift his position. He settled for turning his head a few degrees. "She tell you they're going to cut me open and clear out the plumbing?"

Bev bit her lower lip and watched the muscles work in Jim's face with the effort it took for him to speak. "Yeah, but they've got it down these days to where it's like taking out your tonsils – a piece of cake for a guy like you."

He couldn't manage a smile. "Yeah, so they say. Hey Kid, I hate to admit how hard it is for me to talk, but I know you were hot about me and Claude talking yesterday."

Bev tugged at her ear and felt a stab of guilt - if Jim's attack had been more severe, her last words to him might have been her angry departure from the station. That would have been a terrible way to remember him.

"Come on Jim, you know I get carried away sometimes. We don't need to get into that right now."

He spoke so softly that Bev had to practically put her ear to his mouth to hear him. "It's important, but it wasn't

Shades of Murder

what you think, Kid. Ask Claude about it."

He closed his eyes again and Bev wasn't sure what else to say. She looked around and saw Myrtle standing in the hall with Chief Taylor.

"Sure Jim," she said. "I'll talk to him. You just take it easy and pay attention to the doctors for a change."

Myrtle finished her conversation and rejoined Bev. The women hugged goodbye under the observation of the nurse and Bev promised to contact her parents. She lingered for a moment with her hands pressed against Myrtle's forearms and insisted that she call no matter what the hour if there was anything that she could do.

Chief Taylor waited quietly until Myrtle nodded in agreement and then he and Bev walked out into the parking lot with their private thoughts of the man lying inside. The morning sky had lightened and pinkish clouds were splashed across the expanse of a pale gray sky.

The Chief lit a cigarette as soon as he passed the last *No Smoking Permitted* sign.

"Christ Chief," Bev said in exasperation. "You'll be in there before long if you don't quit those damn things."

He stopped at her car and propped one foot on the front bumper.

"Bev, I'm more aware than you that it could be me or your dad just as easily as Jim and we've all reached the age where these things can happen. Your good intentions are noted, but don't bust my ass about what you consider my bad habits." He smiled to take any sting out of his comment. "Did Jim say anything to you?"

Bev pulled her keys from her purse and held them in her hand. She fingered the silver metal disk with her initials engraved on it. The key chain had been a high school graduation present from the Osborns.

"He wasn't up for much chit-chat, but he told me to ask you about yesterday."

Chief Taylor blew a tiny cloud of smoke into the air. "I'll get to that in a minute. I was with Myrtle when the doctor gave her the news about taking Jim up to Miami for the surgery. He should come through it all right, but he'll need recovery time and who knows what shape he'll really be in."

Bev tilted her head back to scan the Chief's face. Was he saying what she thought he was saying? Was Jim not coming back at all?

"Jim hadn't said anything to you yet because he wanted to discuss it with me first," he continued. "The doctor had warned him that his blood pressure was elevated and he was at risk of a heart attack or stroke. That's what his new pills were for and we were checking to see if he had enough sick days built up to qualify for early retirement."

Bev inwardly flinched at how quickly she'd jumped to a negative conclusion when she'd seen the two men together. "That's what the deal was yesterday?"

The Chief nodded and pinched the cigarette out. The red tip fell to the asphalt and he slipped the butt into his jacket pocket. "That plus the fact that Jim wanted me to bring in someone who's been around, but would be willing to accept you as the senior detective."

Bev almost dropped her keys. "What?" She couldn't have heard him correctly.

Chief Taylor ran his hand across his bald spot. "I had the same reaction. I mean shit Bev, I was friends with your folks before they were married for crying out loud. Hell, I remember when your mother delivered you and I helped your dad take the training wheels off your bicycle. The two of us got drunk together the night he told me you'd decided to be a cop and neither of us thought you'd go through with it. I'm not as much of a dinosaur as you youngsters think sometimes and the truth is, you're damn good at this, but I'm not sure I'm ready for my head detective to be a woman still in her twenties."

Bev could hear him, but it was hard to absorb the words – this was too far off base from what she had imagined. "Well Chief, it's not like you have to make a decision right now," she said, uncertain of what the appropriate response might be. Was she supposed to be excited? Overly modest?

Forcefully confident? Guilty because this wouldn't be happening if Jim's heart was healthy?

Chief Taylor sighed. "We're not exactly in the midst of a crime spree, but no matter which way I decide, I've got to get another detective in and that means you'll be on your own for maybe as long as a month. You up to handling it?"

Bev blinked her eyes and answered as honestly as she could. "I don't see a problem with it, Chief, although I've got to say that I'm puzzled about how I'm supposed to be feeling. I'm not going to pretend that I didn't expect to take Jim's place some day – I just didn't go to bed last night thinking that it would be this morning."

The Chief smiled and turned toward his own car parked nearby. "Bev, don't get ahead of yourself on this one because we both need to think seriously about it. What I need more than anything is for you to keep your cool and not go into some over-achieving frenzy to prove how competent you are. Can you do that for me?"

Bev bit her bottom lip to keep from protesting his painfully accurate point about her character. "I'll try to hold myself back," she said and glanced away to the hospital. "I'd rather not have it come about this way, though."

Chief Taylor paused at his car with his hand on the door handle. "Like I said Bev, we're all getting older and there's not a hell of a lot we can do about it. See you at the office."

Bev watched him drive out of sight and then slid behind the wheel of her sports car. Her vision blurred and tears dribbled down her cheeks before she found a tissue. She wiped her eyes, blew her nose and struggled with a swirl of emotions.

What an incredible break for her and why did it have to be like this? Jim was only a year older than her father and it took little imagination to replace Myrtle with her mother and herself and her brother for the Osborn children. It wasn't something she wanted to experience any time soon - your grandparents were the ones who became frail, not your parents.

And what would Chief Taylor decide about a new

detective? Bev had already made department history, but to actually be in charge, notwithstanding the small size of the department, was an exhilarating thought. She deserved it, no matter how immodest that might sound, but the Chief could let her age, even more than her gender, sway his selection.

She gripped her hands around the steering wheel, leaned deep into the leather seat and tilted her head up. The sun broke free from the horizon - an orange tinted sphere suspended in a faint oval of clouds. She watched several cars filter into the parking lot and thought about the Chief's leadership style – old-school, not afraid to make tough calls and fair for the most part.

She sat up straight and cranked the car. She was doing exactly what she'd told Chief Taylor she wouldn't – trying to get ahead of him and predict what his decision might be. Time to get herself under control and think through things logically.

She'd have to focus on the work at hand and not expend a lot of energy worrying about what was going to happen in the next few weeks. They might not be overrun with crime at the moment, but she and Jim both kept busy with a lot of things that had nothing to do with solving cases.

Well, she wasn't going to get any of it taken care of if she didn't get her ass moving. She passed Bojangles on her way to the office and compressed her lips at the memory of Kyle's admission to her. What a disgusting, infuriating thing! And what in the hell was she going to do about it anyway?

She flexed her hands and slowed to let a jogger cross in front of her. Her disrupted relationship with Kyle would just have to wait for a while – she had more important matters to deal with than her personal life.

Chapter Twenty

Word about Jim had already spread through the station and dominated most conversations when Bev walked through the outer bay area. She heard the same words she'd said, "*Hadn't looked good...; ...not the best shape...*", but no one stopped her to talk - the Chief must have either told everyone what he knew or passed the information to Sheila.

Bev flicked the lights on in the office, looked around and thought about straightening up Jim's paper-strewn desk. She wasn't sure if there was anything in the disorganized stacks that needed immediate attention, but decided to leave the desk alone for a day or two. If something important was behind schedule someone would ask about it.

She booted up her computer and found an e-mail message from Dr. Cleary, the physiologist she'd talked to at the Scarlet Macaw. He'd attached a file with some articles about free diving, although the first one Bev checked was a copy of one she had previously downloaded from the Internet. She dumped the entire message into her electronic file when her telephone rang. Her parents. Christ, they weren't even in the same state; how had they heard so soon?

She gave them as much information as she could and wondered why she was apologizing to her mother for not having called them at 5:30 a.m. to tell them about Jim. She replaced the receiver and made another mental note of things she would never say to her own children if she ever had any.

The second light on the phone blinked and Kyle's voice caught her cold. She rubbed her eyes and briefly thought of hanging up without hearing what he had to say.

"Bev, I know you're upset, but I heard about Jim and I

wanted to ask if there was anything I could do," he said.

"Look Kyle," she said bluntly. "I appreciate you checking about Jim, but I've got too much to deal with right now and I need some time to think. I'll call in a few days if I'm ready to talk."

Kyle hesitated as if he wanted to say something else, but his reply was business-like. "Sure, I understand. Take it easy and I hope I see you around soon."

Bev tugged her ear when she hung up. If only she hadn't gone to Bojangles - what a mistake that turned out to be! Just more proof of the consequences of acting impulsively. Well, there was nothing she could do to change what had happened. Karen Silsby of all the women in town! Christ, it would have been better if he had laid her best friend. She did a couple of neck and shoulder rolls, but no good ideas leapt to mind as a result.

Kristie poked her head into the office. "Excuse me Detective, there's some lady on the telephone who won't give her name," she said. "She insisted on speaking with Detective Osborn and said it was important."

Bev completed one more neck roll and picked up the telephone as it rang through.

"Detective Henderson," she said crisply.

"I told that girl who answered that I wanted to talk to Jim Osborn," a wheezy woman's voice said.

"I'm sorry ma'am, but Detective Osborn isn't available," Bev said and thought the caller must be one of the only people in town who hadn't heard about Jim. "I'm sure I can help with whatever you need." Bev silently tapped her pen against the edge of the desk.

"It's about my ex-husband," the woman said. "The bastard is back and I want him the hell out of my house. Him and his two asshole pals. Jim told me that if the son-of-bitch showed up again I could call and he'd take care of it. Well, I'm calling."

Bev stifled a groan. She hated domestic situations and she had no idea why Jim would have been involved in one. "Excuse me, ma'am, but do you mean you have a restraining order that your ex-husband is violating?"

The woman's voice rose several decibels. "Listen, I don't have a goddamn piece of paper! He's been gone almost two years and then he shows up last night with these two scumbags tagging along and acts like he can waltz in here like we're still married. I want him the hell out. Jim promised me."

The woman's comment about two extra men caught Bev's attention. "Ma'am I didn't get your name, but we do want to help. I just need some more information."

There was another moment of silence and then the woman's voice lowered. "My name is Vera Newly, but my married name was Brewster. Look, Ray Bob and these two other guys are conked out and I was going to leave and go to my sister's, but damn it, it's my house and he's the one who doesn't belong. I want someone to come get all three of them the hell out," she repeated. "Ray Bob's probably got a warrant out on him from somewhere and the other two don't look any better."

"Okay Ms. Newly, I'll bring a couple of officers and we'll take care of it like Jim promised you," Bev said and scribbled the address on a pad. She wanted to ask about the two extra men, but she wasn't sure how long the woman could talk. *Who were they and where did they come from?*

She replaced the receiver and went into Chief Taylor's office. He looked up, closed the file he was reading and pushed it to the side of his desk. You couldn't tell he'd been up since early morning.

"Chief, you know a woman named Vera Newly or a guy named Ray Bob Brewster?"

He pushed his chair back and frowned. "Vera and Ray Bob? He's been gone a couple or three years. Why do you ask?"

Bev propped her hip against the arm of the chair centered in front of the Chief's desk. "This lady, Vera, just called and wanted Jim. She said her ex-husband was at her place with two guys and she wanted him out. Do you know the story, or is she some nut case?"

Chief Taylor grunted and swiveled his chair toward the door. "Vera's okay and it was a case Jim handled," he said simply.

Bev frowned. She couldn't recall any such case or Jim ever mentioning it. "That doesn't make any sense," she said and noticed that the Chief had rolled his eyes. "I would remember a case no older than that."

"Well, let's say it was an unofficial case," he said. "If Ray Bob is back, I imagine Vera wants him out alright. Take a couple of the uniforms. If he's been drinking, he'll be mean."

What was the Chief not telling her? Bev narrowed her eyes. "She said he'd brought two guys with him, Chief and she didn't sound very happy about it. In fact, she said something about checking for outstanding warrants."

Chief Taylor shrugged. "Vera could be right about that. Did she tell you who the other guys were?"

Bev shook her head. "No, but what's the story here, Chief? Is there something I should know? I mean, is this guy dangerous?"

Bev wasn't about to mention that she was intrigued with the idea of two suspicious men suddenly showing up in town. The chances of them being the Devil's Duo were remote, but it wasn't impossible.

The Chief reached into his desk drawer for his roll of antacid tablets. "Look Bev, Vera is an okay lady who's got lousy taste in men. She works at Gill's place and Ray Bob used to rough her up sometimes. I don't try and get inside women's heads, but she wouldn't press charges and there was nothing we could do about it. She finally decided to kick him out and he smacked her around when she told him to get lost. Jim had what you might call a long, personal talk with him and he agreed to a divorce, packed up and left. Ray Bob isn't dangerous most of the time, but he's got a mean streak that comes out when he gets too much booze. And there's no telling about the two he's got with him."

Bev bit her bottom lip. This was the kind of situation that generated mixed emotions. She couldn't agree with what she suspected Jim had done, but domestic violence cases were almost always frustrating. Jim wouldn't have been the first cop to try and get the point across to an abusive husband that getting knocked around by someone bigger or tougher wasn't a pleasant experience.

"I understand Chief," she said. "I'll get some of the guys and have Ray Bob's name run through the system. We might need something because if he was never formally charged and there's no restraining order, we're not exactly on firm legal ground in going after him."

Chief Taylor chuckled. "Ray Bob never has been the sharpest knife in the drawer. A cop shows up and he's liable to take a swing, which gives you assaulting an officer at a minimum," he said. "And since whoever he's hooked up with is probably about the same, take an extra car with you if there's one available."

Bev gave Chief Taylor a half salute, consulted quickly with Earl and was soon on the way to the address that Vera had given her. Earl and Kevin followed her and another patrol car was to meet them.

A woman was sitting on the hood of a dark blue, older model Malibu when they parked along the curb. She was of that indeterminate age between late thirty and early fifty depending on what light she was in and dressed in a pair of shiny gold tights, a leopard print tunic and wore gold leather sandals. Her makeup was surprisingly artfully applied considering how many layers there appeared to be and her red hair didn't match any natural shade that Bev was familiar with.

The woman scooted her wiry body forward to the edge of the car, inclined her head to the cops and quietly appraised Bev.

"You're the lady policeman I talked to?" she asked, unaware of the contradiction of her question.

"Yes ma'am, I'm the detective you spoke with," Bev corrected firmly. "Are Mr. Brewster and the other two inside?"

Vera curled her upper lip and jerked her thumb over her

shoulder. "I been sitting here since I called and nobody's been out the door. The three bums may still be asleep for all I know."

Bev had brought along the photographs of Willie Denton and Hal Grayson and handed them to Vera. "Do these look like the men with your ex-husband?"

Vera studied the faces and shook her head. "No. Are these guys important? Is there some kind of reward?"

Bev took the papers and was glad she hadn't gotten her hopes up, but before she could answer Vera one of the officers pointed to the house.

"We've been made," he said and unsnapped the holster of his weapon. That seemed a bit unnecessary.

Bev pivoted and saw the blinds in one of the front windows sway from side to side. She watched as two officers made their way to the back of the house from opposite directions and when they disappeared around the corners, she beckoned Kevin forward with her.

They stood on the cracked concrete stoop and she rapped sharply on the door with the tarnished horseshoe doorknocker. There was no sound at first and then she saw the barrel of a shotgun protrude from an opened window to her left at the same time they heard a shout from the rear entrance.

They leapt to the ground as she silently cursed the awkward position. Bev's stomach contracted when the shotgun blast seared overhead and she heard glass shatter street-side. Damn, what was this turning into? They pressed into the side of the house and she whipped her head around to see that everyone had ducked behind the cars. A ragged hole had been blasted through the rear passenger window on the first black and white. More muffled shouts echoed from the back, but no one else was shooting so far. She and Kevin flattened closer against the house as they looked at each other. He wiped his hand across his mouth and exhaled a long breath.

"What now, Bev?" he asked in a low voice. He had drawn his gun, but held it down waiting for her answer.

Bev shook her head and angled sideways to peer over the stoop.

The shotgun had been withdrawn and a momentary, eerie silence was broken when a man's voice shouted from inside, below the window where the shotgun had been fired from.

"Leave us the hell alone! You got no business here!"

Bev had pulled up into a crouch and she watched the movements behind the police cars. Earl had a bullhorn and was shielded by the hood of Bev's car. One of the other officers was behind the trunk and he pointed one hand at Earl and waved Bev and Kevin forward with the other.

Bev glanced at Kevin, who had also taken a low sprinter stance, and she nodded their understanding. Earl was close to the front fender of the car so any attention would be directed at an angle away from where Bev and Kevin would be running.

Bev signaled that they were ready and his voice crackled through the bullhorn. "Ray Bob? Ray Bob, don't shoot again, if you know what's good for you!"

A sharp pain streaked up Bev's calf when she launched across the yard, but she pushed forward and one of the officers reached out and pulled her in as she stumbled behind the car. Kevin was on her heels and he gasped that he was okay. Bev heard the broken conversation of the other officers talking on their radios and couldn't make out the words. She caught her breath and worked her way to the front of the car to speak with Earl. *What was going on in the rear of the house? And the neighbors – where were they?*

"You got no right being here! Just go away!" the man shouted again.

Earl lowered the bullhorn when Bev came alongside. He grinned and shook his head. "That's Ray Bob, all right. He sure as hell woke up cranky."

Bev pressed her lips in a straight line. *This wasn't funny for Christ's sake!* "Okay, what's the deal out back?" she asked to keep from snapping her irritation.

"The door opened when the guys first got there, but

whoever it was ducked inside real fast. No sign of guns yet, but they didn't respond when they were told to come out, either." Earl swept his arm to the right. "We got folks shooed back in their houses and Vera's behind the third car. We'll get her out of here in a minute."

"Hey Bev," Kevin said from the cover of the second car. "The station called and there's warrants out on these three – some kind of attempted robbery charge."

Earl nodded knowingly and Bev groaned. Well, at least that explained the reaction. Earl raised his torso slightly above the hood and used the bullhorn. "Come on out, Ray Bob! We've got three cars here!"

"Go fuck yourself!" he shouted. "Me and Vera can work this out ourselves!"

"Does he really think we don't know about the warrants?" Bev asked with a frown.

Earl pulled his hat off and hunkered down again. "Ray Bob is pretty much what you'd call stupid, Bev. He probably figures he can bluff his way out," he said. "How do you want to do this, or do you want to call the Chief first?"

Bev tugged her left ear and thought for a moment. The situation was contained, but it seemed obvious that the men inside weren't anxious to come out. "I imagine the Chief already knows what's going on, but we could get tear gas out here. That might be the best bet."

"Oh give me that damned thing," Vera said, coming up behind Bev.

Bev jumped at the unexpected sound. *Why was she still in the area?* Vera held her hand out to Earl and she seemed remarkably calm for someone with an armed ex-husband and cops surrounding her house. On the other hand, if she'd worked for long at Gill's, she would be accustomed to similar scenes.

Bev strained to be polite. "Ms. Newly, we really need to move you out of here and we'll take care of this," she said. She motioned to one of the officers, but Vera looked her up and down with a stern stare.

"Missy, it took me long enough to come to my senses

over that son-of-a-bitch and I'm not letting my house get messed up because of him. You give me that thing and let me talk to him."

"Ms. Newly...," Bev started, but stopped when Earl touched her elbow.

"Bev, it probably wouldn't hurt," he whispered in her ear as Vera tapped her foot impatiently and continued to hold out her hand.

Bev shrugged and stepped back to let Earl give the woman the bullhorn. He showed her how to depress the speaker button and Vera shrieked so loudly that Bev cringed at the chalk-on-the-blackboard effect.

"Ray Bob, you get your stinking ass out here right now! If they have to bust up my house and they don't shoot you then by God, I'll do it myself! And I'll shoot your worthless dick off too, while I'm at it!"

Bev grabbed for the instrument as Earl looked like he was trying to keep from laughing and Vera started to scream another threat.

"Ms. Newly, please let us take care of this," Bev said and held the bullhorn to her chest.

"Hey look," Kevin said and lifted his gun toward the house.

The front door opened part way even though no one was coming out. The officers stayed behind the vehicles, but trained their weapons in almost one movement.

"Throw the gun out first," Bev shouted. "And then walk out slowly with your hands on top of your head."

Sweat popped out along her hairline as she waited tensely. Bev was halfway through repeating herself when she saw the shotgun slide across the stoop as though it had been shoved with a foot. The door swung fully open and a man cautiously stepped out with his empty hands in front in plain view. A second man was behind him and Bev heard someone say, "They've got the other one."

"Down on the ground," Bev instructed. "Lay flat and put your hands on top of you head." The officers waited until the two men were on their knees and they rushed in to take control of them. The third man was cuffed and being marched to a car. Bev looked closely, but Vera had been correct about the extra two men not matching the photographs. The one in handcuffs had a long scar across his right cheek and one of the men laying in the grass had the build of a football player gone to fat.

Earl took Vera's arm and inclined his head down the street where the Chief's sedan was inching through the neighbors who were clustering around to find out what the commotion was all about. The driver stopped at the end car and the Chief climbed out to speak to Vera. She shook her head at something he said, kissed him on the cheek, waved to Bev and walked away to a knot of women huddled nearby. Chief Taylor dangled his cigarette between his thumb and forefinger and waited for Bev to come within speaking distance.

"Everyone is okay, I hear," he said and surveyed the tempo of the scene.

"I suspect this isn't how Ray Bob and his pals feel," Bev said and raised her eyebrows. "It would have been nice if we'd known about the warrants before we came out," she added.

Chief Taylor shrugged his wide shoulders, ignored her comment and waved away the newspaper reporter who was moving rapidly toward them. "Damn, I'd better go talk with the newshound before he finds the youngest rookie to fill him in. Anyway, the deal is that these yahoos tried to heist an armored car in Saratoga a few days ago. It wasn't a big haul, but they got a couple of bags and wounded one of the drivers. Ray Bob must have figured they could lay low here for a while. I guess he thought Vera had either changed her mind or would feel sorry for him. By the way, she'll come down to the station and give her statement when you're ready. She didn't see the bags, but they're probably around."

Bev blotted her forehead with the back of her hand. "We'll check the house, but we probably should have waited until we'd run the names before we came out."

The Chief twitched his mouth. "It doesn't really matter,

considering that we have them now, but I've got to say that I think we've all had enough excitement for one day." He pushed away from his car. "Just do the minimum report today Bev, and you can get the rest later," he said.

Bev nodded and stood for a moment to catch her breath. She watched the reporter speak briefly with Chief Taylor and then move to Vera.

Bev found Earl and talked to him about searching the house. She would have to interview the three men, but liked the Chief's advice about writing a quick report and knew it would be a good idea to go by the hospital to see Jim. It would be better if he heard the story from her before he got some wildly exaggerated version.

She slipped into her car and glanced in the rearview mirror. Vera was making broad gestures while trying to simultaneously fix her hair. Bev would have someone check with the armored car company to see if they had offered a reward for the culprits' capture. They usually did and if the money was recovered, it would be because Vera had called. That was probably the only good thing Vera would have gotten from her time with Ray Bob, but at least he should be gone for a long stretch of hard time.

Pain throbbed in her left ankle and Bev saw that her pants leg was streaked with dried mud from the flowerbed. She'd run by the house, pop a couple of over-the-counter pain relievers and change clothes. The Chief was right when he said they'd all had enough excitement for the morning – this kind of thing hardly ever happened and especially not within days of something like the standoff at Haughton's. Well, one thing was for sure - the town's quota for gunplay should be maxed out for a while.

Chapter Twenty-one

It took Bev until mid-afternoon to make it to the hospital and she was glad to find that her name had been added to the short list of authorized visitors. She approached the glassed-in room and Myrtle raised her hand in welcome.

The older woman was now dressed in a blue and white seersucker pantsuit and even though she looked tired, the fear that had shown in her eyes early that morning had receded. Bev knew it wasn't that she was in denial about Jim's health, but like Bev's mother, she would doggedly project her steadfast strength outwardly and save her misgivings for private sharing. Bev quietly entered the room and gave her a comforting hug.

Jim's appearance hadn't improved dramatically, but he was slightly elevated in the bed and the electronic monitors hummed in what sounded like a low, normal pitch.

"Bev, how are you?" Myrtle asked with a small smile. "We heard bits and pieces about the fracas and weren't sure who was involved."

Jim cleared his throat and moved as if to sit upright, but Bev wagged her finger at him while keeping one arm across Myrtle's shoulders. "You stay still," she said. "I'm fine and part of why I came by was so you wouldn't get the wrong idea about what happened."

Myrtle stepped away and patted the back of the chair where she'd been sitting. "Your mother and I learned a long time ago that it was easier to be a cop's wife if you don't know too many details. Jim will want a blow-by-blow description so if you don't mind, I'll take a break while you fill him in."

She didn't wait for a reply, but leaned across the bed,

pecked Jim on the cheek and laid her hand on Bev's arm in a gesture that conveyed both thanks and relief that she was all right.

"So none of our guys got hurt?" Jim asked as soon as Myrtle was through the door.

Bev pulled the chair closer to prevent him from straining forward. "Nothing more than a busted out window on a squad car," she said and explained everything that happened.

He nodded approvingly when she mentioned that in all likelihood, Vera would get the five thousand dollar reward that had been offered. The two stolen bags had been found intact in a closet in one of the bedrooms and the armored car company was inclined to be grateful.

The only part she left out was her fleeting suspicion that the two extra men might have been the Devil's Duo. It had been a long shot and Jim would no doubt have teased her about it.

"Well, Ray Bob never was too bright, but I didn't think he'd ever get involved in anything more serious than beating folks up when he got drunk," Jim said. He blinked his eyes and changed the subject. "Did you and Claude talk?"

Bev nodded and caught her lower lip between her teeth. "Uh huh."

Jim slowly turned his head and gave her a look that reminded her of when she started out as a rookie. "Don't make me ask a lot of questions, Kid. You were surprised, weren't you?"

Bev hesitated. This was a man she remembered from her earliest years, whether it was the extra present at Christmas or a game of catch at the summer cookouts that alternated between the Osborn and Henderson backyards. It had been awkward for her to come directly under his supervision when she made detective even though she knew Jim was a stalwart supporter who had quietly chastised some of his peers for their initial skepticism of her. During the past four years they had developed a bond that nearly equaled that between her and her father. And, as with her father, there had been flashes of irritation with what she took as an overly protective attitude and occasional embarrassment when she was forced to acknowledge that Jim's experience sometimes produced more accurate results than her carefully reasoned analysis.

"Yes I was surprised," she said. "I guess there are times when you still make me feel like a rookie," she continued, "and I wouldn't have thought you'd recommend that I be in charge."

Jim's look bordered on somber. "Bev, it isn't the easiest thing to think of you as a cop, let alone a detective. Your dad and I talked about it when you were up at Jacksonville and to be honest every now and then we hoped you weren't serious about it; that you'd decide to switch to being a teacher or something. We may not have widespread violent crime down here, but this business is never really safe and it took time to get used to the idea of having you on the force. Like I told you the other day though, you're as good as any cop I've known and you're still young, but it wouldn't be right to bring an outsider in without giving you a chance. I know Claude isn't quite convinced yet, so let him come to the decision on his own. Don't try and push him on it."

Bev felt her throat constrict at the unaccustomed and undisguised praise. She briefly squeezed Jim's hand. "Yeah, well maybe the doctors will have you back before you know it," she said with a smile. "It'll be good practice for me and then the Chief won't have to worry about a replacement."

The lines around Jim's eyes crinkled. "That's not going to happen, Kid. I'd pretty much made up my mind before last night and I'm taking this as a sign. Once the surgery is over and I get cleared by the doctors, I'm booking that cruise I've been promising Myrtle and then I might get around to re-landscaping the yard like I've been talking about."

"Good, you can start with having someone build us a bigger deck and you can supervise," Myrtle said as she returned with several magazines in her hand. "By the way, Bev, your mama called to check on us and said that between Jim and the goings-on this morning she didn't know who to worry about the most. I told her everyone was okay and not to get into a tizzy."

"I knew she wouldn't be happy until she talked to you herself," Bev said.

Her mother's tizzy had occurred during the thirty-minute telephone conversation they'd had at noon. She had covered everything from how Jim should get more rest to how if she'd made Bev take ballet lessons when she was seven years old, she never would have turned out to be such a tomboy and would have become a teacher or a nurse instead of taking after her father who, by the way, certainly shouldn't have encouraged her in the first place. Bev had tucked the telephone against her shoulder and read her e-mail until the tirade had passed. It was the simplest way to handle conversations like that.

She rose to give Myrtle the chair. "I'm going to head out unless there's something you need me to take care of."

Myrtle smiled. "No, the children will be by soon and we'll swap out and take turns making sure Jim behaves himself. Now you tell Claude to get you some help in the office and don't be trying to do two people's work. You've got a lot of energy, but even you have your limits."

Bev gave her a quick hug, waved to Jim and exited before the well-intentioned maternal advice could gather steam. She couldn't take two such lectures only hours apart.

As she walked to the parking lot, she thought about what Jim had said and her conflicting sense of concern for his heart attack and a growing desire to wipe out any doubts the Chief might have about accelerating her career. Senior detective at her age! Why shouldn't she be excited?

After all, Jim was out of immediate danger, bypass surgery was commonplace and he was going to an excellent hospital in Miami. He had said himself that he was the one who had broached the subject of retirement and the attack had only reinforced his decision. Her parents were enjoying their second career and there was no reason it shouldn't be the same for Jim and Myrtle. In a way, this could turn out to be the best thing for everyone.

Bev turned left instead of right out of the hospital grounds and went by her apartment building to check on the repair work. It was one of the older places in town with limited amenities, but it was located near a small park and was easily accessible to work. The two three-story rectangular red brick structures were divided by a wide breezeway.

The assistant manager gave her the welcome news that except for some minor cleanup work, the apartment was ready. Bev drove into her designated carport and went inside for a quick inspection.

The flames had started in the apartment next to Bev's and while they had not penetrated her interiors walls, the water damage from the powerful fire hoses and the smoke had permeated the combination den and dining room as well as the kitchen.

The odor of a fresh coat of paint blended with a strong disinfectant smell had replaced the previous smoky stench. Bev rubbed her hand across her nose and hoped that opening the windows and turning on the ceiling fans would solve that problem within a few hours. The new carpet was the same dappled beige as before and the padding underneath had a nice spring to it.

The management had either felt guilty about the delay in the repairs or more likely, was concerned they might lose tenants, but Bev saw that even the areas that had sustained no damaged had been professionally cleaned and repainted. It was almost like moving into a new place.

She calculated the effort it would take to pack up her belongings and transport them and decided that spending one more night at her parents' house made a lot more sense.

The pre-dawn scare with Jim and then the unexpected encounter at Vera's were starting to catch up with her. Fatigue rolled through her body and pain stabbed behind her forehead. Or maybe it was fumes from the new paint. In either case, it was time for the day to be over.

She made arrangements to have the apartment aired out early the next morning and concluded that her headache was probably as much from not having had a chance to eat as anything else. She was too tired to even consider cooking and stopped on the way home to pick up a roasted chicken dinner. By the time she parked in her parents' driveway, she was ready for a quiet evening. She changed into a pair of sweatpants and a long sleeve T-shirt, washed the chicken down with a couple of beers and then found herself staring at the telephone. The sight of Karen at Kyle's side replayed in her mind like a video and her anger and disappointment bubbled hotly to the surface.

Her carefully trained, analytical side tried to rationally explain that it was just one of those things and that maybe Kyle could explain. Her emotional side swiftly told the analytical side to go to hell and she went to bed early. She had wrestled with enough emotion for one day.

Chapter Twenty-two

Willie poured straight bourbon into the plastic glass and watched Hal switch back and forth between channels to see how many stations were carrying a piece about the two brutal killers who were staying ahead of the police. Sometimes the television people used words Willie didn't understand, but Hal seemed to think it was funny when they talked about the Devil's Duo.

"Listen to them, Willie. We're fucking famous and they don't even know who the fuck we are," he said when the man from the Florida State Police Headquarters office admitted they had no firm suspects under investigation.

Hal turned the volume up as the spokesman was trying to answer questions as to why there had been no progress in the cases. He laughed at the pained expression on the man's face.

"Now do you understand why we shoot everyone? The guns can't be traced, we don't leave fingerprints and there's no one left around to give a description. There's nothing for them to go on. All those fancy forensic techniques don't mean dick if we don't give them anything to work with."

Willie nodded and washed down the last bite of a ham sandwich with a large swallow of bourbon. He was tired of sandwiches and small dark motel rooms and not knowing what was going on. He didn't have much education, but he figured Hal was crazy. It didn't take some head doctor to understand that.

It wasn't just that he killed people; it was the way he walked right into a store as friendly as could be, always smiling and talking to Willie real casual like. Then a six pack or something in hand, get the cash register open and a shot with no warning. Goddamn, the last guy had been in the middle of a sentence about the weather when Hal had killed him. And then it was the way Hal looked afterwards, real pleased with himself like he knew things other people didn't. That had to be crazy. What was he supposed to do about it though?

He could probably kill Hal in his sleep, but then what in the hell would he do with himself? He had money, a stash of drugs in a bag, and no damn idea of where to go. They were too far east in Florida to make it to Mexico easily and too far south to get to Canada. And even if he could get there, he wouldn't fit in and he didn't know anybody who could help him. Hal was crazy, but at least he was smart and seemed to have some kind of plan for getting them out of the goddamn mess they were in.

Willie sat up and stared when one of the younger reporters asked if the Florida police had been notified to be on the lookout for two men from Mississippi. Shit!

The guy who answered the reporter made a brushing motion with his hand. "There are two men wanted for questioning for a triple murder in Mississippi that appears unrelated to the other cases," he said. "Naturally we've issued an alert, and we always cooperate when other states are seeking fugitives. At this point, there's no compelling reason to think it's the same men."

Willie twisted the bottle of whiskey on the bed and felt his hands go clammy. He turned to look at Hal. "Did you hear them, Hal? Maybe they do know who we are. Who else would they be talking about?"

Hal lit a cigarette and flipped the burned out match onto the floor. "Listen to what the fat fuck just said, Willie. If someone in Mississippi figured it out, the asswipes here aren't buying it."

"But you said no one would know," Willie said and swallowed hard. "Maybe this guy is just saying that to the reporters. Maybe they do know. They must have our names or they couldn't know who to be looking for."

Hal shrugged and used the tone of voice that made Willie

feel stupid. "Even if they have put it all together, all they have to go on is some bad photographs of us, Willie. We don't look much like that now and unless the Florida cops agree to stop every white man our age and question him, we don't have anything to worry about. We don't stay in the same motel more than a couple of nights and we don't cause trouble. There's nothing to make anyone suspicious."

Willie plucked the bedspread with his hand. He always stayed in the car when Hal checked them in, so he hadn't had a conversation with a single person other than Hal since they robbed the pusher. He thought of the bottles of whiskey, cartons of cigarettes and magazines stashed in the car. He knew Hal kept the drugs and extra gun in with the spare tire, but the other items were just lying under a piece of old tarp.

"But wouldn't it be a good idea for us to get wherever we're going? I mean, we've got all that stuff in the trunk and what if the cops do put up a roadblock or something? If they start looking around, they'd find everything. That would make them ask questions. I mean, you do have a plan, don't you, Hal? You said we were going to some special place. How come you haven't told me where?"

The other man narrowed his eyes and then opened them wide and grinned. "Yeah Willie, we're going someplace real special. You ever been on a boat?"

Willie was confused at the change of subject. He wished Hal wouldn't do that to him. "You mean, like fishing?"

"I mean like one of the big boats you see on television. On the ocean, Willie, have you ever been on the ocean?"

Willie shook his head. "I was gonna go to Biloxi one time, but something happened," he said. "I've been fishing on the Mississippi a couple of times. Are you saying we're going somewhere on a boat? Where are we gonna get a boat?"

Hal laughed and it was an ugly sound, the creepy one that Willie hated. "We're going to the Caribbean, Willie. We'll head out and find ourselves a fucking tropical island with palm trees and pretty girls with big tits. There's hundreds of islands we can pick from that have only maybe three or four cops. We show up, pay a little bribe money and no one cares who we are or where we came from. After a while, they'll forget about us over here and we'll be home free."

Willie wrinkled his forehead as Hal talked. "But how are we gonna get a boat? And who's gonna to drive it?" he asked.

Hal thumped his chest. "I'm going to drive it," he said. "My old man used to be a mechanic at a marina in Biloxi. I grew up tinkering around the boats and started driving them when I was a kid. My old lady buried a knife in my dad's chest and killed him one night when he got bombed and started beating on her again. She wasn't much better than him, though, and the state sent me and my sister to foster homes after she was arrested. My sister liked the family she was with, but the ones I got were real preachy and a pain in the ass. I woulda been gone as soon as I hit eighteen, but got into trouble and they talked this old fart judge into letting me go in the Navy. They said it would straighten me out."

Willie stared at him. "You were in the Navy?"

Hal chuckled and lit a cigarette. "Not for long – it was a crock of shit like everything else. I made it through basic and was assigned to Norfolk. I got busted once for possession and then we were getting the barracks ready for inspection one day and this nigger mouthed off about how I wasn't doing my share." Hal sucked deeply on the cigarette and exhaled. "I nailed him right across the jaw. Woulda' beat him to a pulp too, but this other guy, Tom Farmer, pulled me off. Then the son-of-a-bitch rolled over on me when I got hauled in front of the commander. Shit, you'd think a white man would take up for another one, but Farmer was too much a kiss-ass guy. Anyway, I got time in the brig and they discharged me – *unable to adapt,* or some bullshit thing like that."

Willie was trying to follow the story. "But what's that got to do with getting a boat?"

Hal settled back into the pillows he'd propped against the headboard. "I'm getting to that. A few months ago I was reading this magazine and bigger than hell, there was this piece about some guys in Florida working to save some damn fish or reef or whatever and one of the guys they wrote about was good old Tom Farmer. Must of got out of the Navy and got himself set up down in the Keys with his own diving business and everything. And get this, his business is right in this marina – surrounded by all these boats. They had pictures of it."

Hal waved his cigarette back and forth. "That's what got me to thinking. Here I was stuck in that shithole town where you and me were and here was good old Tom, living it up in the Keys. And it's practically no time at all from the Keys out into the Caribbean. Plus, this other guy I know can get us the documents we need – passports and all – and he's in Florida. So it all fit together just perfect. It's Fate, Willie – Fate smiling on us."

Willie was starting to get the idea, but part of it didn't make sense. "That's where we're heading – to this guy's place? He'll help us get a boat? But if he didn't stick up for you before, why would he help?"

Hal dropped the glowing cigarette into a beer can and lit another one. "Hell no, he wouldn't help, but it doesn't matter. Timing is what's important. It isn't the big tourist season right now, so marinas like that close up early. We roll in late at night, break into old Tom's place and use it as a base to check out the boats in the marina. We pick the one we want and then we're out of there. The fishing boats won't be around until sunrise and we'll be long gone by then."

Willie took another swig of bourbon. It sounded okay, but could it be that easy? This wasn't in and out like the stores.

"But won't there be guards for the boats?"

Hal shook his head. "Nah, I looked this place up on the Internet and it's not like it's a rich man's marina. There are some big boats, but if there's a guard, it'll be some old geezer who probably hits the sauce and goes to sleep as soon as everyone is gone. Look, stealing a boat is no harder than boosting a car – you just have to know what you're doing. It'll be a piece of cake – don't worry about it." Hal waved his hand to cut through the cigarette smoke. "Paradise, Willie. We're going to find a tropical paradise. Nothing but beach, pretty girls, rum and big lobster. We've got money and we'll sell the drugs and get more money. That's what I've been telling you, we're going to start a new life. Our next stop is for the passports and stuff and then we drive south, right to Farmer's and we're on the way. Fate is on our side – I always knew it would work out my way someday – I just had to be smart enough to see the chance."

The news show was over and Hal switched to a wrestling match.

Willie wasn't sure he understood everything, but it sounded like Hal had worked it out in his head. He hoped Hal was serious about making their break in a few days. Maybe the Florida police weren't looking hard for them, but he didn't like the idea that they had been mentioned on the TV, even if they hadn't said their names.

"Oh man, what a slam," Hal said and Willie looked at the screen.

The referee pulled the wrestlers apart and the cameraman swung away from the ring and panned the crowd. There was a good-looking blonde sitting ringside yelling her support and wearing a tight pale pink shirt and no bra. Willie stared as the camera focused on her. Her nipples showed like hard little lumps and every time she jumped up and down, her large boobs jiggled. The shirt was almost the color of her skin and it made her look nearly topless.

If she looked like that from the top up, how would she be all naked on a sandy beach? He bet she had a nice round ass, the kind a man could grab hold of. He emptied the bottle of whiskey, and thought about sticking it to the blonde while palm trees swayed overhead. He hoped they would head to the marina soon and that Hal was right about how easy it would be.

Chapter Twenty-three

Bev flattened the last empty box and put it on top of the others. What a relief to be back in her own apartment with her belongings in their assigned spaces. She looked around with satisfaction and congratulated herself one more time for successfully resisting her mother's decorating suggestions. The simple lines of Danish modern and color coordinated mini-blinds and valances were infinitely better than overstuffed floral upholstery and floor length chintz drapes.

Some upscale apartments in her price range had been built over the last few years, but she preferred the character that came with the older building. She liked the bank of windows in the dining area that overlooked one section of the park and the big bay window in her bedroom that opened onto another section. The pass-through in the galley kitchen was designed to carry on a conversation with someone while keeping him or her out of the way. Not that she spent much time cooking, but when she did she didn't want anyone underfoot.

Surveying the kitchen reminded her that she needed to make a trip to the grocery store to restock. A six pack of diet Coke, one of beer, half a turkey sandwich and a box of baking soda pushed to the rear were the lonely contents of the refrigerator. The thought of food led to the thought of not having dinner with Kyle. She sighed at the idea and wandered in for a diet Coke.

She had deliberately concentrated on visiting Jim, work, and anything else that had blocked the fifteen minutes at Bojangles.

Kyle was honoring her request not to call, but how was

she supposed to interpret that? If he really cared, then wouldn't he at least try to contact her? Well, he had telephoned the one time. So he was going to give up with no further effort? What did that say about him? And what had he done after she'd left that night? Returned to the bar for another drink? Returned and let Karen comfort him? Bev shuddered and sucked an ice cube into her mouth. Surely he wouldn't have done that. Shit, she was right back where she started – better to think about something else.

Bev crushed the ice cube, swallowed the slivers and flopped down on the navy and forest green striped couch. She pressed the remote control of the television and surfed the channels. Slowly, the correct way, pausing long enough to actually see what a show was, rather than speed past with a momentary glimpse of images.

She took her finger off the channel button when she saw two scuba divers exploring a reef system in clear blue water surrounded by colorful fish. The narrator was describing the large green eel that one of the divers had coaxed out.

Diving and the case of Wiley. She was bumping up against the deadline the Chief had given her and if she couldn't make some progress, he was going to insist that she accept it as an accident. She hadn't had any spare time the last two days and Monday's schedule would be full with closing the report on the incident at Vera's and she should go through the stack of papers on Jim's desk. She could spend Sunday in the office – it would be quiet and she'd be able to focus on just the case.

The chiming of the doorbell surprised her and she jumped at the sound. She clicked the television off, got up, opened the door and reached quickly for the plastic bag that was dangling from Aunt Lorna's wrist. Her arms were filled with two paper bags that looked heavy.

"Sorry I didn't call first," she said and let Bev also take one of the paper bags. "I talked to Myrtle and she said you were moving back in today and I missed you at your folks' place. I figured you hadn't had a chance to buy groceries with everything that's been going on, so I picked you up a few things."

Bev nodded her head toward the kitchen. "That's awfully sweet of you and you're right, but I really was going to take care of it."

Lorna grinned and set the bag on the counter next to the ones Bev had put down. "You have beer, Coke and cold pizza in the refrigerator, I bet," she said.

Bev laughed. "It's part of a sandwich actually instead of pizza. Can I get you a Coke?"

Lorna grimaced. "Not if it's diet. I'll take a beer instead. I brought you one meal too, although I imagine you have plans for the weekend."

"Uh no, nothing big. In fact, I'll probably go into work to try and get caught up," Bev said quickly.

"I see," Lorna said and began to unload the bags. "Well, we have some staples and somewhere in the plastic bag are some satchels of potpourri I made during the holidays. I thought the rooms might need freshening."

"And you wonder why you're my favorite aunt," Bev said and pulled out a package of prepared salad, a roasted Cornish game hen, a loaf of sourdough bread and a container of scalloped potatoes.

"Everything can pop in the microwave," Lorna said as she lined the rest of the groceries along the counter. "I'll put these away if you'll tell me where. And don't forget my beer, young lady."

Bev paused and slipped her arm across Lorna's shoulders. She squeezed lightly and let go when Lorna smiled in response. Bev was suddenly glad to have some company and she stepped toward the refrigerator. "Coming right up, but why don't you take a seat and let me put things away?"

She took a bottle of beer out, twisted the top off, tilted it, and watched the golden liquid rise to the top of a pilsner glass. Lorna moved around to the other side and hoisted onto one of the cane bottom, high back stools and Bev set the glass on a navy blue gingham place mat on the breakfast bar.

"I know it bothers you when I sound like Emma, but have

you taken the time to figure out how tired you probably are?" Lorna asked with a gentle smile.

Bev put the bag of Colombian coffee in the freezer and shrugged. "Not exactly and it's only been a little over forty-eight hours since Jim's attack," she said with more energy than she felt. "I'm good for at least ninety-six."

Lorna made a clucking sound with her tongue. "Bev honey, you do like to throw the bullshit around, don't you? Well, I'm not enough like Emma to sit here and badger you. That stubborn streak is part of what's gotten you where you are. And with that said, why don't you swap to a beer and come sit down? Let's move to the couch though; I need something soft to sit on."

That did sound inviting. Bev dumped the ice from her glass, rinsed it and poured carefully to get the half-inch head she liked. She joined Lorna on the couch and almost let out a groan at how good it felt to sit still. She'd been in motion lifting and stretching most of the day.

"So now that we have you off your feet, did Jim have that much work piled up, or do you not have plans with your lawyer friend?"

Bev winced at the question before she stopped herself.

"Ah," Lorna said quickly. "Or should I not ask?"

It was a little late for that.

"I'm not going to be a busybody, but I'd be glad to listen if there's something you want to talk about," she continued quietly.

There was no confidante in Bev's circle of friends; at least not since Helen had gotten married. They lunched occasionally, although their conversations now seemed to center on work and Helen's new life with her husband. Maybe another perspective would help, and it wasn't like she had to give all the details.

Bev tugged her ear. "Oh, it's just that Kyle and I had sort of a major disagreement and it took me by surprise. I told him to give me some time to think things over, but with Jim's heart attack and all, Kyle hasn't been my top priority. And I don't know, sometimes I think it would be easier to not mess with men. I mean, it's not like I don't keep busy."

Lorna patted her knee and smiled. "You're a little young to be throwing in the towel and while I'm not in the love life advice business, I do have one piece for you if you want it."

Advice from Lorna about something other than plants was unusual. Bev took a sip of beer and nodded.

"I got the impression that you like this young man and a lot of disagreements can be resolved with a little compromise," she said with a smile. "Remember, I have folks coming in the shop all the time looking for special arrangements that say 'I'm sorry'. This is hardly what you'd call profound, but if Kyle is as nice as I think he is, he's probably worth a telephone call."

Bev rocked her head back and forth. "Yeah, I've been thinking about doing that." The beer suddenly reacted with a lack of sleep and she yawned.

"Aha, you are tired," Lorna said and drained her glass. "Now that you can hold off grocery shopping, I think your idea of taking it easy this evening is a good one. And look, I have to make a run down to Key West tomorrow to check on a new hibiscus hybrid a woman has been cultivating if you'd rather take a trip than go into work. We could swing by the hospital on the way out to check on Jim and then hit the road. I don't have to bring anything back, so you could even drive if you'd like."

She stood, motioned for Bev to stay seated and retrieved her purse from the dining room table. Bev rose too quickly and the muscles in her lower back twinged.

She opened the door and bent her head to kiss the cheek Lorna offered. "A drive to Key West does sound tempting," she said. "Let me think about it and I'll call you later. Hey thanks again for everything, to include the advice."

Lorna laid her hand on Bev's shoulder. "You're welcome and do get some rest. That way I can be truthful with Emma when she nags me about how you're doing."

Bev laughed, closed the door, hunched her shoulders and relaxed them to try and relieve some of the tightness. A good set of slow stretches was the other thing she needed.

Maybe a day off wasn't a bad idea and a leisurely drive could help clear the mental cobwebs. She picked both glasses up from the coffee table and her stomach rumbled. It was too late for lunch and too early for dinner, but Lorna had included a bag of corn chips and a jar of salsa in the provisions. That and another beer would sustain her.

Bev looked at the telephone hanging on the wall and thought about what Lorna had said. The problem was that she didn't know what she wanted to say to Kyle yet. Then what good would it do to call? Hope that something would come to mind if he answered the telephone?

Another yawn started and her stomach rumbled louder this time. It was easier to think about a snack than Kyle or her murder case for that matter. Food, some stretches, a little couch potato time and then she'd decide about Lorna's offer. The two of them riding along with the top down on the car was sounding better and better. And why not? She might get inspired and everything would fall into place while they ate cheeseburgers and Key Lime pie.

Chapter Twenty-four

Monday began as fast-paced as Bev had expected and she was glad she'd taken the day off. She and Lorna had gone by the hospital to check on Jim and then enjoyed the drive to Key West with the top down on the convertible and the volume up on Jimmy Buffet. Bev had relaxed for the first time in days and finally gotten a restful night's sleep.

She fielded several telephone calls from people asking about Jim, finished the report on the incident at Vera's and worked through most of the jumble on Jim's desk.

Despite the fact he'd told her he wouldn't return to the office, she didn't want the finality of boxing up his possessions. That was for Jim to do when he was ready. The Chief hadn't said anything more about a new detective, so there was no need for the desk space.

She drank a large bottle of orange juice for lunch and quickly worked through the papers in her own in box. There was a remarkably uninformative report on another liquor store robbery-murder that was attributed to the Devil's Duo. The time of death was placed at around two o'clock in the morning which meant the manager would have been in the final moments of being open and, according to the owner, would probably have had the evening's sales bagged up for deposit.

The pattern was identical in that the security tape was missing and manager had two bullets in him; one to the stomach and one to the chest.

The local patrol had discovered the body around three o'clock. Once again there were no fingerprints and no witnesses since the only other business close by was a gas station across the road that had closed at midnight.

Bev sympathized with whoever was in charge of the investigation since it looked like nothing less than a multiple day, full scale series of road blocks and a check of every backwater motel across the center of the state was likely to uncover the Devil's Duo. No one would realistically expect the state to commit those kinds of resources; the tourist industry hadn't been affected yet.

Bev tossed the report in the trash and was reviewing a proposal for mobile data terminals for the patrol cars when the insurance claims agent handling Wiley's policy called.

They spoke for a few minutes and Bev regretfully told him that she couldn't provide any hard evidence to support her belief that the death was a homicide. He might have been more disappointed than she was at the idea of writing a substantial check for the small number of premiums that had been collected.

Bev replaced the receiver and looked up when Sheila stuck her head into the office without knocking. "Bev, a delivery came while you were on the phone." She grinned and held it out. "Kind of nice, don't you think?"

Bev frowned for a moment and stared at the object she was holding. It was a tulip shaped, clear glass like the ones used for exotic drinks. There were two pale yellow roses with a sprig of baby's breath enclosed in a plastic water tube in the center of the glass and the rest of it was filled with gold foil wrapped candies.

"There's a card," Sheila said, as if Bev couldn't see it, and set the glass on the desk where Bev pointed. "And it's not even your birthday."

"Maybe it's a thank you from Vera Newly for helping her get the reward," Bev said and tried to look as if she meant it.

"Oh sure, that's what I would have guessed," Sheila said and laughed. "Okay, I won't ask, but no holding out if there's anything good I should know."

She left with a tiny shake of her head and Bev tugged the small card loose.

I'm not trying to rush you, but I forgot to tell you that

I make a great pina colada. Give me a call if you'd like to try one.
Kyle

She smiled in spite of herself, reached into the glass, pulled out a candy, unwrapped it and popped it into her mouth while she pursed her lips and re-read the card. The candy was a butterscotch toffee - the expensive kind.

It was an interesting gesture. Not flashy, yet it made a statement. Should she call to let him know she got the gift or wait?

Chief Taylor's shout for her put a stop to either plan. Puzzled as to what could have the Chief in such an uproar, Bev walked into his office as he was swearing at one of the junior members of the mayor's staff. The young man in his early twenties was nervously trying to explain some sort of document the Chief was waving around.

Bev took the letter the Chief thrust at her and scanned it as the young man looked relieved at the presence of someone closer to his own age. Bev recognized him from the last town hall meeting. Jay Caldwell, she thought his name was.

"What in the name of Jesus Christ do they mean about having to justify our budget for next year and what the hell is this bullshit with breaking expenses into all these categories?" Chief Taylor snapped. "I do my goddamn budget the same way every goddamn year. I put down what we got the year before and throw in a little to spare. Who in the hell dreamed up this bookkeeper's idea?"

Bev suppressed a grin at his outrage. The mayor's office had published new budget guidelines right after the first of the year. With the growth of the town, the city council wanted to adopt some standard business practices and get a handle on how the municipal dollars were being spent. The Chief and the deputy had refused her suggestions when she had tried to talk about developing a spending plan, so she'd quietly installed a simple accounting program on Sheila's computer.

"Chief, you really don't need to worry about this," she

said and smiled at the uncomfortable messenger. "I can take Mr. Caldwell in my office and we'll get it settled."

Chief Taylor narrowed his eyes and poked his finger in the air in the direction of Mr. Caldwell's chest. "I've been running this department since you were in kindergarten," he said. "I don't waste money around here and I'm not going to spend one damn minute explaining myself to a couple of pencil-necked, wet-behind-the-ears accountants."

Jay Caldwell started to respond, but Bev shifted so the Chief would focus on her and waved her hand to indicate the triviality of the administrative requirement.

"You're not going to have to do that, Chief. Seriously, this is a paperwork drill that you should let me handle. I'll have it done in no time, it won't affect our funding and you won't even notice."

Chief Taylor frowned, but settled back in his big brown leather chair, rubbed his bald spot and stabbed his finger in the air again at the same time he pulled a cigarette from the pack lying in front of him. "All right, you take care of it, but I swear to God, if we get one dime less that I usually do, you tell the mayor that I'll come into that frufru office of his and take it out of his hide."

Bev motioned for Mr. Caldwell to keep quiet and follow her while Chief Taylor busied himself with finding his lighter. The cops in the large outer office pretended they hadn't heard the Chief's diatribe. These were the times that everyone tried to stay clear of the bursting radius of his temper.

Bev offered Mr. Caldwell a butterscotch to make up for the verbal abuse and nodded sympathetically when he expressed regret that the police chief and the mayor had a friendship that extended back for four decades. She soothingly agreed that the older generation could indeed be resistant to change and then promised the budget forms would be filled out and delivered by the next afternoon.

Bev sighed when Mr. Caldwell left and she spent another thirty minutes with Sheila to make sure they could meet the deadline. She didn't bother to tell Chief Taylor that she had already been assured that the department would actually get a increase in their budget that would cover the mobile data terminals. With those, the officers could check information directly from their patrol cars and send preliminary reports to the station.

She returned to her desk and called Kyle's office before she could change her mind, but the secretary told her that he was out of the building until six o'clock. Bev thanked her and left the message that she had received the article he'd sent. That put the ball back in Kyle's court and gave her more time to think about what she would say if and when he called.

Enough was enough and the Wiley case was next on her agenda. Her best approach would be to gather Jim's files, combine them with what she had and use the white board that took up half of one wall. She'd list out the witnesses, the events, what was known and her remaining questions. She hadn't followed up on the cancelled dive nor had she re-read her notes from the second interview with Farmer. She'd start there and see if that generated any new questions.

She pulled the Wiley folder from the drawer and had no more than sequenced the notes the way she wanted when the intercom buzzed again. Christ, no wonder she couldn't focus on the case. She grabbed the telephone and tried not to bark a response.

"Bev, I know you're busy, but a Miss Silsby is here to see you," Sheila said.

Bev stiffened, straightened up, and thought about telling Sheila she was too busy. "Ask her to come back here," she said instead and looked at the file spread in front of her. What in the hell was Karen up to?

Karen appeared in the doorway almost immediately. "Well, I see that you're hard at work. I do hope you have a few minutes to talk."

Bev didn't bother to try to be gracious. "Is there something you need?" she asked. Karen was dressed in a sleeveless denim dress that reached the top of her knees for a change and it had a neckline that actually covered her boobs.

"I know I'm about the last person in the world you want to see right now, but I need to speak with you," she said and glanced at the flowers.

Bev tapped the back of her chair with her fingertips. "Any chance you've come to tell me how you and Farmer pulled it off?"

Karen shook her head and didn't seem to take the offense that was sincerely intended. "I will say that you are persistent, but no, that's not the reason." She nodded toward the glass without commenting about it. "Is this a private enough place or should we go somewhere else?"

Bev shoved the papers back into the folder and reached for the telephone. "Let me put a block on any more calls," she said and when Sheila answered, she asked her to make sure there were no interruptions until her meeting was over. Then she got up and closed the office door before she returned to her desk.

Karen stood quietly until Bev was seated and then she took Jim's chair and draped her expensive looking leather purse across the back.

Bev took a deep, silent breath and waited for Karen to begin.

Chapter Twenty-five

Karen pointed at the black plastic ashtray that Jim kept on his desk for the Chief. "Mind if I smoke?"

Bev shrugged. The hell with waiting for Karen to start. "If you're not here to talk about the case, what is it that you want?" she evenly.

Karen lit her cigarette and curved her lips in a half-smile. "I'll get to that in a second," she said. "I heard about Jim Osborn's heart attack. Is he going to be okay?"

Bev was taken aback by the question. "Yeah. As a matter of fact, he was pretty lucky. They're going to have to go in and perform a bypass, but they'll take him to Miami where they do them all the time. It just took us all by surprise."

Karen nodded. "I'm glad to hear it. He impressed me as a decent kind of guy. Anyway, the reason for my visit. The insurance company called this morning and I'm sure they're pissed off, but I'll have my check soon. Greg's father already got an offer on the condo and it should be sold within two or three weeks."

Bev arched her left eyebrow. "And you'll be leaving town?"

Karen ran a beautifully manicured dark pink nail along the edge of the table. "Yes. I spoke with the university and there's no requirement for me to hang around to attend some ceremony after I've completed my course work and have my grades. The job interviews that I have lined up are contingent on my final transcript, but I don't foresee any problem with that."

She stared at Bev in a direct way that was either entirely sincere or incredibly duplicitous. "I trust that no matter what your personal feelings are, there's no problem with me moving on?"

Less than a minute passed as Bev silently ran through her possible responses. She fought to acknowledge her lack of objectivity about this woman who had stood provocatively in the bar at Bojangles and the woman who had expressed little sorrow at the death of her boyfriend. This was business and Karen's legal standing was the only issue that was important - except that Bev had no viable case yet and Karen's legal status was merely that of a fortunate beneficiary.

"I've made no secret of the fact that I don't buy accidental drowning, but I can't hold you here," Bev said bluntly.

Karen took a drag from the cigarette. "Look, I've told you all along that I'm not involved and I have a hard time believing Tom is, but I've already said everything I care to about that topic," she said. "And now that I have my major concern answered, I think that we should talk about Kyle."

The benefits of Bev's day off with Lorna virtually dissolved as her anger sparked so quickly she had to clench her jaw to keep from lashing out – she'd be damned if she was going to react openly. She swallowed and pulled her feet underneath the chair so she could stand. "I don't think that's necessary," she said.

Karen pressed her index finger against the desk. "Do you think it's possible for you to climb down off that judgmental pedestal and listen to me for a minute, please?"

Karen's tone puzzled Bev - it wasn't her usual mocking one.

Bev paused and Karen spoke quietly. "You know, you're such a sanctimonious tight-ass that I genuinely enjoy fucking with your head, but by the same honesty, from what little I know of Kyle, I think he's a pretty nice guy. He was really upset the other night when you stormed out and he couldn't talk to you."

"And when he came back in there you were, all ready to offer him solace," Bev said before she could stop herself.

Karen inspected the red tip of the cigarette and grinned. "I hope you're not trying to kid yourself into thinking that you don't care about him, unless, of course your reaction is just because it's me. But before I stray too far from the point, what I want to tell you is that as strange as it may seem, he didn't hang around long at all and he simply wasn't interested in me. To use an old-fashioned parlance, I do believe the man is smitten with you."

Bev was torn between a skeptical response and a desire to say, "Really?". She settled for keeping her mouth shut.

Karen unhooked her purse from the back of the chair and rested it on the desk. "I don't know why I'm going to bother to tell you one more thing, but I suppose it's because Kyle is probably the kind of man I should be attracted to if I wasn't always going for the bad-boy type," she said.

Bev rose as Karen stood and she locked eyes with her. "Look, the night I met Kyle he'd only been in town for a little while and he didn't know anyone," Karen continued. "I was, quite frankly, out to get laid because Greg was off on some jaunt or the other. Kyle was cute and available and if I recall correctly, talented in the sack, but I told him up front that I was involved and had no interest in any kind of relationship. I saw him maybe twice after that, but it was the same kind of deal - no questions, just a little fun sex. The other night was the first time I'd seen him for a while."

Bev tightened her mouth. "And that's not supposed to matter?"

Karen shook her head, stepped to the door, paused and turned with her hand on the knob. "I have no problem at all believing that you've never picked a guy up in a bar for the hell of it or because you were drunk, but unless you're a born again virgin or some shit like that, I think you should give the guy a break. Like I said though, it's not really my business, so if you want to dump him over what is essentially bullshit, that's up to you. Take care, Detective, and I'll find my own way out."

She slipped through the door and left it ajar as Bev gripped the back of her chair. She stood for a moment until she noticed an odd sensation and realized her nails were almost piercing the fabric. She loosened her grip with an impatient shake and breathed shallowly, alternating between anger and the embarrassing acknowledgement that Karen was right.

Did she want to walk away from Kyle because of Karen? She never drank enough to lose control and jump into bed with a man she didn't know, but a couple of her friends weren't so cautious and while she thought it was a bad habit, she still enjoyed their friendship. Couldn't she excuse it in Kyle, or at least listen to what he had to say? She'd been furious with the idea that he might have considered her to be a quick tumble, yet didn't the fact that he'd asked her out again negate that image? That wasn't the way a man behaved if all he cared about was how many women he could score with.

As much as she hated to agree with Karen about anything, she probably had overreacted. She looked at the candy-filled glass and smiled again. If the idea of Lorna and a woman like Karen giving her basically the same advice about Kyle wasn't irony, she didn't know what was. If he called, and there was no reason to think he wouldn't, she'd agree to get together for a talk and see how she felt when she saw him.

Bev sat down at her desk and rearranged the papers that she had shoved into the folder when Karen arrived. Maybe Karen didn't have anything to do with Wiley's death, but she wasn't ready to say the same for Farmer; not until she'd gone through everything once more in excruciating detail and made another call or two. All she had to do was find the thread to unravel his story.

She thought back to the conversation she and Jim had had over apple pie when he'd told her that sooner or later she had to come across a case she either couldn't solve or couldn't prove. His idea that she didn't want to admit that she might have made a mistake had been particularly grating. Was that possible? Could she have become convinced of her own infallibility? She was on the verge of admitting that she might be off base about Karen. Was it so much more difficult to re-think her view of Farmer? Could her desire to be correct blind her to what was right? Was she deliberately stirring up the situation with Farmer just to support her own ego?

She didn't think so, although if she couldn't find the thread soon, she'd be out of ideas. In a way she didn't know which would be worse – admitting that she'd been wrong or holding to her theory and being forced to accept that she couldn't prove it.

She slapped her open hand against the desk and turned to a clean page on the writing pad. She didn't like either of those options so she'd better get busy before they were her only two choices.

Chapter Twenty-six

Bev stared at the blank notebook page for a moment and then wrote TIMING in all caps. The timing of Wiley's drowning was what bothered her the most. Initially it had been Harry's comments about the conflict between Farmer and Wiley that had alerted her, but it was Dillworth's information that had really raised her suspicions. Okay, what was in the notes that had to do with timing?

She started with the interviews and highlighted the items she would transfer to the board, but she couldn't concentrate between thinking about what Karen had said and listening for the telephone to ring. Kyle called a few minutes before six and Bev suggested that they meet at Paradisio's. It was public, but not a spot she frequented so maybe they wouldn't be interrupted by a string of acquaintances.

She put the Wiley file away and drove slowly enough to make sure she kept Kyle waiting ten minutes or so. She wanted him to be slightly anxious, not think that she was standing him up.

The stucco building that housed Paradisio's wasn't close enough to the water to draw the tourists. It had originally been a Chinese restaurant and then a short-lived attempt at a seafood buffet place. It had sat empty for over a year before someone looked at the market closely enough to recognize that Italian cuisine beyond pizza and spaghetti was what the town lacked.

Bev paused briefly at the entry and noticed that Kyle had taken a table in the far back where he could watch the door. Polished wooden tables filled the bar area and the hostess station was positioned between it and the larger dining room. Most of the people who weren't in the qeue for dinner were clustered around the television behind the bar.

Kyle stood as she approached and signaled to the waiter at the same time. His glass of red wine looked as if he hadn't taken a drink yet.

"I'll start with a cappuccino," Bev said and took the chair Kyle held for her. He smiled tentatively when the waiter departed.

"I'm glad you came," he said. "Any chance it was the flowers? I was going to send a dozen roses, but I thought that might seem a little needy."

Bev shook her head and pursed her lips slightly. "Like I told you, it was a nice gesture, but I'm here mostly because I decided we should try and see how we wanted to handle this."

Kyle moved his glass slightly to the right and rested his arm on the table. "Can I take that to mean you want to handle it or were you just speaking in general terms?"

Bev drew a deep breath and forgot what she had rehearsed on the drive over. The appearance of the waiter with her cappuccino bought her a few minutes and Kyle didn't rush her. She wasn't sure if she wanted to take the lead, but maybe it was best.

She looked at him. *Oh hell, go for the direct question.* "Did you go with Karen after I left the other night?"

"Not on a bet," he said with enough surprise that it was probably the truth. "The idea never occurred to me. Is that what you thought happened?"

Bev shrugged and blew a stream of air across the cinnamon flecked white frothy top of the coffee. "It could have," she said.

He shook his head and lifted his wineglass. His eyes were steady. "Bev, it's what I told you that night. I don't think you want a lot of details, but Karen, which I admit sounds more reasonable than Monique, and I weren't together much and even if you hadn't come into Bojangles, I had no intention of going with her again."

Bev raised her eyebrows. "A woman who looks like that and comes onto you the way she did and you don't give it any thought? That's what I'm supposed to believe?"

Kyle set his wine down without taking a sip and pressed his fingertips together. "Bev, it wouldn't make sense for me to say Karen isn't appealing, but I really wanted to catch you for dinner that evening. Karen was not the woman I was interested in."

God, he sounded sincere.

Kyle started to speak again before she could respond. "Listen, we haven't known each other all that long, and maybe it's just me, but I thought that you and I had something going, something that we could spend some time exploring. If I'm wrong about that, please say so because I'd just as soon you tell me now."

Bev shook her head and then realized she may have sent an incorrect sign. "The 'no' means you're not wrong, not that I think we didn't have a connection," she said quickly. "But it's not like I'm in a big hurry either," she added, lest she give the impression of trying to pin him down. The last thing she wanted was to act like she was angling for some kind of commitment.

Kyle smiled as if he understood the kind of limit she was trying to establish. "I know what you mean, but I've been doing a lot of thinking over the last few days and if you have the time, I'd like to tell you why I broke up with the woman in Chicago. It wasn't quite the way I explained it and while as a rule, I'm not into talking about former lovers, it might get my point across."

Bev was puzzled at the direction the conversation was taking, but nodded for him to continue - she *was* curious as to why he was still unattached.

Kyle shifted his chair closer so he could speak quietly, but he was careful to not crowd Bev. "Her name was Jasmine, she was in advertising and we met at a party. We hit it off right away because, like with you, it doesn't take me long to figure out that I enjoy someone's company."

He paused as if to gauge Bev's reaction to the comment and she lifted her hand a couple of inches off the table in acknowledgement. She noticed the waiter in her peripheral vision, although he was either experienced enough to figure out they needed some privacy or indifferent to the fact they were sitting in his section and not drinking much.

"Anyway, Jasmine and I had a lot in common, even though our working lives didn't cross paths. Without getting into this too deeply, we dated for several months and finally decided to move in together."

Bev sucked her bottom lip between her teeth. She hadn't gotten the impression that they had been that serious. Living together was hardly the same thing as merely dating.

Kyle took a sip of wine and if he noticed her expression, he didn't say anything. "I mean, we weren't making any promises, or at least we said we weren't, that it was just a practical living arrangement. She'd lost her roommate, I'd been thinking about getting a new apartment, etc.,. Things went pretty well for a few months and then one day she asked me for a favor."

Bev noted that an edge had crept into his tone and his jaw tightened. He looked away from her briefly and then resumed the story.

"One of the junior vice presidents in her company, a real arrogant son-of-a-bitch, got stopped during a traffic violation and they added possession of an illegal substance. What he had with him definitely exceeded a personal use amount, although it wasn't a huge bust."

"A little extra for distributing to good friends?" Bev asked quietly. It wasn't too difficult to guess what favor Jasmine had asked for.

Kyle nodded. "Yeah, not to mention the protégé of the advertising company's Chief Executive Officer."

"So your girlfriend figured that if she could get you to intervene, then gratitude from the company would follow?"

Kyle shrugged. "When she asked me the first time, I wasn't too upset because I figured, what the hell, she didn't realize that this was more serious than fixing a traffic ticket. She didn't let up though, so I finally told her to drop the subject. She was pissed and it got pretty frosty around the apartment."

Kyle stopped talking and drained his wineglass. He set the glass down carefully and gave Bev a lop-sided smile. "I thought she'd gotten over it though and it was maybe a week later that I found out that Jasmine arranged to have dinner with the most senior guy in my office and to cut to the chase, they heated up the sheets and she got the favor she was looking for."

Bev winced involuntarily. "Ouch."

Kyle rocked the empty glass on its base. "Yeah, aside from the fact that she turned out not to be the person I thought I knew, it made work kind of dicey," he said and looked at Bev. "It did, however, make it real easy when I was offered the job down here. I don't mean I was running away," he said hurriedly, "I mean I had never planned to stay in Chicago permanently and it seemed like a hell of a good time to leave."

They both fell silent for a moment and the waiter stepped over from a nearby table. Kyle motioned to his glass and Bev handed her empty cup to the young man.

"I'll have a red wine also," she said and waited for Kyle to finish whatever he had to say. Her anger with him was dissolving, but that still left the question of what was to happen next.

He shifted in his chair again and rubbed the back of his neck. "I wasn't looking to get involved with anyone again too soon, but I didn't have a routine established when I first came to town so I did the singles scene for a few weeks," he said and glanced over as another couple took the table next to them. He looked back at Bev and lowered his voice to where she had to lean forward slightly to hear him.

"Listen Bev, I wasn't lying when I told you that I don't usually move as fast as I did with you. I know the deal with Karen made you wonder about that, but I guess I was feeling sorry for myself the night I met her and one thing led to another and I don't know, it was just – just something that happened. I know it seems dumb about the name and all and I'm not going to act like the fling with her was the smartest thing I ever did in my life. I want you to understand though that there's no way I think of you as just someone to jump in the sack with."

Bev stopped herself from nodding and he cleared his throat, apparently unsettled by her silence. "Okay, the truth is that I don't know where you and I might be going, but from the first night we had dinner, I knew I wanted to get to know you better. You're a special lady and I enjoy being with you. I don't want to rush anything between us, but I'd sure as hell hate to stop under these circumstances."

The waiter reappeared and Bev took the glass as she sorted through Kyle's words.

Kyle cleared his throat again. "Uh Bev, a little feedback would be okay," he said.

He wasn't quite squirming, but he was close and Bev smiled. "All right, it's my turn," she said. "I do understand about Karen and I've probably been pissed off about it long enough. You're right about it making me wonder if you'd just spun me a line, though. I don't have to tell you that I'm no prude, but I've got no patience with guys who use sex as a scorecard. And you're also right about us taking some more time to find out how compatible we are, or aren't, for that matter."

Kyle grinned and touched the rim of his glass to hers. "Does that officially take me off the hook, and if it does, can I buy you dinner?"

Bev shook her head, but kept her voice light. "Yes to one and no to the other." He looked startled and she smiled. "Kyle, it's been a tough few days and I've got a full schedule tomorrow. I don't need a late night and I figure if I have more than one glass of wine, I'll decide two would taste good and then there's no telling what would happen."

Kyle reached his hand out and touched her forearm. Bev instantly remembered the feel of his body against her and she nearly lost her resolve. She quickly took a sip of wine to break the physical contact, but smiled to let him know that her rejection was only momentary.

"Then can we make a date for Friday?" he asked and moved his hand. "I grill a great steak if I do say so myself or I could take you some place fancy."

Bev wiped away a drop of wine that was clinging to the stem of the glass. "Let's plan on Friday and I'll think about where."

He nodded and changed the subject. "That sounds good and I can imagine that things are hectic at the office. Is Jim going to have to retire or will he be coming back?"

Bev ran her finger around the top of the glass. "It's possible that he'll retire, although some of it will depend on how the surgery goes," Bev said and felt a little uncomfortable with her lie.

It would be nice to be able to tell Kyle, to tell him about the extra pressure she was under, to have someone to talk to about the professional opportunity that was hovering within her grasp, but this was neither the time nor the place. If things worked out Friday, then she could explain.

Bev motioned to the clock on the wall. Her desire to not allow her emotions or her hormones to control her decisions edged out her desire to see Kyle naked. "I'm glad we got together and talked about this, but I do need to get home," she said. "I'll call you about Friday."

The waiter may have been more observant than Bev had given him credit for because he slipped the check to Kyle as Bev pulled her keys from her purse. She paused long enough to let him settle up and escort her outside to the car.

They stood without speaking for a moment and then Kyle bent his head to give her a light kiss on the mouth. It was a kiss filled with desire, but not impatience. It was the right kind of gesture, sort of like the flowers. She felt a warning flutter in her stomach, turned her head gently and smiled a good-bye.

"I'll call you," she repeated and slipped into the driver's seat before she could change her mind.

Kyle nodded in understanding, stepped back and lifted his hand in farewell. Bev drove away and thought about what he'd told her about his ex-girlfriend. At least their breakup had been something easy to understand.

She passed by the beauty parlor where her mother had had a standing Thursday morning appointment for nearly twenty years and suddenly realized a downside of repairing the relationship with Kyle - convincing Emma Henderson that she should not jump to conclusions.

Well, she had another few days before her parents returned home and maybe she could suggest that she should plan a huge retirement party for Jim. Once the news was made public, everyone would be expecting some kind of farewell ceremony. That would keep her busy and be a big help to Myrtle.

The smells from Paradisio's kitchen inspired her taste buds for Italian and when Bev arrived at her apartment, she zapped a better than average frozen lasagna in the microwave, but limited herself to one glass of red wine. She wanted to go in early and finish the review of the Wiley file. She knew better than to attempt to ignore the Chief's deadline and she had one less distraction now that the situation with Kyle was cleared up.

She'd been allowing her emotions to interfere too much lately and it was time to get herself under control and find proof against Farmer. There would be no more worrying about Kyle and she would unplug the telephone at work the next morning if she had to.

Chapter Twenty-seven

Willie Denton stared at the door as a key turned in the lock. He was certain it was Hal, but his fingers rested on the pistol lying on the bedspread next to him in case he was wrong. He relaxed when he recognized Hal's silhouette in the door.

Willie was startled when he realized Hal was talking to another man standing behind him. He wondered what the fuck was going on.

"Yo Willie, this is Dwayne," Hal said and jerked his thumb at the man who entered carrying a partially filled, faded olive drab duffel bag. He propped the bag against the wall, lowered himself onto the arm of the stained, orange plaid chair and nodded in greeting without making a move to shake hands.

Willie swung around to sit on the edge of the bed and returned the nod as he and the stranger looked each other over without speaking. Dwayne was a little taller than Hal and had his black hair pulled back into a short ponytail. He wasn't fat, but had a beer gut that hung slightly over the worn pair of jeans that were streaked with what appeared to be dried paint. His dark brown eyes were squinted and his nose looked as if it had been broken at least once.

"What's going on?" Willie asked and focused on the new man instead of Hal.

Hal took off the lightweight windbreaker he'd been wearing and pulled his pistol from the waistband of his jeans. He laid it on the nightstand next to his bed and waved his hand between the two men. "I've known Dwayne for a long time. He's the one who'll get us the papers we need and he's done a lot of boat running down south. He can get us away from the coast without drawing attention and we need one more hand for the boat. I mean for us to get a nice one, big enough so we don't have to worry about the open water."

Willie shifted his gaze back and forth between the two men. He didn't much like the idea of bringing in someone new, but the truth of the matter was he didn't know much about boats and he wasn't sure if Hal did or if he'd been bullshitting him. It sure as hell wouldn't do them any good to grab a boat and then sink it.

"You did time in the Navy too, or something like that?" he asked Dwayne.

Dwayne snorted. "Do I look like some fucking swabbie? There's folks around here who like to avoid the Coast Guard and I help out. I'm in between jobs right now," he replied and turned his head toward Hal. "Is this some goddamn interview?"

Hal waved his cigarette in an arc and blew a trickle of smoke into the dimly lit room. "Willie, Dwayne's okay, don't worry. He's the one with the contact for the passports and his part of the take is that he keeps the boat when we get to where we're going. And Dwayne, Willie's gotten pretty good as a back-up man, so don't think he can't handle himself. The three of us will take off day after tomorrow and head out. An easy drive down the Keys, we heist the boat and we're on our way. You want a beer, Dwayne?"

Dwayne shook his head. "No, I need to go wrap up a couple of loose ends. I'm not planning on coming back for a while." He stood, reached into the bag and pulled out a camera. "Sit up straight, Willie and then I'll do Hal."

Willie didn't like having his picture taken, but the flash popped in his eyes before he could protest. The little dots lingered and blurred his vision. Dwayne snapped three shots of him and of Hal and then slipped from the room without so much as a goddamn word.

Hal walked across the room and lifted the lid off the white Styrofoam cooler they'd stolen from the last liquor store. He pulled a beer out, tore the metal tab off and pitched it on the floor. "Damn Willie, we're getting low on beer; we'll have to make another stop."

Willie groaned silently. "Man, we're on our way out of the country," he said quietly. "Don't you think we ought to just buy a couple of six packs and get the hell gone? We've got plenty of cash for beer."

Hal grinned, but there was neither humor nor warmth in the action. "Come on, Willie, you're not getting nervous are you? We've been fine up to now and besides, I explained to you that's why we went back northeast and then south again; the cops will figure we're on our way out of state and won't be looking in this direction. We take off when no one is paying attention, do one more quick job on the way to restock supplies, drive straight on to the marina, grab the boat and then we're out into the big blue ocean with our next stop on an island somewhere in the Bahamas. You know there's more than seven hundred islands in the Bahamas?"

"Seven hundred islands?" Willie said in disbelief. "How can there be that many if it's only one country?" He found the bottle of whiskey he'd set on the nightstand and poured a shot into his glass.

Hal found the remote control at the foot of Willie's bed, dropped onto his own bed and began to quickly move through the limited number of channels. "Just one of those things, man, but that's good for us because like I told you, there's practically no police on those small islands. Nothing but sun, rum and more pussy than you can handle. It'll be perfect, you'll see."

"Won't they wonder why we're there? I mean, won't we look out of place? Aren't those natives black or something? It's not like we'll fit right in."

That had been bugging him ever since Hal told him where they were going. The idea sounded good, but what if it didn't go down the way Hal thought? And if the new guy took off with the boat, they'd be stranded, wouldn't they?

Hal doubled his pillow up and shoved it behind his back. "It's not a problem. Americans and Europeans show up on the islands all the time looking for a little piece of paradise. I'll figure out a story for us before we get there and nobody will be suspicious. I'll make it something simple so you won't have trouble remembering it. We'll just be two more guys that got pissed off at our bosses and ex-wives and hit the seas looking for adventure."

Hal tuned into one of the business shows and Willie thought about them making another stop. He didn't want to do another job. There'd been too many already and no matter what Hal said, they'd been lucky as well as smart.

He was anxious to move again; this was their second motel since the last robbery and he had a disturbing feeling in his gut that sooner or later someone would start to ask questions.

Willie swished another mouthful of whiskey and felt the sting of it on the roof of his mouth. Whether Hal wanted to admit it or not, they could make a mistake in something they said or did; something unexpected could give them away. All it would take was one phone call and a visit from the local cops who were probably like cops everywhere. A cop gets an idea in his head and wants to know something and he could work on a man until he told everything. Sure, if they were hauled directly in for questioning, then they might get a by-the-book type who'd let them call a lawyer first, but it was a lot more likely they'd try and sweat them first and with no witnesses around, any seasoned cop could claim attempted escape with a straight face. No one was going to argue over a busted lip or some bruised ribs if it meant the Devil's Duo had confessed.

Willie closed his eyes for a moment to get rid of the image of the last time a burly sheriff's deputy had jammed a nightstick repeatedly into his kidneys until he was gasping for breath and puking between gasps. Hal had done hard time and might be able to take a beating and still refuse to talk, but Willie knew he wasn't that strong. And he suspected that Hal knew it, too.

Maybe the guy, Dwayne, was exactly what Hal said he was and maybe Hal was thinking about leaving Willie behind if he had someone else to help out. The way Willie figured it was if Hal left him behind, it would be with a slug to the back of his head. Willie took one more swallow of whiskey, capped the bottle and set it on the nightstand.

He didn't want to think about Hal turning on him; he just wanted to head south and not stop until they were out on the ocean. Besides, didn't most marinas have their own stores? They could grab whatever they needed there along with the boat and not take a chance on a last job along the way. He'd take a nap and then tell Hal about it when he woke up.

Chapter Twenty-eight

The next morning Bev stopped first at Sheila's desk and opened a super-size box of doughnuts. Sheila took a plain glazed one and grinned. "This is not your usual juice and muffin. What's the occasion?"

Bev set the box on the adjacent table. "I'm trying to keep everyone occupied so I can get a little quiet time. Can you help keep the calls down for me?"

Sheila nibbled the edge of the doughnut and nodded. "Sure, I'll tell Kristie and run interference with folks - genuine emergencies only," she said and paused before she took a bigger bite. "And what do want us to do if, oh let's say, the Assistant DA wants to talk to you?"

Bev pursed her lips and thought about brushing it off, but that would be unfair to Sheila. "I guess I can be interrupted for that," she said and escaped into the office before Sheila could extend the conversation.

Bev set up the coffeepot and pulled the Wiley files from the drawer. She quickly sorted the papers into separate piles for the work Jim had finished, her notes, the coroner's report and the articles on shallow water blackout that she'd gathered.

As she neatly aligned the papers she remembered that she hadn't read the articles that Dr. Cleary had transmitted via e-mail. She attached a bright blue square of paper to them as a reminder and centered the notepad on the desk as a point of reference. She wiped the white board clean and put two brand new pens in the tray. The neatly organized array would surely lend itself to tidy answers.

She started where she'd left off and cross-referenced the documents looking for references that dealt with the timing of Wiley's death since that was the thing she kept coming back to – the coincidence she couldn't resolve. *Happened after morning dives. Farmer started mouth-to-mouth. Marine Patrol took over rescue. Wiley died. Afternoon dive trip cancelled. Happened before investigator arrived. Wiley to be out of town that day.* Bev stopped at the last note.

Farmer had said Wiley had planned to be out of town so he wouldn't have met with the investigator. Now that was something she hadn't thought through at the time – would the investigator have been satisfied with that response? Wouldn't he have insisted on making another visit? Well, maybe if the absence was supposed to be a long one he wouldn't have. She ran back through the interviews with Karen. No mention of Wiley planning to be away, but there had been no reason to ask that specific question.

Bev found Karen's number and punched it in. She kept the conversation brief and didn't elaborate after Karen said she didn't know what Bev was talking about. *Okay, had Farmer lied about the out of town trip or had Wiley not told Karen?*

Bev refilled her mug, leaned against the small table and stared at the white board she'd left blank. She thought back to the visit with Farmer at the dive shop when she'd met Danny. What had he said? *Regular customers, more experienced divers or that maybe there wouldn't have been time for the free dive that morning. Another reference to timing.*

Bev wandered back to the desk and sat down. She started again with the first interviews with Dillworth and found the entry about having one safety diver instead of two - she'd written *Novice in water, not good idea.*

She thought for a moment, dialed Adventures Below and kept her fingers crossed. Danny answered the phone.

"Oh hi," he said when she identified herself. "Gee, Tom isn't here right now, but he should be back late this afternoon."

Thank God. "No, that's okay, you should be able to answer my question," she said nonchalantly. "Do you remember when we were talking about the group that you had to reschedule? The day of the accident?"

Danny paused and Bev wrapped the telephone cord around her finger to keep from rushing him.

"Uh yeah," he said. "Some of the regular customers. That's why Tom figured they wouldn't mind rescheduling."

Bev unwrapped the cord. "So, they weren't like students?"

"Gosh no," Danny said. "They were all advance level divers and two, or maybe it was three, of them were either dive master or assistant instructor qualified – you know, like lots of dives and trained in rescue. I mean, if Greg had waited to do his free dive with them, it might not have made a difference, but maybe they could have helped. Of course, Greg might not have gone out at all and then it wouldn't have mattered," he added after a tiny pause.

Bev squeezed her hand around the receiver. "Excuse me, but what do you mean?"

"Well, the morning guys were pretty new to diving and Tom had recommended they do a guided dive and he couldn't be the guide and handle the boat by himself. That's why Greg went along. The afternoon group wouldn't have needed him, so I don't know if he would have gone or not. He did doubles some days, but not always." Danny said something Bev couldn't understand as though he was talking to someone else.

"Hey, a lady just came in. Can I call you right back?" he asked. "Or did I answer your question?"

Bev scrawled the note on the pad. "Actually yes, I got what I needed," she said, although she still wasn't completely sure of what she had.

She moved to the board, transferred the key words in block letters, stepped back and looked for the link. Okay, if Farmer had lied about Wiley being out of town, then he would have been there to talk to the investigator and from what she'd learned about Wiley, he probably would have caused problems. But being out of town didn't matter since he was dead. Now, if Danny was right about the afternoon group, Greg might not have gone and if he had, Farmer would have had help with the rescue.

Bev rubbed her hand across her eyes. The problem was that even if Farmer had lied about Wiley and why he cancelled the second group, that didn't explain what really happened to Wiley. If Farmer didn't actively do something to him – and there was no evidence of physical or substance interference, then logically the worst thing Farmer had done was make sure he was alone in the water with Wiley. Why? On the off chance that there would be a problem on the dive, there would be no one else to help and he'd be deliberately slow to react? She'd been down that path already.

The disturbing thought that she could be wrong tumbled around inside her head. The promise she'd made to herself to accept that answer had been easier to handle when she hadn't honestly thought that she would draw another blank. Damn, what am I missing?, she thought.

She walked back to the desk for her coffee mug and saw the blue paper stuck on the magazine articles that she hadn't looked at yet. She lifted her head when Sheila pushed the door open far enough to stick her head in.

"Bev, I don't want to distract you, but you've been in the office all morning and I was wondering if you wanted Kristie to pick you up some lunch," Sheila said. "Oh, I checked the Chief's calendar. He'll be gone this afternoon and no crisis have cropped up so you should be able to keeping going on whatever it is you're doing."

Bev pushed back from the desk, sighed and stood up. "Thanks for the offer, but I've got some yogurt here. I think I will take a stretch break, though."

Sheila nodded and left the door open. Bev went outside for some fresh air and did some slow stretches to ease the tension in her neck and shoulders. When she returned to the office she took a container of peach yogurt and a diet Coke from the refrigerator, sat down and read the articles while she ate.

The first one was a rather dry five-year statistical review

of recreational diving fatalities with no emphasis on any particular cause of death.

Bev was mildly surprised to discover that unlike the movie versions of great white sharks dismembering people or faulty air hoses, the highest percentage of deaths was attributed to human error that often involved panic.

The second, shorter article was devoted to an update about shallow water blackout. Bev read through it quickly and stopped at the last paragraph with the author's warning to avoid a deep free dive after scuba diving.

She read the one and half pages carefully again to make sure she understood what he had written. She spooned the remaining bite of yogurt into her mouth, then reached for the interview with Dr. Cleary. She grabbed a blue highlighter and marked the passage when he had mentioned that Wiley's dive had been to eighty feet.

Next Bev went back to her initial conversation with Dillworth. She scanned twice until she found what she was looking for - his comments about free diving not being a big sport in the area. Another swipe of the highlighter.

She ran her fingers through her notebook to the very first interview with the two young divers that had been witnesses to the incident. It was the one named Bibbins whose response tracked with what she was rapidly formulating as a theory. Her luck held and within an hour she completed telephonic interviews with Dr. Cleary and Dillworth. Dillworth verified that he didn't know Wiley's dive was to eighty feet and Dr. Cleary acknowledged that he hadn't been aware of the contents of the article he'd sent her when he had looked at the report on Wiley.

Bibbins was the last on the list and she jiggled her foot as she waited for him to come to the phone. Okay, stay calm, she told herself and asked Bibbins if he had time to answer a few follow-up questions.

"Sure," he said enthusiastically. "But I haven't thought of anything new."

"Actually, I'd like to ask if you booked your dive in advance with Adventures Below or did you wait until you arrived?"

"Oh no, a friend of ours had recommended them and I called at least two weeks in advance, maybe a little longer than that," he said without hesitation. "I talked to Tom and he told me about the dive sites and all and we talked about us using a guide since we'd never been to the Keys and we'd only logged eight open water dives."

"Sure, that would make sense," Bev said. "Now I'd like to talk about when Mr. Farmer asked if the two of you minded staying out while Mr. Wiley did his free dive. Was that the first time a free dive was mentioned?"

Bibbins hesitated and Bev tried not to squeeze the receiver too hard. *Come on, come on!*

"The first time it was mentioned?" he repeated. "Uh no, I mean we'd been talking about it before that – how you did it and all. I'd seen it on TV, but hadn't met anyone who'd ever done it. The conversation started when Tom was talking about some guy around there who'd made it to almost eighty feet. I guess Greg hadn't heard about it because he said he didn't think so."

Yes! "And then what happened?" Bev asked and leaned forward in her chair.

"Uh well, Tom said the guy's name and then he said that maybe he could give Greg some pointers or something like that and then Greg said something like *bullshit*, excuse me, but he did, and that he could do eighty feet no sweat."

"And that's when they asked if you and Mr. Matson would mind waiting?"

Bibbins paused again and Bev wished she could see his face. "Well, sort of," he said at last. "Tom said something like that it had been a while since Greg had done a free dive and he should probably wait until he could ask this guy's advice about going deeper. Greg started laughing and said he didn't need anybody's advice and that if we weren't in a hurry, he'd show Tom. And that's when Tom said they didn't have another dive that afternoon so if we didn't mind, he'd go in the water with Greg. Oh man," Bibbins said with a little gasp. "I guess maybe Tom was right. I hadn't even thought about that until now."

Yes, yes, yes! Bev thought, but quickly said, "Well, that's not something you could have known about and there was no reason for you to have thought about in all the excitement."

They spoke for another few minutes and Bev thanked Bibbins when he offered to write down everything he could remember, talk to Mr. Matson as well and e-mail it to her.

She gently replaced the receiver, flexed her shoulders and breathed a long sigh. She'd found it and goddamn, she had to give Farmer credit for an intricate scheme! She walked to the board, wrote EIGHTY FEET and underlined it. Farmer had set the whole thing up from beginning to end.

He'd read the article about the risks of shallow water blackout being increased if a deep free dive was done following a regular deep scuba dive. He had booked Bibbins and Matson and worked it so that Wiley would dive with them. And Farmer was the one who initiated the conversation about doing the free dive, not Wiley. And the eighty foot depth was beyond what Wiley usually did and well beyond the author's caution.

Bev paced back and forth between the board and her desk. Okay, there was no guarantee this scheme would work, but Farmer had arranged the precise conditions the article had warned about, and Bibbins and Matson made for perfect witnesses to innocently report that Farmer had done everything he could for Wiley. It might not be a conventional murder, but it sure as hell hadn't been an accident either.

Chapter Twenty-nine

Bev started to dash out of the office to tell the Chief and then remembered that Sheila had said he'd be out. Damn, wouldn't you know it.

Well, the delay would give her time to re-write her narrative, look for any possible holes and be ready to arrest Farmer as soon as the Chief gave her the nod. Okay, maybe she wouldn't be able to arrest him immediately, but definitely haul him in for intense questioning.

Questioning when she already knew the answers; the satisfaction of seeing a suspect recognize that he, or she, no longer had the upper hand. Or at least not unless they had the money to hire a lawyer whose sense of justice was for sale.

She resisted the urge to do a little victory prance in front of the board, lifted her can of diet Coke in salute to her cleverness and grimaced when she took a lukewarm sip. Oh well, she could celebrate later, but was she ever going to enjoy the look on the Chief's face when she laid out the details she'd pieced together!

The only part where she was going to have to concede she was in error was about Karen. The set-up was genuinely complicated and unless Karen knew a hell of a lot more about diving than she seemed to, she wouldn't have known anything about Farmer's plot. It was still possible that she had asked him to get rid of Greg, but the timing was more closely aligned with Farmer's need because of the impending investigation of the dive shop.

The ring of the telephone startled her. "Bev, Sheila said you were taking calls from the DA's office," Kristie said with what was probably a smothered giggle. "Mr. Stewart is on hold."

"Thanks, I'll pick up," Bev said and depressed the blinking button.

"Hi Bev, it's Kyle. How are things going?" he asked.

She smiled at the sound of his voice. "Uh really well," she replied. Maybe she shouldn't say anything to him until she talked to the Chief. Oh hell, she'd have to consult with the DA's office anyway.

"I've been going over the Wiley case again and I've got it figured out. I know how Farmer killed him and it was no goddamn accident." She knew her tone was smug, but she was entitled considering the amount of shit she'd been taking from everyone.

Not unexpectedly, Kyle paused before he responded. "Um that's great, Bev," he said. "So what's the deal?"

Bev looked at the spread of paper across her desk and at the board. "It's pretty tricky. Chief Taylor is gone for the day, but how about if I swing by and fill you in unofficially?"

Kyle's hesitation surprised her. She thought he would have welcomed an excuse to see her. "Look I'd like that, but I had the Explorer serviced today and I've got to pick it up before the shop closes," he said. "Do you mind coming by the condo instead in about an hour? I can meet you back at the office, but I'd rather get comfortable and have a cold beer unless you have some objection."

It was a reasonable suggestion, but Bev paused. Was she ready to go to Kyle's place? Did it matter one way or the other? She was over being angry with him, so what difference did it make where they met?

"I almost never turn down a cold beer," she said before he could misinterpret her brief silence. "I'll see you at your place."

They said good-bye and Bev replaced the receiver with one hand as she clicked on the *Open File* icon on the computer to bring the report up on the screen. She wanted to fill in the blanks with what she'd worked out.

She shook her head slightly to clear away the sudden mental image of Kyle's naked body and the way they had tumbled into his bed. There would be time enough for that later - she'd finally solved what could have been a perfect murder and that needed her full attention.

Bev used the hour to complete her narrative and make an extra copy of it and some selected notes. She shut the lights off when she was finished and told Kristie that she wouldn't be back after her errand.

She detoured into the ladies room and let go of any pretense that her visit was strictly professional. She re-braided her hair into a softer look, freshened the light makeup she wore and applied a dot of perfume between her breasts. When she got to her car, she draped her jacket on the passenger's seat and undid the first button on her blouse.

Kyle had considerately parked along the curb so she could use the driveway and he must have been watching for her because he opened the front door as soon as she switched the ignition off. He had already changed into a pair of jeans and a short sleeve knit shirt that brought out the blue of his eyes.

"Hi," he said with a grin and Bev suddenly couldn't remember why she'd been so angry with him. What woman wouldn't try to pick him up in a bar?

"I see you got your truck okay," she replied and stopped short of giving him a kiss - business first.

"It's a sports utility vehicle, otherwise known as an SUV, or a UTE if you prefer," he corrected. "If you call it a truck, then in this part of the country I might have to buy a gun rack for it and that just doesn't seem to be me."

Bev laughed and followed him inside. He waved her toward the couch and went into the kitchen to get the beers. Bev extracted the papers from the file folder, laid them out sequentially on the coffee table and waited for Kyle to join her.

"I guess congratulations are in order", Kyle said as he filled two frosted glass mugs.

Bev flipped back the strand of hair that had slipped loose and decided to answer the unasked question first.

"Once you see what I've got, it's easy to understand why

I missed it, but I have to admit that I'm no longer inclined to think that Karen was involved except maybe to strengthen Farmer's motive. She's not a diver and I don't see how anyone who isn't could have come up with this idea. There's still the angle that maybe she wasn't actively a part of the plan, but did convince Farmer to do something, although it's more likely Farmer came up with it on his own. I think that what happened is he figured this out and it was so damn close to perfect that he couldn't get it out of his mind."

Kyle handed Bev one of the mugs and sat next to her on the couch. His grin was lopsided. "Well it makes this less complicated if Karen's in the clear and you've given it a great buildup, but before you get into the whole thing, am I out of the doghouse?"

Bev smiled and touched his cheek with the tip of her finger. "Yes you are or I wouldn't be here. Now pay attention and let me show you how it went down."

She took one sip of beer, grabbed a coaster from the stack on the end table and set the mug on it. She tapped her finger on the narrative and waved her hand across the documents.

Bev gave Kyle the highlighted copy of the short article about free diving. "This is the key," she said. "But before I go any further, I assume you don't know much about scuba diving."

Kyle shook his head. "Not to speak of, although I was planning to take it up now that I'm living here. Should I change my mind?"

"I don't think so," Bev replied. "According to the dive experts I've been talking to, and from what I've been reading, diving is pretty safe if you have the right equipment and follow the proper procedures. Read the last couple of paragraphs of that article, though. There's a very clear warning for free divers not to mix a deep free dive after a deep scuba dive because of the increased risk of suffering shallow water blackout."

Kyle held his hand up as he quickly read the article and then looked at Bev. "Okay, I've got this part. And the

Shades of Murder

connection is what?"

Bev stood up and started to pace back and forth. It was hard to hold back her excitement.

"Farmer is the one who originally booked the clients and had recommended they use a guide, which is why Wiley went with them. They did a wreck dive at about ninety feet and then a shallow dive of about forty feet. Farmer stayed on the boat and that's all perfectly normal. After the two dives were over with though, Farmer is the one who made a comment to Wiley about doing a free dive."

Bev pointed to her notes. "Bibbins, one of the clients, remembered it because he asked some questions about it. Neither Jim nor I thought anything about it when we started the investigation since everyone was acting like Wiley doing a free dive was commonplace. Anyway, Farmer was talking about how some other local guy had logged a dive to nearly eighty feet. Now as it turns out, that's not particularly deep for free divers, but according to Dillworth, free diving isn't that popular in this area and when you start diving like that you need to have some special training. He's pretty tuned into what goes on around here and he doesn't know of anyone who trains for the deeper dives."

Kyle's forehead creased as he listened to Bev and she could tell he hadn't made the leap. "The depth is an important point," she continued, "and so is the fact that Farmer had intentionally cancelled a dive group for the afternoon. The people in that group were all experienced divers and included at least two that were rescue qualified."

Kyle laid the paper on the coffee table. "Wait, I don't know what that's got to do with anything."

Bev paced past the couch. "I'll get to that in a minute. So, according to Bibbins, Farmer mentioned that maybe Wiley shouldn't be trying to break records since he hadn't been free diving for a while. Bibbins said Wiley blew that off and it was maybe half an hour at most when Farmer and Wiley got into the water. Now look at the date on that article."

Kyle glanced down and then back at Bev. "Three months

ago, but I'm still not with you," he said. "And what about the cancelled dive?"

"Okay, we've found out Farmer and Wiley were basically complete opposites. Farmer kept up on all the latest dive information and Wiley could care less about it. Farmer probably knew about this guy's research and with Wiley being the competitive person that he was, he set Wiley up to do a dive that if this guy is right, had a high probability of ending just like it did. Remember that Farmer is the safety diver and he's the only other person in the water. Bibbins and Matson don't have a clue that there's a problem until they see Farmer dragging Wiley. Four or five minutes could have easily passed before Farmer started the resuscitation and they wouldn't have noticed. Not to mention that if you don't have a good seal while you're administering mouth-to-mouth, you can look like you're doing it correctly and it's a waste of time. By the time the Marine Patrol shows up and takes over, the chances of Wiley recovering are virtually nonexistent."

Kyle had moved forward on the couch until his knees were touching the edge of the coffee table. "And if the other group had been there, someone else might have jumped in on the rescue piece?"

Bev stopped and ticked off her fingers. "That, for sure, but part of why Wiley went on the morning dive was to be a guide for Bibbins and Matson. If they'd had to get back to prep the boat for a second trip, it might have looked odd for Farmer to have delayed coming in and the chances are that Wiley wouldn't have gone on the second trip considering the level of divers that were involved."

Bev caught her breath, took a drink and searched Kyle's face. His eyes moved back and forth rapidly and she was prepared for his questions.

He nodded tentatively. "Damn, that could work, but aren't you hanging a lot on this one guy's theory?"

That was the easy one. She resumed walking back and forth the length of the couch.

"Yes, but aside from the fact that I called the dive

physiologist in North Carolina to double check that the guy who wrote the article is apparently highly regarded, it all makes sense if you think through it. Shallow water blackout is not that uncommon and even with appropriate rescue action, the person doesn't always pull through. A few minutes of delay is all it would have taken to almost guarantee Wiley can't make it. Now I know you're wondering if Farmer could actually have arranged this, but if you talk to people who knew the two men, you'll see it wouldn't have been difficult. Farmer gets rid of Wiley and in the process saves Karen from what he considers an abusive relationship, and I'm willing to bet he knew about the policy Karen had. Even if she wasn't a part of it, he would have thought he was doing her a favor from a financial point of view."

Kyle rubbed his hand across his chin. "And there was the investigation of the dive shop dangling over his head."

Bev stopped pacing and balanced sideways on the edge of the couch. "Exactly, and that's what was bothering me all along. Farmer was working to buy Wiley out, but there was no way he could make it happen before these dive industry folks showed up. I mean, from what I've heard of him, Wiley might have told them to take a leap just because he felt like it and Adventures Below wouldn't have gotten off with only a warning. The bad publicity could have put a hole in the business that they couldn't recover from. Farmer told me that Wiley had agreed to be out of town when they came, but I asked Karen about that and he hadn't told her about taking any kind of trip. Bibbins and Matson presented the perfect witnesses for what Farmer had planned and the second group booked their dive after them. That could have ruined the whole thing and Farmer was the one who cancelled – well, postponed the dive, but made sure he had the scene set the way he needed it."

needed something to tide her over until dinner.

It was surprisingly quiet at the hospital and Bev had no problem finding a parking place. She tossed the empty cup into the trash barrel and quickly chewed a breath mint to cover the smell of the milkshake out to day movements. As best as Bev could explain it, it was like the worn pair of jeans that was maybe a little frayed in places, but it was the pair you reached for first.

Jim nodded slowly, lifted one hand and let it drop to the bed. "I've got enough life insurance and the house ain't much, but it's paid for, so Myrtle would be okay for money. It's like I told you the other day though, I want to be able to take her on that cruise, be around to help with the grandkids and all that stuff. I owe her that and a lot more."

Bev reached over and straightened out a non-existent wrinkle in the covers. "Is there anything I can do for you?"

Jim swallowed hard, glanced around the room and then brought his gaze back to Bev. Not surprisingly, his moment of vulnerability had disappeared and his tone was normal. "Well, if you could sneak me in a dozen doughnuts..."

Bev understood what he really meant and the brief excursion into maudlin revelation was over. She laughed and held out her hands to ward off the suggestion. "Even if I managed to get by the nurses' station, Myrtle would kill me," she said.

As if on cue one of the nurses stepped inside the room with a paper pill cup in her hand. She didn't say a word, but it didn't take too many detective skills to read her body language.

It could be fun to stay and fluster the nurse. Bev hadn't told Jim what she'd discovered about the case yet, although as she watched him dutifully swallow his medication she could tell he was more tired than he wanted to acknowledge. If she started in about Farmer, they were liable to get into a lengthy discussion and get carried away with planning a strategy. That couldn't be good for him.

"Hey Jim, it's late and I need to head home," she said and was given an *It's about time* kind of smiles by the nurse as she pointedly looked at her wristwatch.

Bev projected a smile of complete innocence in return, stood and picked up her purse to prove that she was in the process of leaving.

She leaned across and gave Jim a peck on the forehead. "By the way, in case you hadn't heard, the guys gave so much blood to the hospital that the doctors should be able to drain you dry and refill you."

Jim grinned. "Yeah, the Red Cross lady gave me the news. She said even Claude came by, but he was so damn thick-skinned they couldn't get a needle in him."

Bev stepped away and patted Jim's arm. "That's the rumor. Get some rest, big guy, and we'll check on you tomorrow after you get settled in Miami."

Jim blinked his eyes rapidly. "Sounds good and Bev, thanks for everything. You take it easy and don't be too stubborn to ask Claude for help if you need it."

Bev nodded in agreement and slipped out the door. She walked down the corridor and when she saw the sign to the hospital chapel, she turned on impulse and entered the small, quiet room.

Bev's church attendance was erratic and usually directly proportional to her mother's reminders that the pastor had inquired about her welfare. Religion wasn't something she thought a lot about and felt only minimal guilt when she requested God's assistance and then didn't follow through with whatever promise she'd made. After all, God was pretty understanding and as long as she lived a good life, that was the important part, wasn't it?

She sat in one of the pews for a few minutes and didn't try to make any bargains for Jim's sake. He was a decent man with a loving family and they could all use some more time together. She knew that didn't always count in the balance of human life, but it couldn't hurt to mention it.

A cool breeze lifted loose strands of her hair as she exited the building and clouds almost obscured the waning moon. The smell from a nearby Mexican restaurant carried down the street and a sizzling platter of fajitas suddenly seemed more appealing than a quick sandwich. It had been a full day and sitting down while someone waited on her wasn't a bad idea at all. Besides, after a couple of cold beers she'd be able to mentally map out the presentation to Chief Taylor that she was planning to have waiting for him in the morning.

Kyle stared at the sheet of paper he was holding and shook his head slowly. "Bev, I don't want you pissed off at me again and you're right, I can see how it might have happened this way, but this is going to be damned hard to prove. And if I do get enough to sell a jury this isn't murder from a legal definition. Farmer didn't force Wiley to go on the dive."

Bev could tell Kyle was trying to be supportive, but she didn't want him to get caught in legal hair-splitting. "Look, Bibbins will testify that Wiley hadn't said anything about doing a free dive and that Farmer initiated the conversation. It'll be easy to find out if anyone local had made a seventy-plus foot free dive like he told Wiley and this article was published three months before it happened. At a minimum, you should be able to go with attempted murder. I agree it's not a conventional weapon, but we do have a corpse."

Kyle sighed and exhaled a long breath. "There have been attempts at prosecution in similar cases such as when someone knew another person had a heart condition and they deliberately provoked a confrontation that then resulted in a fatal heart attack, but I've got to tell you it's tough. There are too many variables that a defense attorney can argue."

Bev knew it was an unusual case and she wasn't distressed with Kyle's position. "I understand what you're telling me, but my point is now that I've figured it out, I can turn the heat up on Farmer," she said. "Look, he thinks he's gotten away with this, but we're not dealing with a professional in spite of the fact it was a clever plan. I'm convinced that I can get a confession out of him. All I need you to do is get permission for us to put him and his business under a microscope. We check his computer, his bank accounts, talk to enough people around town and I don't think he can take that kind of pressure. His reputation is important to him and I bet he'll fold and tell us everything."

Bev watched comprehension replace the doubt on Kyle's

face and he whistled softly. "You may be onto something," he said. "I'll have to talk to the boss though because we'd need to be careful how we proceed."

Bev took the paper from him and replaced it in the folder. "You see it now though, don't you? Farmer set it all up."

Kyle closed the small distance between them and slipped his arm around her waist. "If I tell you I do will you believe it's true and it's not that I'm trying to get in your pants?"

Bev caught her breath at the feel of his arm and she twisted around to face him. Was the desire in her eyes as intense as it was in his? "And are you trying to get into my pants?"

Kyle put his other arm around her, pressed his lips against the side of her neck and lowered his voice. "Very much so, but I'm not using this as an excuse. I mean, asking you to come here today wasn't exactly subtle and if you want to leave I'll understand, but I can't think of anything I'd rather do than get you naked and make love to you until you can't see straight."

He reached down, tugged Bev's blouse loose from her slacks and slid his hands underneath. She offered her mouth to him and felt her breath catch in the back of her throat at the passion in his kiss.

The exhilaration of solving the case and her pent-up emotions melted together so that Bev couldn't separate one giddy feeling from the other.

She returned Kyle's urgent kiss as she felt him push the coffee table away and they were stretched out on the couch before she could say anything else. How could he have this kind of effect on her and what was she doing?

She moaned slightly and pushed her hand weakly against his shoulder. He loosened his grip, but kept his arms around her as they both breathed heavily. His face glistened with sweat and Bev could feel her hair sticking to the back of her neck.

"Kyle," she started, "I'm not..."

He moved one hand and put his forefinger gently to her lips. "Sssh," he whispered. "It's okay, I understand."

Bev looked into his eyes, but didn't see even a hint of

irritation. Did he really understand? Chagrin started to replace the light headedness that had gripped her. Christ, how was she supposed to handle this?

Kyle propped up on one elbow and stroked her cheek. His voice was soft and low. "Bev, it really is okay. You drive me so crazy that I keep getting ahead of myself, but that doesn't mean I can't wait until Friday, or the time after that, or whenever. I meant it when I told you I don't think of you as someone just to jump in the sack with."

He dropped his finger and traced the outline of her bottom lip. "But, if you don't mind, let's sit up and let me kind of recover," he said gently. "It's a little tough in this position."

God, she wanted to tell him not to stop, but she needed some time to think. She nodded silently instead and he rolled off the couch to his knees. He stood, swaying slightly, took her hand and pulled her up. Her face was hot and she wondered if she was blushing.

"Are we both okay here?" he asked with a grin that held more humor that she had a right to expect. "I mean, we're still good for Friday, aren't we, or do I need to send more flowers?"

Bev smiled and tucked her blouse back into the waistband of her slacks. "No more flowers are required, but you could hand me my beer."

"I don't think it's still cold," he said. "I'll get you a fresh one." He took the mugs and walked to the kitchen.

Bev took a deep breath and gave him serious points for style.

Kyle returned with the full mugs, handed her one and pulled her close when he sat down. "Okay, so how about you tell me what time to pick you up on Friday and where you'd like to go."

Bev cradled the icy mug in both hands, took a sip and looked over the rim at Kyle. "Thanks for what just happened," she said quietly. "I appreciate it."

He touched his mug to hers and smiled without saying anything else.

Bev cleared her throat and was genuinely surprised at how quickly her feeling of awkwardness had faded. Most other men she knew would have at least treated her to a pout under the circumstances. "I don't mind going out," she said, "but you did mention something about grilling a mean steak and making great pina coladas or for that matter, I have a couple of dishes that I do pretty well with. You could come for dinner at my place. What are you in the mood for?"

Kyle wiped the froth from Bev's upper lip and smiled. "I'm sure you're great in the kitchen, but I don't want you to do any work. If you come over here Friday I promise to behave like a perfect gentleman."

Bev laughed this time, reached out and ran her free hand through his hair. "Well, let's don't define that term too narrowly," she said and then realized that might sound like she was being a tease. God, why couldn't she get herself under control with this guy?

Kyle grabbed her hand, kissed the palm lightly and then gently placed her hand onto his knee. "Fair enough and I'll try to make it past dessert anyway. Now, not that I'm not enjoying this, but take me through a couple of points on your case again – I have to admit that I got distracted toward the end."

Chapter Thirty

Bev covered the key areas with Kyle again and then glanced at her watch. Damn, she was running late if wanted to make the hospital and the scent of Kyle's cologne was rousing her senses. She mumbled about the time, told Kyle he could keep the copy she'd made, kissed him quickly on the cheek and let him walk her to the car.

"Good luck with Chief Taylor," he said with a grin. "Call me when you finish."

Bev nodded, backed out of the driveway and drove slowly down the block shaking her head at how quickly she had responded once more to Kyle. It was the sort of excitement that she'd known was missing in her life and she might as well face it – she liked the way he made her feel and being around him. It was as simple as that and she could work through the emotions of it later.

Everything was finally coming together in the Wiley case and even though it would take a few more days or maybe as long as a week, Bev was on the verge of breaking through Farmer's story and she'd have that wrapped up neatly before he knew what was going on. What a coup that would be! The Chief might even be forced to give her an out and out compliment instead of a left handed one the way he usually did. Not that she would hold her breath waiting for that to happen.

Bev made one brief stop for a chocolate milkshake and sucked the cold mixture through the straw. She needed something to tide her over until dinner.

It was surprisingly quiet at the hospital and Bev had no problem finding a parking place. She tossed the empty cup into the trash barrel and quickly chewed a breath mint to cover the smell of the milkshake out of consideration for

Jim's enforced diet restrictions.

He was still in intensive care, but that was due more to the fact that the patient load was light than it was to Jim's medical condition. They were moving him to Miami in the morning and would perform the bypass surgery within a day or two. His color had improved and when Bev walked into the room he was complaining to Myrtle about the lack of real food such as doughnuts and chicken fried steak.

Bev suppressed a smile as his wife told him to quit being a baby. "And this from a man who was at death's door only recently," Myrtle said and rose to accept Bev's hug. "I'm glad you made it by. Jim is ready for some police gossip and I need to go to the house to pack a few things. We have an early start tomorrow."

Bev winked at Jim and helped Myrtle gather her oversize purse, assorted magazines and a canvas bag that contained skeins of green and white yarn and a partially crocheted item that had not yet taken identifiable form. She offered to carry something to the car, but the older woman shook her head and stepped forward to give Jim a kiss on the forehead.

"No, you stay and keep him company for a little while and then convince him that he really does get a decent night's sleep here." She smiled affectionately and patted Bev's shoulder in parting. "He's a mite grumpy, so don't mind his fussing," she said and trotted out the door as Jim rolled his eyes.

"Grumpy my ass," he grumbled and shifted his bulk in the narrow bed. "I haven't had a decent meal since I got here, every time I try to sleep some nurse comes in to poke me with a goddamn needle and this snot-nose doctor who doesn't even shave yet lectures me about changing my lifestyle. I've got a right to complain."

Bev reached over and straightened the cover that Jim had kicked loose. She folded it neatly across his abdomen and he sniffed loudly.

"You had a chocolate milkshake and you look like you just got laid," he said enviously. "That's a hell of a thing to flaunt around."

Bev laughed and pulled up the chair that Myrtle had vacated. "The milkshake is correct," she said and felt the flush start across her cheeks.

"And you're saying I'm wrong about the other?" Jim asked with a grunt and ran his hand across his jowls. "I swear, you look like you might have knocked off an afternoon quickie. Why have you been holding out telling me the good stuff?"

It was comforting to see that Jim's powers of observation were almost back to normal. Bev cleared her throat and shrugged. "Well, you've had a lot on your mind lately."

Jim looked forlorn and sighed. "Bev help me out, will you? After they carve me up, it may be months before I can use my pecker for anything worthwhile; I need some excitement to keep me going."

Bev shook her finger at him. "Actually, you don't need excitement at all," she said.

He sighed again and she gave in. "Okay, all I'm going to tell you is that Kyle and I are seeing each other. We hit a little bump that I think we've gotten past now. Neither of us is a kid and neither of us knows what's going to happen and we aren't worried about it. We're going to have a good time and see what develops and not rush anything. Satisfied?"

Jim nodded and smiled. "I am, but Emma's not going to let you off that easily."

Bev gave an exaggerated shudder. "Well, I figure she'll be worried about you and Myrtle and that will keep her occupied for a few days. And speaking of which, tell me honestly how you're doing."

Jim hesitated for a minute before he spoke and gave Bev a half-smile that heralded one of his sporadic serious moods. He dropped his bantering tone. "Relieved, grateful as hell and just as nervous," he said.

"They've gone through the procedures with us and I guess I'm ready for this, but I've got to tell you Kid, it makes a man wonder about what he's done with his life. You think about all the moments when you put off doing something because you think you have plenty of time. They can give me all the shots and pills in the world and I still wake up in the middle of the night with these damn machines humming and sure hope the snot-nose doctor is right about my chances. I'm not ready to check out of the net just yet if I get any say so."

Bev scooted the chair closer to the bed and remembered the times that she'd thought of this man as indestructible; when as a child she saw both Jim and her father as strong, awesome, heroic men in their blue uniforms with shiny badges and holstered pistols.

"You worried about Myrtle?" Bev asked quietly.

Of all the things he would be most concerned about, Myrtle's welfare would be at the top of the list. The Osborns were like her parents in that they didn't have a openly demonstrative relationship, but rather one of comfortable closeness that could be seen in their day to day movements. As best as Bev could explain it, it was like the worn pair of jeans that was maybe a little frayed in places, but it was the pair you reached for first.

Jim nodded slowly, lifted one hand and let it drop to the bed. "I've got enough life insurance and the house ain't much, but it's paid for, so Myrtle would be okay for money. It's like I told you the other day though, I want to be able to take her on that cruise, be around to help with the grandkids and all that stuff. I owe her that and a lot more."

Bev reached over and straightened out a non-existent wrinkle in the covers. "Is there anything I can do for you?"

Jim swallowed hard, glanced around the room and then brought his gaze back to Bev. Not surprisingly, his moment of vulnerability had disappeared and his tone was normal. "Well, if you could sneak me in a dozen doughnuts…"

Bev understood what he really meant and the brief excursion into maudlin revelation was over. She laughed and held out her hands to ward off the suggestion. "Even if I managed to get by the nurses' station, Myrtle would kill me," she said.

As if on cue one of the nurses stepped inside the room

with a paper pill cup in her hand. She didn't say a word, but it didn't take too many detective skills to read her body language.

It could be fun to stay and fluster the nurse. Bev hadn't told Jim what she'd discovered about the case yet, although as she watched him dutifully swallow his medication she could tell he was more tired than he wanted to acknowledge. If she started in about Farmer, they were liable to get into a lengthy discussion and get carried away with planning a strategy. That couldn't be good for him.

"Hey Jim, it's late and I need to head home," she said and was given an *It's about time* kind of smiles by the nurse as she pointedly looked at her wristwatch.

Bev projected a smile of complete innocence in return, stood and picked up her purse to prove that she was in the process of leaving.

She leaned across and gave Jim a peck on the forehead. "By the way, in case you hadn't heard, the guys gave so much blood to the hospital that the doctors should be able to drain you dry and refill you."

Jim grinned. "Yeah, the Red Cross lady gave me the news. She said even Claude came by, but he was so damn thick-skinned they couldn't get a needle in him."

Bev stepped away and patted Jim's arm. "That's the rumor. Get some rest, big guy, and we'll check on you tomorrow after you get settled in Miami."

Jim blinked his eyes rapidly. "Sounds good and Bev, thanks for everything. You take it easy and don't be too stubborn to ask Claude for help if you need it."

Bev nodded in agreement and slipped out the door. She walked down the corridor and when she saw the sign to the hospital chapel, she turned on impulse and entered the small, quiet room.

Bev's church attendance was erratic and usually directly proportional to her mother's reminders that the pastor had inquired about her welfare. Religion wasn't something she thought a lot about and felt only minimal guilt when she requested God's assistance and then didn't follow through with whatever promise she'd made. After all, God was pretty understanding and as long as she lived a good life, that was the important part, wasn't it?

She sat in one of the pews for a few minutes and didn't try to make any bargains for Jim's sake. He was a decent man with a loving family and they could all use some more time together. She knew that didn't always count in the balance of human life, but it couldn't hurt to mention it.

A cool breeze lifted loose strands of her hair as she exited the building and clouds almost obscured the waning moon. The smell from a nearby Mexican restaurant carried down the street and a sizzling platter of fajitas suddenly seemed more appealing than a quick sandwich. It had been a full day and sitting down while someone waited on her wasn't a bad idea at all. Besides, after a couple of cold beers she'd be able to mentally map out the presentation to Chief Taylor that she was planning to have waiting for him in the morning.

Chapter Thirty-one

Bev was at the cash register paying her bill when she saw two patrol cars speed by with lights and sirens on. Neither her cell phone nor her beeper had gone off, but at the rate the cars had been traveling they'd be anywhere within the town limits in a few more minutes and if it was important, they would be calling her. She grabbed an extra peppermint and walked outside to see which direction they'd taken at the intersection.

The patrol cars had turned left. That was on the way home and Bev watched for them as she drove. She was half a block away from Paradisio's when she saw the blue and red lights. An emergency response vehicle was angled next to them and the back doors were open as one of the emergency technicians was working on a man who was sitting in the rear.

A knot of people milled around near the door and two of the cops were in the process of putting a handcuffed man into the back seat of one of the cars. The fact that he was wearing a suit caught Bev's attention. His coat was hanging askew and he looked like he'd taken a couple of punches. She swallowed the last sliver of the peppermint and swung into the lot.

"Oh hi, Bev. Did someone call you?" Kevin asked and slammed the door before Bev had a chance to see if she recognized the man in custody.

Now that she was closer she could see that the man in the emergency vehicle was holding a bloodstained cloth in one hand as the technician examined his face. The bleeding seemed to be under control although his shirt might be a loss – head wounds were always messy.

Bev shook her head. "No, I was just down the street and saw the cars. Anything serious?"

Kevin grinned and tilted his head toward the injured party. "He probably thinks so, but it's not too bad. The guy we've got in here started busting up the place and whacked a few folks around before we got here. Earl's inside and can give you the details. No knives or guns though, so this should go quick once we get him back."

His partner had moved to the opposite side of the car and was dispersing the crowd with the standard line about the show being over.

Bev strolled past them and took in the scene of what appeared to be a relatively small brawl. One side of the lounge was intact while tables and chairs were scattered and overturned in the section to the right of the bar. Four people were standing by the bar as an officer with a notepad took statements.

The second paramedic had his back to Bev and was blocking her view of the woman he was attending to. She could see a mass of wavy dark hair draped across a bare shoulder.

Earl was off to one side speaking with the gentleman that was probably the manager from the agitated look on his face. "Hey Bev," Earl said. "I didn't know they'd called you. It's pretty straight forward."

Bev moved close to talk without shouting. "I was in the neighborhood," she said. "What's the deal?"

He waved his arm in the direction of the paramedic. "The lady was over there with some guy. Another guy came in, was drunk, started raising hell with the lady, calling her names and all. Then it kind of went downhill from there. He grabbed a beer bottle, started knocking things around and caught everyone by surprise. Some of the guys at the bar jumped in to subdue him, one of them got smacked and the lady got knocked around before they got the other guy pinned down," he explained in virtually one breath. "That about it?" he asked the manager.

The manager nodded in agreement. He was in his mid-fifties and looked like he spent most of his time indoors – soft, but not to the point of folds of fat. His ash blonde hair was thick enough to be styled and his clothes had the coordinated effect of an outfit put together by a salesman in a clothing store – one of the reds in his tie precisely matched the thin red stripe of his shirt.

"Yeah, a hell of a thing," he said and twisted the gold tiger's eye ring on his right hand. I mean, this isn't some redneck bar where this shit happens all the time. Anyway, I don't know the guy's name, but he's been in a few times. The woman is a regular and plays pretty fast and loose if you know what I mean," he said and winked unnecessarily. "I came out of the office when I heard the commotion, but nobody was expecting this."

"Okay, so just the woman and the one guy hurt?" Bev asked before the manager could waste her time defending his reputation.

"Yep," Earl said. "The guy had kind of a nasty cut, but I don't know about the lady. She was giving the paramedic kind of a hard time."

Bev turned to look and confirmed the suspicion she'd had the moment she'd heard there was trouble over a woman. Her line of sight was clear and she saw Karen run her hand down the arm of the paramedic.

Bev lifted her hand in a good-bye gesture to Earl and walked across the room to check the damage to Karen. Her upper lip was almost double the size, her left eye would be a grotesque color within an hour or so and the paramedic had applied a butterfly bandage to her left cheek.

"I think you should let us take you to the hospital ma'am," he said. "That cut could use a stitch or two to be on the safe side."

Karen stroked his forearm again. "Thanks for your help, but I'm okay," she said calmly. "If it starts to bleed I promise I'll come in. Right now you'd better get a move on with your other patient. He looked like he really will need stitches."

The young man clicked his bag shut and looked at Bev.

"Any chance you can tell her that I'm right?"

Bev shrugged. "You probably are, but I've seen worse," she said.

He left without a response and Bev and Karen were silent until they were alone. Bev pulled a chair out and sat facing Karen. She pursed her lips and slowly shook her head. "You starting to hurt yet?"

Karen lightly touched her cheek and flinched. "No, and I don't intend to press charges so there's no sense in me taking up your time," she said evenly.

Bev rolled her eyes. "Yeah well, the owner and the other guy may not feel as charitable. The troublemaker was a jilted lover I presume?"

Karen reached into her purse and extracted an oval gold compact with her initials engraved on it. "Some men have a hard time with rejection," she said and opened the compact.

Bev watched the dismay cross Karen's face when she saw her reflection. "Damn," she said softly. "This will take a while."

Bev sighed. Karen might be worthy of disdain, but not a beating. "Look, we can get this guy for disorderly conduct, criminal mischief, public drunkenness and assault on the other party, but a double assault charge will carry more weight."

Karen closed the compact. "Actually, I suspect when the dust settles, you won't have any charges at all," she said. "You may not know him, but the man in question is the nephew of the president of the Chamber of Commerce. I'm willing to bet you that restitution for damages will be made, the gentleman with the head injury, who happens to work as a lowly assistant in the city's budget office, will receive an early promotion, and the nephew will receive little more than a slap on the wrist."

She raised her undamaged eyebrow. "Care to guess how I would be presented by the defense attorney? Care to guess who would be made out to be the real injured party? You know, temporary loss of judgement due to terrible treatment by a cold-hearted floozy sort of thing. It's a very popular attitude in the good old boys' circle."

Bev tugged on her ear. What good would it do to argue the point? "So that's it?" Bev asked. "An ice pack and a couple of aspirin?"

Karen glanced toward the bar where Earl was finishing up. "That and some medicinal scotch," she said. "After all, it's not like I've never been hit. It's not something I get off on, but this looks worse than it is." She dropped the compact into her purse. "Now if you'll excuse me, I need to go home, pour a scotch, find some aspirin and locate an ice pack."

Bev rubbed her forehead and sighed. "Look Karen, there's no sense in us pretending that we like each other, but for the life of me I don't understand how someone with your looks and obvious intelligence can be this stupid about men. You have to care more about yourself than this, for Christ's sake."

Karen plopped her purse onto her lap and hesitated, an internal mental debate obviously underway. She winced slightly when she made the mistake of trying to smile.

"I told you before that I don't give a shit about your opinion, but for some goddamn reason there is something that I'd like to explain to you. On the other hand, I don't want to delay that scotch too long."

Bev pulled her lower lip between her teeth. Maybe she was more tired than she realized and her guard was down or maybe it was just seeing Karen looking about as vulnerable as a woman can. "I tell you what," she said. "I'll get you a scotch and we'll talk for a few minutes. Then you can decide if you want to go to the hospital after all."

Karen inclined her head and Bev went to the bar. The customers were beginning to trickle back in and they carefully avoided the area of the confrontation.

Bev took a moment to wrap up the conversation with Earl. She told him that he could leave and she would take Ms. Silsby's statement. The bartender put a small round tray on the bar and set a double scotch and water and a tall club soda on it. He took a hand towel, dropped ice cubes in the center and added it to the tray.

"It's on the house," he said when Bev pulled a ten dollar bill from her pocket. "Tell Karen she can have as many of these as she wants."

Not the best way to get free drinks, but Bev nodded her thanks and carried the tray to a table by the far wall. Karen had moved to let them wipe up the spilled drinks and clear away the broken glass. Funny, it was close to where she and Kyle had talked only the day before.

Karen took the scotch and sipped it from the undamaged side of her mouth. She almost smiled when Bev opened her purse and pulled out a small bottle.

"It's close enough to aspirin," she said and tapped two pills into the Karen's open hand.

Karen closed her eyes briefly, swallowed the pills with some more scotch, picked up the makeshift ice bag and held it gently to the battered portion of her face.

"Look, it's not that I'm actually stupid about men," she said without preamble. "I don't want to get wrapped around armchair psychology, but it's a basic defense mechanism. I pick guys who are no good for me and that way I can't possibly be disappointed when they aren't. It's a pretty common tendency that's rooted in abandonment and other such issues. A standard neurosis as these things go and normal for someone with my background."

Bev stared and absorbed the words. "Okay, wait a minute. If you know this much, then why in the hell don't you change your behavior? Go into therapy or whatever? You've been around enough to know there's help available."

Karen sighed and for the first time since she'd met her, Bev saw a measure of fragility replace cynical bravado. Karen's voice dropped low and for a moment Bev saw someone she could sympathize with.

"One thing at a time is why. It's like I told you, I know the way out for me is to finish my degree and get far enough away to leave all this behind. I'll have a good job and a new beginning and I'll find a therapist; preferably a woman, I think, to help me work through all this. It's not something that you fix without serious intervention and it takes a while. I should be able to get it all together under those circumstances, don't you think?"

Bev was having a hell of a hard time holding onto feelings of animosity. Maybe this and what Karen had said before about how she grew up was bullshit, but it had the timbre and feel of truth. This was not a bid for pity.

Bev picked up the club soda and nearly dropped it from the moisture that had accumulated on the sides. "Yeah, that sounds like a decent plan," she said. "How's the medicinal scotch doing?"

Karen held the glass up to the light and sloshed the ice cubes in the golden liquor. "Between this, the pills and the ice I'm not in much pain. As you may have noticed, my original escort for the evening is nowhere to be found. I do believe he slipped out in the confusion and managed to not make a statement to the police. Probably had something to do with the wife he has back in Cleveland or wherever it was. At any rate, if we can get me a cab, I think it's time I make my way home."

Bev glanced around the room and back at Karen. "Oh what the hell, you're not much out of my way. If you really don't want to go to the hospital, I'll drop you off," she said.

Karen drank the rest of her scotch and shrugged. "I bet that's one of the last things you'd expected to do this evening, but like you say, what the hell."

She stood and wavered a bit. She held her hand up when Bev automatically reached to steady her, drew a deep breath and straightened her shoulders. "I'm okay," she said and stepped forward with what was an obvious effort. She blew a kiss to the bartender and Bev shook her head at the gesture.

Neither of them spoke on the drive to the condo. Bev pulled alongside the sidewalk and Karen opened the door and hesitated. "By the way, did you and Kyle talk?"

The question startled Bev. "Uh yeah we did," she said. "We're okay for right now and we'll see what happens."

Karen swung her legs out and turned her head to look at

Bev. "That's good. I suspect if you give it a chance the two of you might work out. Look, I don't think it will do any good, but I'll write up a statement and drop it by the station in the morning."

Bev nodded and Karen climbed out and shut the door. Bev waited until she was inside and then made her way to her own apartment. Christ, another day that had more action packed into it than most entire weeks had. And what a bizarre encounter with Karen. If someone had told her that the two of them would have had the conversation that just took place, she would have laughed it off as impossible. Funny how things turn out sometimes.

Chapter Thirty-two

Bev arrived at the police station early the next morning in time to re-organize her files. She added a few extra notes to the ones she'd written and shamelessly brewed a fresh pot of a French roast coffee she'd brought in. It was a better brand than the Chief would get from the café where he met every morning with a regular group of his buddies.

Chief Taylor entered the building within his well-established fifteen-minute window and Bev waited patiently for him to chat with Sheila and read through the log of the evening's activities. She'd already checked and there was nothing that was likely to put him in a bad mood. The ruckus at Paradisio's wouldn't interest him in the least.

Bev laid everything out neatly on Jim's desk and within ten minutes of his usual schedule, the Chief wandered into her office and leaned against the door jam.

"I swung by the hospital this morning," he said by way of greeting. He scanned the papers on the desk, but didn't mention them. "They should be headed to Miami about now."

Bev stood and walked toward the coffeepot. "Yeah, I spoke with Myrtle last night. The surgeon they have is supposed to be one of the best in the state and he'll operate tomorrow or the day after if Jim is stable. How about a fresh cup, Chief?"

He raised his eyebrows, moved to behind Jim's chair, pulled it out with one hand and extended his mug with the other. The heavy mug with a chip on the rim was stained from years of coffee and infrequent rinsing. Maybe she'd get him a new one for Christmas. God knows washing this one was apparently out of the question.

"And I'm supposed to sit down while you tell me what?" he asked to clearly signal that she needn't bother to try and manipulate him.

"The Wiley/Farmer case," she said and curbed the excitement she felt with the damn fine job she'd done. "I've got it."

Chief Taylor took the mug from her, lowered himself into the chair and paid no attention to the squeak. He blew air into the steaming brown liquid. "Have you now? Well, give it to me in simple terms because I don't intend to listen to some long drawn out version at this hour of the morning. If I want details, I'll ask for them."

Bev took a sip of coffee to hide her grin; so far his reaction was right on target. She leaned her hip on the corner of the desk and extracted a single piece of paper that she'd typed up into a *What, Who, When, How, Why* format.

It was the way Chief Taylor processed information and the format Bev had decided on the night before. One page was adequate as a starter. The rest of the documentation would serve as back up for the Chief's inevitable string of questions.

It was a strain to sit quietly, but Bev didn't interrupt as the Chief digested the page he was holding. When he read it the second time Bev found herself gripping the handle of her coffee mug to keep from delving into the folders to find the appropriate passages to reinforce her position.

Chief Taylor lowered the sheet of paper with no discernible expression on his face. He stared at the top of the desk and took another swallow of coffee. "You can back up this diving gobbledygook with what you've got in there?"

Bev inhaled silently and gave herself a pat on the back. The Chief got it or otherwise she would have been treated to an immediate barrage of profanity.

"Absolutely," she said. "It took me this long because neither Jim nor I knew anything about dive procedures and we didn't know to ask for some of this information."

He frowned, but it wasn't his pissed-off frown. "So why the hell didn't those diver guys at the research place catch it? Didn't you say all this was reported to them? If this theory about the potential danger in free diving after regular scuba diving is right, wouldn't they have noticed it?"

Bev pointed to the second folder and shrugged. "This theory is just now be looked at, so not a lot of people are familiar with it yet. The diving expert I've been talking with didn't know about it until I asked him for general background and he found the article he sent me. And from their perspective, all it would mean is some more data to support the idea of not combining a deep regular dive and a deep free dive. There wouldn't have been a reason for them to think of a set-up."

The Chief put his tongue to the front of his top teeth and made a sucking sound. Then he pushed back in the chair and stretched his legs out. "And what you want is to go after Farmer with what you've got? Squeeze him and see if he comes clean?"

Bev nodded eagerly. There was no longer a need to act as if this was routine. She stood up and paced a few steps away and moved back and forth as she spoke. "That's what I think is the best idea. I remember seeing some dive magazines at his shop and it would be easy to find out if he subscribes to the one the article was published in. I mean, it was a hell of a plan and it's a little on the complicated side, so I realize it might be tough to present, but if we can get under Farmer's skin and let him know that he's not as smart as he thinks and then dig into his business, we ought to be able to rattle him enough so that he'll make a mistake, or we can find where maybe he did some research on his computer about this or…" Bev stopped and trailed off when the Chief held up his hand.

Shit, what did she say wrong? He pointed to the chair and in an automatic sort of response Bev sat tensely on the edge.

Chief Taylor set his mug on the desk and rubbed his bald

spot with his other hand. "Bev look, what you've got makes sense, and to tell you the truth, I did wonder when it turned out that Farmer had a strong motive for getting rid of Wiley. What you also have is a hell of a lot of circumstantial evidence without any real proof."

Bev lifted her hands in protest. "Chief I know that, but what I'm telling you is that we can get the proof - I know it as sure as I'm sitting here. I was right about this not being an accident when everyone else was willing to accept that line of bullshit," she said before she could stop herself. Damn. That was probably the worst thing she could have said.

To her surprise the Chief let that slide by without comment and then leaned forward with his hands clasped together on the edge of the Jim's desk.

"First, settle down and don't get defensive," he said calmly. "Second, I'll give you that it looks like you called it correctly and yes, it's a solid piece of detective work. The problem is that right, wrong, or indifferent, this is going to be next to impossible to prosecute. You've got a couple of diving experts you can bring in, so Farmer gets a decent lawyer and he'll get experts to testify just the opposite. You think you can pressure Farmer to confess and I'll tell you right now that maybe you can, but I doubt it."

Bev rotated her fingertips against her temples and shook her head. "So we don't even try? We say, what the hell and let it go? We let Farmer get away with murder, or conspiracy, or whatever the right goddamn legal term is? Wiley is dead and Farmer gets not a single day of jail time?" She could hear her voice rising and she suspected it carried into the open station house, but the Chief let her finish this time.

He blinked his eyes slowly while she struggled to get herself under control again. His tone was deliberate, neither condescending nor sharp as he so often chose to be.

"Bev, there's a couple of pretty important points I need you to pay attention to. I'm not trying to tell you this is the way things should be, but as good as you are, you're still one of these people who think everything can be right or wrong, good or bad, black or white. Damn few things in life are like that and the things that people do to one another sure as hell aren't."

He released his hands and swept one across the desk. "You've got a man who seems to be a pretty good man for the most part. He gets jammed up on a business deal, maybe he loses his head over a woman and he's dealing with some arrogant asshole to boot. The way it sounds, this Wiley guy probably was living on borrowed time and it doesn't look like the world is a worse place with him gone."

Bev started to speak, but the Chief stopped her with a look. "I'm not done yet." He jerked his thumb over his shoulder to the outer room. "Now on the other side of the coin, you take those two nut jobs running around shooting up convenience store clerks. It's embarrassing that they haven't been caught yet and we can only hope someone nails them soon, but they're genuinely bad guys you can hang something on. You can link weapons and probably stolen goods. Sure, maybe they suffered some damn childhood trauma that a lawyer can argue to sway a jury, but at least a prosecutor has pictures with someone's brains blown out and a jury can understand that. The case that you want to bring doesn't have a particularly likeable victim, the method is unusual, not to mention hard to grasp, and all Farmer has to do is stick to his story. We'd be dealing the DA a lousy hand to play."

Chief Taylor paused and lifted his mug in a semi-salute. "You're smart Bev and you did a good job working it out, but this one isn't going to fly even if that's not what you want to hear."

Bev inhaled deeply two or three times, centering herself and hating to listen to what she knew was sound advice from his perspective. On the other hand, the Chief didn't know that she'd already had this same discussion with Kyle and she was too close to give up now.

She softened her tone - she wouldn't get anywhere if the Chief thought she was trying to overcome reason with emotion. "Okay Chief, I know it won't be easy, but if the DA's office is willingly to go further with it you'll back me, right?"

Chief Taylor raised his eyebrows again and pulled a cigarette from the pack in his shirt pocket. He lit it, took a long drag and stood up.

"Bev, don't bother to tell me that you don't have anything going with the new assistant DA. If he's willing to take this on and his boss lets him, then I won't pull the plug. I'm just telling you not to hang everything on getting this to trial, much less getting a conviction."

With that, he left the room and Bev flapped her hand to clear the lingering smoke. She walked over, poured another mug of coffee and was only marginally disappointed with the Chief's assessment. The mere fact that he understood and finally believed her very nearly offset his irritating reminder that the police held only half the equation for punishing crimes. Lawyers, courts and loopholes – Christ, it was frustrating at times! Bev sipped her coffee and refused to hold onto the pessimistic view.

She had Kyle's promise of support and yes, prosecution would be difficult at best and while it would have been nice if Chief Taylor had been more optimistic about their chances, she'd overcome more than one obstacle in this case. With just a little luck, she could bring it all the way home.

She returned to her desk and punched in Kyle's office number to see if he'd talked with his boss yet. The secretary told her that he was at the courthouse and Bev left a message for him to call.

She curbed her impatience at the delay and eyed the stack of papers in her in box. There was nothing urgent, but the pile was not going to disappear by itself and working on a tedious task was a good way to occupy her time while she waited. It was hard enough to cover the work of two detectives and she'd be damned if she was going to press the Chief about replacing Jim.

She was down to the last two reports when she heard a

man clear his throat.

"I called the office and thought I'd stop by instead of telephoning just in case I could talk you into having lunch," Kyle said and walked into the room.

Bev scratched a comment on the paper and slipped it into the outbox.

She smiled and motioned him to Jim's chair. "I'd like that," she said. "We're not going anywhere though until you tell me what the DA said about Farmer."

Kyle sat on the corner of the desk rather than in the chair and grinned. "Did you get the go ahead from your boss?"

Bev didn't flinch. "More or less. He even sort of complimented me, but he doubts I can crack Farmer," she said candidly. "So if you guys are behind me, that will help a hell of a lot."

Kyle hesitated in a way she didn't like at all. If he'd struck out, this was going to be very difficult indeed.

He fingered the knot of his tie. "Well, let's say I wasn't entirely persuasive," he said, "but there's no reason to go off on me," he added quickly when Bev glared at him.

"What the hell does that mean?" Bev felt her shoulders tense.

Kyle's voice was level, but he couldn't completely suppress a grin. "The boss told me that if I was thinking with the brains in my skull instead of my dick that I'd realize this was not a winnable case."

"And you think that's funny?" Bev said with a growing sense of anger and shoved her chair back to stand.

"No, but the important part is that he didn't think your theory was wrong," Kyle said matter-of-factly. "Look, I happen to know that Judge Pickett is out of town which means he would have to go to either Judge Claiborne or Newington for the warrants. He and Newington are like oil and water and Claiborne is remarkably liberal for this area. The chances are they'd both turn us down and if we wait until next week, we'll have a better chance with Judge Pickett."

Bev paused and reigned in her exasperation much as she'd

done when talking to the Chief. God, why couldn't they just let her run with this one? She focused on Kyle again as he lightly snapped his fingers to get her attention.

"And the other thing is, I did a little checking for you. One of my tennis buddies is a vice president in the bank where Farmer has his business account. I can get him to make some discreet inquiries and if you're right about Farmer's finances we should have something definitive by the time Pickett is back in town. I know you're anxious to move on this, but I doubt Farmer is planning to go anywhere in the next several days."

Bev paced back and forth the length of her desk for a few minutes.

"Come on Bev," Kyle said invitingly. "The DA didn't completely squash the idea, but he wants to be cautious and you have to admit it's not a bad idea. Let's go have a two martini lunch and you'll feel better about it."

Bev rolled her eyes. "I don't drink martinis," she said and pulled her purse from the bottom desk drawer. "But if we go to the Fish Hut, I could soothe my frustration with some blackberry cobbler."

Kyle stood and bowed toward the door. "Okay, cobbler instead of martinis. And then if you'd like we can swing by my office afterwards and I'll outline the other information that I think I'll need to convince the boss. There are some areas where we can do preliminary work."

That was more like it and on their way out of the station Bev was keenly aware of the glances exchanged by everyone who saw them. It was pretty obvious that their relationship wasn't going to be a secret and she still wasn't sure how that would be perceived. Would it affect how the men viewed her? Well, she didn't have time to worry about that right now.

Bev climbed into Kyle's Explorer. Christ, she was trying to cover both her job and Jim's, plan the tactics in a complicated murder case, potentially become the youngest ever, not to mention first female, senior detective in the police department and work out the ground rules of a relationship. But other than that, she didn't have a thing on her mind.

Chapter Thirty-three

Willie closed the trunk of the car and noticed that Hal had mounted the set of Arkansas license plates. That meant they were down to the other set of Louisiana plates, but they wouldn't need them if the plan for the boat worked out.

He still wasn't comfortable with the idea of breaking into a place and hanging around. Hal was always saying how it was important for then to get in and out of places quickly. Would it really be quiet like he said? Would there be a guard around? If there was, wouldn't Hal shoot him just like he had everyone else?

Willie bit a ragged piece off his thumbnail, spit it out and stared at the trunk of the car. The problem was that if it came down to making a clean escape or having a witness, they wouldn't have a choice. There'd been too many murders to expect any kind of mercy if they were caught and nobody was going to care that Hal had done all the killing except that one guy. They would both be looking at the death penalty. Goddamn, it wasn't right that he'd get blamed along with Hal when he hadn't wanted to shoot anybody in the first place!

Willie turned when he heard a noise and looked over to see the old man who ran the motel locking up the office right on schedule. At nine o'clock sharp every night he put out the sign that told folks to come to the small apartment behind the motel and for guests departing before eight o'clock in the morning to leave their keys in the box attached to the wall.

Once the manager had jiggled the door to make sure it was shut, he shuffled away without so much as a glance around. The motel was quiet with the other occupants already inside their rooms with the blinds and curtains closed. The café down the street had been dark for half an hour and the gas station at the intersection would lock up at ten o'clock.

Willie turned in the opposite direction at the sound of footsteps on the gravel parking area and saw Dwayne approach. At least the man showed up on time and hadn't hauled along extra baggage. The duffel bag he'd brought that afternoon was stuffed in the trunk of the car and the small backpack he had slung across one shoulder wouldn't take up much room. The two men exchanged nods without speaking and Dwayne followed Willie into the room.

Hal was double-checking the drawers to make sure they had everything. The only items left in the room were the nearly empty cooler and the briefcase with the drugs and all the cash from the pusher.

"We'll take off after the gas station closes," Hal said to Dwayne. "You got the passports?"

Dwayne dropped the black backpack on the bed and opened the side pocket. He pulled out the documents and passed them to Willie and Hal for review.

Willie had never seen a passport and didn't know if it was any good or not, but Hal seemed satisfied. Willie had selected the name of William Joseph Ryan in honor of two of his baseball heroes; Joe DeMaggio and Nolan Ryan. He was using William so he could still be called Willie and not be confused with a complete new identity. Hal had thought it would be easier for him.

"Let me hang onto yours," Hal said and took the passport from Willie. "We wouldn't want to take a chance on losing them."

Willie didn't object, but he noticed that Hal didn't take Dwayne's document. He wasn't sure how long it would be until they made it to the Bahamas, but he was thinking about not sleeping until then and for damn sure he intended to have his pistol tucked into his waistband. He'd stopped sucking on the whiskey bottle and was completely sober for the first time in days.

"Turn to channel six," Dwayne said, slumped onto the orange chair and threw one leg over the arm. "The Mountain Man is up against Doctor Doom tonight. He ought to kick his ass right outta the ring."

Hal switched shows and they settled in to watch the wrestlers take turns with body slams and headlocks as they waited until time to go. Hal hadn't said anything else about making one last hit on their way to Verde Key and maybe he'd changed his mind. Willie was kinda pulling for Doctor Doom, but Dwayne was right and the Mountain Man had him down on the mat pretty fast. Good thing he hadn't put any money on him.

Willie had studied the map that afternoon for the quickest way to Highway 1. There shouldn't be much traffic after ten o'clock on a week night and he'd drive just enough over the speed limit so as not to attract the attention. They would be at their destination in only a hour or so if they didn't stop.

The way Willie had it figured they should be out on the water before daylight. What kind of boat would they take - one with a hot tub like the fancy ones he'd seen on television? Hal said they would get a big one and with three of them, they ought to be able to handle one like that.

Come to think of it, it would be useful to learn how to crew a boat and if Dwayne really knew what he was doing, he could teach him during the trip. He didn't mind working hard and the only reason he ever had trouble on the job was because he was always getting stuck with some prick boss. It might be different working around boats.

Willie had been thinking that if he offered to take only a small cut of the money and none of the drugs, then Hal would probably let him go on his way. He didn't know for sure, but with his new passport then maybe he could even go off to a different island than Hal. There had to be lots of boats if they were in a group of islands and what he didn't learn from Dwayne, he could pick up on his own. He wasn't smart about books, but he wasn't stupid about everything.

All he was asking for was a chance to start over; a chance

to forget about the string of bodies they'd left in their path. He was sorry it had turned out the way it did, but what was done was done and it wasn't like any of those people could be brought back.

He wasn't the one who started it and it wasn't fair to blame him. If folks hadn't fucked him over all his life, then he never would have gotten mixed up with Hal in the first place and if he'd known how crazy Hal was, he wouldn't have agreed to go along with robbing the pusher. Things had just gotten out of control and he was going to go straight now, honest to God he was.

And if there was a guard at the marina, maybe he would be some old boozer who wouldn't come around and they could make a quiet getaway. It would be over with no more killing; six or seven hours and they would be out of the country with new lives ahead. That's all he was asking for now; less than twelve hours and they'd be in the clear.

Chapter Thirty-four

Bev sat on the couch in her apartment with the television tuned to a show that she wasn't actually watching and tried to curb her restlessness. She'd spent the afternoon with Kyle researching precedent for cases similar to the Wiley one and outlining the best approach to use to assuage the District Attorney's concerns.

The work had been gratifying and it gave her a chance to see Kyle working in his prosecutor environment. It was impressive to watch him take her files and call up case law from judicial rulings made in different parts of the country over the past several decades.

They made decent progress and shared a mutual understanding of the elements of proof to pursue. Bev was a bit disappointed to learn that the District Attorney would personally handle the case instead of Kyle if they could bring it to trial. It was a logical move since aside from the fact that Kyle was a newcomer to the area, she couldn't expect the DA to pass up the opportunity to present an unusual murder. They had spoken briefly when he stopped in the office, bemoaned the complicated nature of the case and adamantly refused to ask for a search warrant until Judge Pickett returned to town. He'd left them with the closing statement of wanting every detail checked and double checked before he hung his ass too far out.

Bev didn't mind the extra effort, but the idea of waiting even another few days to get the green light to proceed gnawed at her. Farmer's roots to the community were strong, but what if he took off on a dive trip to Fiji or some damn place like that?

Bev sighed, stretched her legs out to rest her feet on the coffee table and felt the tightness in her calves. She'd been so busy over the past few days that she hadn't worked out. It was pushing eleven o'clock, but a seven or eight-mile loop on her bicycle always helped when she was tense and sitting around wasn't doing her much good.

She was lounging in her favorite pair of pale blue, lightweight sweats so all she had to do was retrieve her shoes from underneath the table and grab her fanny pack. She tucked her weapon into the specially designed pack along with her badge and cell phone. She occasionally rode late in the evening and had never had any trouble being out alone.

She pedaled down the quiet streets as the family neighborhoods prepared for bed and she could hear music from the bars along the waterfront. She wasn't disturbed by the clouds that diminished what little light reflected from the crescent moon; the streets were well-lit and there wasn't enough traffic to worry about. A flash of lightning in the distance seemed far enough away to be unimportant and she didn't think a thunderstorm had been predicted on the morning weather report.

The breeze was invigorating and she re-played the day's events starting with her discussion with the Chief. She reached her turn-around point and hesitated. Jackson's Marina where Farmer's Adventures Below dive shop was located was only another couple of miles and the extra distance would be good for her.

Bev passed by the Scarlet Macaw and looked through the large windows. There were no more than half a dozen people scattered around the bar and Dillworth was behind it pulling a pitcher of draft beer.

She looked across the parking lot and noticed a light on in Adventures Below. Farmer was alone and moving around with a clipboard in his hand as if he was taking inventory. Bev dismounted the bicycle, walked it to the dive shop, set the kickstand and carried on a quick argument about why she should go home. The Chief and Kyle would both have fits if they knew she was here. On the other hand, maybe an unexpected visit like this would throw Farmer off guard.

And what would that accomplish? Suppose he slipped up or had a sudden surge of conscious? She had no other witness, no notebook and no reason to be having a conversation with him that would stand a cross-examination. Well, if he said something he shouldn't she would certainly remember it and if he gushed forth a confession she would just call for a squad car and then politely ask him to repeat everything when they got to the station.

The debate became a moot point when Farmer turned to the window and saw her standing outside. He understandably looked puzzled, unlocked the door and stepped back to let her in.

"I thought I heard something," he said. "It's a little late for a business call and I wouldn't think you had a sudden, irresistible impulse to check into scuba lessons."

He wasn't nervous, but the lines in his face seemed deeper than they were the last time they'd talked. Maybe a guilty conscious was nagging at him.

"Kind of late to be working, isn't it?" Bev asked pleasantly.

"No more so than to be out for a bike ride," he replied. "And should you really be out at night like this?" He gestured for her to move further into the shop and he closed the door behind her.

Bev patted the fanny pack. "I've never had a problem, but my dad feels the same way and he gave me one of these. One quick pull and a flip and badge and gun are at hand."

Farmer nodded and lifted the clipboard. "A wise precaution and to answer your question, I learned when I first opened this place that it was easier to do these things at night and I've never needed much sleep anyway. Danny, the young man you met, is very efficient, but I like to spot check on a random basis."

"That sounds like a good business practice," Bev said and looked around the open room. "And now that it's all yours again you wouldn't want to fall behind on the housekeeping tasks."

"Do you mind if I finish this display case?" he asked

instead of responding to her comment. He turned his body so he could count and talk to Bev at the same time.

"I don't know if you've ever thought of running your own business," he said after a moment. "You soon discover that it is precisely the tedious, boring tasks that must be done on time and done correctly. If my only job was to dive and teach diving, it would be all fun and very little work."

He finished annotating the page, set his clipboard on the glass top and slipped the pen into the front pocket of his shirt. "By the way, is there something in particular that I can do for you or is this simply a general conversation?"

Bev kept her voice low with no inflection. "You know, when Jim and I started on this case neither of us knew much about diving. I've had some pretty interesting conversations with a number of people since then."

Farmer showed no emotion. "I'm sure that you have. Steve told me that he introduced you to Mike Cleary and from what little I know about you, I would assume you've done other research as well."

He pointed to the table near the coffee stand. "Would you care to sit down or would that be ill-advised on my part?"

It would be if she were lucky. She smiled disarmingly and stepped toward the table, but cut too close to a pair of mannequins and bumped the closest one with her upper arm. She jumped at a movement and Farmer's hand shot past her to grab the figure before it fell.

"Sorry," he said and righted the gear-laden form. "This got knocked over yesterday and I've got to put a new support in to stabilize it before someone gets hurt."

He propped it back into place while Bev moved the fanny pack around from the small of her back and took one of the chairs.

"Well, do you think you shouldn't talk to me?" she asked. "During our last conversation you were pretty candid and since you think I'm off-base, I would hope that you at least don't mind helping me clear up a few details."

Farmer moved leisurely around the shop, shut off the

display case lights and joined Bev at the table. His smile was enigmatic and bittersweet. "Not at all and I gather that you don't believe in fortuitous occurrences or divine intervention?"

"Do I think God reached down and more or less smote Mr. Wiley in order to save your business and punish him for whatever else he'd done?" Bev shook her head. "No, that's too tough to swallow and when you throw Karen's good fortune into the mix that makes it even more difficult to accept as coincidence."

He had no way of knowing that she had grudgingly accepted coincidence about Karen's involvement. If one of the reasons Farmer killed Wiley was to help Karen, then maybe if he felt she was in danger, he'd go out of his way to divert suspicion from her.

A long rumble of thunder followed a streak of lightning and rain suddenly pelted against the windows. How could a front blow in that quickly? Bev cocked her head to listen, but kept her eyes on Farmer.

He scratched above his left eyebrow and maintained eye contact. "I do understand why you're frustrated with this incident, but the word 'coincidence' exists for a reason. An insurance check to Karen, my intense feelings against Greg and my improved business state don't change the fact that shallow water blackout and death are not uncommon under the circumstances that we encountered. It was all properly reported as you must have discovered in your conversation with Mike Cleary. And I did give you a copy of the report."

Bev tucked a strand of hair behind her ear. "Yes, you did and I read it a couple of times. We didn't know Mr. Wiley of course, but he certainly looked like he was in good shape. Why do you think he had problems on that particular dive?" Bev inhaled quietly and held her breath. Christ, she was on thin ice asking questions like this.

Farmer shrugged. "I haven't the faintest idea," he said without expression. "And don't forget the testimony of witnesses that I administered first aid to Greg. I really have nothing more that I can tell you and I don't know what details you're still unclear about."

Bev flinched involuntarily when rain rattled harder and they both looked over as the water suddenly sheeted down the sides. Damn! If she said much more, she would tip her hand. She didn't want him to know that she had the entire scheme worked out, but a nonchalant exit into the pouring rain was going to be difficult to execute. Surely this was one of the squalls that would stop within a matter of minutes.

Farmer stared at the window and gave Bev a half-smile. "How unfortunate. I don't seem to have told you what you probably wanted to hear and you don't seem to have any raingear handy."

"It's not a big deal," Bev said calmly. "I know you'd like me to close the books on this whole thing, but to tell you the truth, I'm just not quite ready to do that yet."

Farmer blinked his eyes slowly and spoke gently. He didn't sound at all like a man who had plotted someone's death.

"How certain and dedicated you are, how sincere in your pursuit for truth, for what you define justice to be. Those are admirable qualities and I'm sorry that you consider me to be the kind of man that you do."

He pulled a key ring from his pocket. "Listen, I've finished here and I'd like to lock up unless you think further discussion is in order. I have the van so we could put your bicycle in the back and I can take you home."

That was more laughable than her giving Karen a ride, but it was clear that she wasn't going to get anything useful out of the impromptu meeting. "Don't worry about me," she said. "It's not like I'll melt and I think it's starting to slack up."

Bev pushed her chair away from the table and heard an odd, muffled sound from the rear of the building. The wind had died, but perhaps the waning gusts had hurled something into the shop.

Farmer frowned, rose and held his hand up to Bev. "Let me check that and then we'll go out the front. If it's still raining, I really do insist that you let me take you home."

Bev shook her head, but Farmer had already gone through the open doorway. She bent down to retie one of her laces and was double-knotting it when she heard a low voice say, "Just take it easy, Tom and walk back slowly."

Bev jerked upright and sprang to a stand, but Farmer's rigid body was blocking the man talking. Bev caught her breath and watched Farmer half stumble as he backed up against the table. He edged to her right and she saw the speaker – a medium height, bald man holding a pistol with a steady grip. His dark green rain jacket was unzipped halfway down and water droplets dripped from the sleeves and tail.

Bev twitched her fingers to reach for her weapon, stopped and clutched the edge of the table instead. If the man was as composed as he appeared to be, her movement might alert him. Better to act confused until she could get a feel for what the hell was going on.

The man looked at Bev in an appraising way, but his face didn't register surprise. "Well, here I thought the place would be empty and we've got ourselves a party," he said and motioned Farmer to stand next to Bev.

"Dwayne, get the front lights and make sure the door's locked," he instructed without taking his eyes off them. "And yank the phone cord out if you can find it."

A second, slightly taller man, holding an automatic by his side, stepped past them and shut off the first set of overhead lights. Bev heard a door bolt slide into place. The lights from the interior office and the single florescent tube in the back area illuminated the rear section of the showroom, but someone passing by the front window wouldn't see past the rain-streaked glass.

A third man, the shortest of the three, slipped in and stood behind the first man as if waiting for orders. The butt of his gun stuck out of the waistband of his jeans and he wiped the back of one hand across his nose. His denim shirt was wet along the shoulders and he shifted his eyes nervously from the table to the man called Dwayne who was leaning one elbow against the front counter.

"Trying to remember, Tom? Can't put it together?" the man with the gun taunted softly. "It's been a long time."

"Gray, Greer – something like that – it was Norfolk," Farmer said more calmly than Bev expected him to.

Gray? No, not Gray – Grayson! Was it possible? Shit! Bev silently expelled a breath and conjured up the images of the photos. Shave one, put a beard on one and she could see it, but who in the hell was Dwayne?

"Close enough and yes, it was Norfolk, you nigger-loving kiss-ass," the man said coldly. "But I'm not here for a fucking reunion. Dwayne, go pick a boat and Willie, check the office for anything good. I bet Tom hasn't made his nightly deposit yet." He flicked the gun in a slight downward motion. "You two sit – hands up on the table where I can see them." The two other men left the room without question.

Bev and Farmer sank into their chairs as Grayson – it had to be him – pulled a chair out away from the table and sat across from Farmer.

"What, what's this about?" Bev asked plaintively. That's it – pay attention, but act distressed – that was the normal way to behave.

"It's about bad timing," the man said. "You shouldn't be working this late, Tom – it's not good for you," he continued.

"Look, I don't do a big cash business, if that's what you're after…"

"I'm not surprised," Grayson said and cut him off. He tilted his head toward Bev. "Who's she?"

"My niece," said Farmer before Bev could open her mouth. "She was on her way home."

"Not now, she's not," Grayson said in a voice that was as flat as the lines of his face.

Bev shot a glance at Farmer as if she still didn't understand. His face was set hard and Bev wished she knew what their connection was. Did he know how dangerous Grayson was? Bev bit down on her lower lip and raced through her options. *How long would it take to get to her gun? Think. Reach, snatch, aim — no, shit, the safety was on. Twenty seconds? Thirty? Could she move before the others came back? If she moved, would Farmer panic? Probably not.*

Willie reappeared and sidled up to the table with a zippered canvas bank bag in his hand. He laid the bag next to Grayson, but didn't sit in the remaining chair. "There's not a lot in here, but more than some places and there's a safe," he said and seemed twitchy compared to Grayson's stillness. He flickered the tip of his tongue in and out of his lips. "What about them, Hal? What are we going to do with them?"

"Don't worry about it," Grayson replied without looking at him. "They're no different from the others."

Even in the dimmed light, Bev could see the chilly intent that had risen in his fixed gaze. Did Farmer see it, too?

"A safe, huh? Anything interesting in it, Tom?"

"Mostly business documents," Farmer said and shifted in his chair. He pressed his left foot against Bev's ankle and inclined his head almost imperceptibly to the left. "There's no bundles of money laying around if that's what you mean," he added.

Was Farmer trying to tell her something? Bev coughed nervously, covered her mouth and stole another glance. Farmer shifted his chair closer and pressed his foot against her ankle again. She bent forward with another cough and turned her head to the left. *Nothing, nothing she could see.*

"Water," she squeaked. "I need a drink." She started to rise and Grayson angled the pistol toward her. "Stay put," he said and lifted his free hand to the side of his head. "Get the lady some water, Willie. We don't want her to choke to death."

"The bottle," Bev wheezed helpfully and cut her eyes as far to the left as she could without turning in that direction. She caught the edge of the mannequin's hand in her peripheral vision. *The mannequin — the wobbly one — the one that had almost fallen earlier. What was Farmer thinking? Shit, where was Dwayne?*

Willie had taken a cup and filled it to the brim. He stretched his hand out and sloshed some of the water onto the floor. He averted his eyes when Bev took the cup and drank slowly.

Was she guessing correctly about what Farmer had in mind? Was he going to do something or did he expect her to? Shit, they were in a tight group. Bev let the partially filled cup slip through her fingers and it landed under the table. She knelt to retrieve it.

"Leave it," Grayson ordered, but she'd had time to reach in and snap off the safety.

Bev sat in the chair, but this time she poised on the edge with her toes balanced for a quick launch. *Now what, and where was Dwayne? Did he still have his gun drawn?*

"Should I go check on Dwayne?" Willie asked and ended the question with a whine. "Shouldn't he be done by now?" He had begun to shuffle his feet and he shivered as he plucked at the wet shirt clinging to his shoulders.

"He won't be much longer," Grayson said and stood with another slight flick of the pistol. "Willie, you watch her and I'll have Tom show me what's in that safe."

He took one step to the left and Farmer rose smoothly, but abruptly shoved his chair back into the platform with the mannequins. The movement startled the two men and Farmer lunged for Grayson's arm as the mannequin toppled forward.

Bev twisted clear to the left and ripped her pistol from the pack. "Police, hold it!" she screamed to Willie, but she saw a blue blur in the open doorway and heard the shot as something shattered behind her.

She pivoted and fired rapidly as Dwayne exposed himself too long. She saw the body fall and swung her gun back toward Willie. He had dropped his weapon and moved his hands up when the gun in Grayson's hand exploded as Farmer tried to wrench it loose. The round caught Willie in the face and he crumpled in a spurt of blood.

"Drop it!" Bev yelled, but the struggling men had swung

toward her and Farmer was in the line of fire.

She stepped to the right for a better position, but Grayson tore his arm free and thudded two shots into Farmer as he held the slumping body like a shield. Grayson shoved the body away with his free hand and already had the pistol aimed at Bev. She fired a round to his chest, but he wavered and tried to raise the pistol again as she knocked him backward with a double tap. He lay still and Bev stood immobile for a moment trying to get her bearings and clear the ringing from her ears. She stepped to Farmer, rolled him on his back and reached for his pulse, but his eyes were fixed wide open and his limp hands were covered in blood from where he'd clutched at the gaping holes in his stomach.

Bev straightened slowly and realized that someone was pounding on the front door. She stiffly walked to the door, pushed the bolt back and opened the door. Funny, her hand was trembling. A gray-haired man in a dark blue uniform held a nightstick in one hand and a cell phone to his ear with the other hand.

"My God, lady, what's all the racket..." he started and saw the gun dangling at her side.

"Police," Bev said tiredly and fumbled for the badge she hadn't had time to show.

"I..., they're on the phone," the man said cautiously and sniffed the air. The stench of gunpowder and bluish smoke hung in the room and his eyes widened when Bev took the phone from him and stepped back into the shop.

She had her badge out now and he stared at it as though he was trying to figure out what it was.

"Hello, hello, are you there?" a voice on the other end of the phone asked urgently.

"It's me – Bev," she replied wearily and didn't try to stop the guard when he rushed forward to the first of the bodies. She gave instructions in a clipped voice and then disconnected the call – she couldn't take a lot of questions.

"Holy shit, what happened?" the guard asked with a bewildered look on his lined face. He stood by Willie's body shaking his head and Bev fleetingly wondered how she was going to explain.

The guard was saying something else, but his words were lost in the scream of the sirens of two patrol cars that skidded to a stop.

Kevin was the first one through the door and he reached for Bev's elbow as three more officers came in and fanned across the room. The first ambulance swung in next to the patrol cars and Bev began to tell Kevin what had happened. A chill took her by surprise and someone draped a windbreaker around her shoulders. She looked down at the stains on her pants from where she'd knelt beside Farmer. She paused when she saw the blood and Kevin waited for her to continue, but they both turned when the Chief's square frame nearly filled the open door. How had he gotten the word so fast?

He stepped inside, took the baseball cap from his head and shook water to the floor. "You okay, Bev?"

She nodded and moved her arm in what felt like slow motion. "Yeah and I don't know what this will turn out to be, but I'm pretty sure two of them are the Devil's Duo."

Kevin whistled low and Bev bit her bottom lip.

"Farmer's dead, Chief, but he saved my life. They would have killed us both." She swallowed with an effort and watched the paramedics work methodically. Earl had taken the security guard to one side.

Chief Taylor grunted and looked at Bev closely. "Right this minute I don't want to know why you were here at this hour of the night," he said. "We'll talk about that when we're alone."

"He saved my life, Chief," she repeated. "There's a lot to tell, but if it hadn't been for him, we'd both be dead."

Chief Taylor took her elbow and carefully pulled her out of the door. "I hear you, Bev, but come on; let's get you down to the station. Dr. Cooke will be along shortly and they can finish up here. We're going to have a hell of a lot to do on this one and we might as well get started. You feel up to it?"

Bev nodded without speaking and let him lead her to his

car. She climbed in. The rain had become a drizzle and a mist had formed across the hoods of the idling vehicles. The Chief radioed that they were on their way in and Bev listened to the familiar voice of the dispatcher.

The paramedics were unloading the gurneys from the ambulances and Bev stared at the body bags stacked on top. How? How in the name of Christ had it come down like this?

Chapter Thirty-five

It took until nearly sunrise for the three men to be properly identified and the news of the death of the Devil's Duo, with the unexplained third man, to circulate. The telephones rang constantly and by the time most normal people were enjoying breakfast, the station was crowded with officials from the state police, the mayor's office, and even a pair of Drug Enforcement Agency agents that showed up from Miami.

Bev should have been exhausted, but she was fueled by the borderline chaos and projected far more control than she felt. She carefully explained the actions she'd taken and the procedures she'd followed at least four times.

It was only during the first private telling to Chief Taylor that she'd been completely honest about why she was out and how she'd arrived at the dive shop. He'd chewed her out for putting herself in that kind of situation and then agreed that her reason for being at the dive shop didn't need to be repeated.

They held a formal press conference at nine o'clock although the local guys had managed to provide the news services with a morning story of just-breaking, juicy footage of the bagged bodies, an interview with the security guard and a more or less correct account of the shooting.

Kyle appeared at the police station within an hour after the shooting and once he knew Bev was okay, he spent his time helping separate the curious with a legitimate need for information from the curious who just wanted a piece of the action. Not surprisingly, Kyle's boss made himself available to assist with the state police, the DEA agents and anyone else he considered to be important.

The detective from Mississippi who had originally considered Hal Grayson and Willie Denton as possible suspects called and carried on a long conversation with Chief Taylor and Bev. They discussed the items found in the car that would hopefully link the men with the deaths that had started their bloody spree. It wasn't every day that multiple cases could be solved in one forensics sweep.

The DEA agents helped piece together the flow of the two men's movements since they'd left Mississippi with the erratic pattern that had, indeed, served them well. By the time the scenario was completed, the addition of Dwayne Wallace Bolling was presumed to be connected to the presence of the three fake passports. The DEA agents were familiar with Bolling's history of smuggling and other illegal activities and that made it fairly easy to surmise the intent of stealing a boat. The DEA agents also worked through the FBI and they somehow tracked down the Navy connection between Farmer and Grayson. Exactly how that tied in was still a point of confusion, but it seemed to be a point that could be resolved at a later time.

Information from the sheriff's department in Mississippi strengthened the speculation that Hal Grayson was the planner as well as a textbook psychopath and Willie Denton was a basic dumb fuck who would have been better off having never laid eyes on Hal Grayson.

The telephone call from Bev's parents had been one of the trickiest moments and Chief Taylor took over to assure Emma that they didn't have to change their plans and drive immediately to the station.

The excitement finally calmed down around mid-afternoon and Bev was alone again with Chief Taylor. The out of town visitors had accomplished their stated missions and those who wanted it had been interviewed. Bev had less than politely convinced the lingering reporters that no, she would not say anything more to them and Kyle had escorted his boss and the mayor's assistant out of the area. He and Bev had had no private time and she'd nodded tiredly when he whispered that he would call her as soon as he could.

Bev slid into the leather chair in the Chief's office rather than onto one of the straight backed ones that she usually took. Funny, it was the chair that Jim always used. Damn, it was comfortable, too.

Chief Taylor lit a cigarette and allowed the pleasant silence to buffer them both for a few minutes.

"A hell of a busy day, Bev," he said quietly. "So how are you doing now that you've had a chance to think about it?"

Bev closed her eyes briefly. She was astonished at how rapidly her mind processed the scene at the dive store and compared it to the time she'd shot the drunk outside the bar and the stand-off at Vera's.

"I think I'm okay," Bev said after what seemed a long time to her. "But I've got to tell you Chief, Farmer still puzzles the hell out of me. Why? I mean, why did he do it? Wouldn't most folks have tried to talk their way out of something like that?"

Chief Taylor thumped a line of ash into the ashtray and shrugged. "Look, I know you've had your hackles up about Farmer from the beginning, but like I told you yesterday, I think he was fundamentally a good guy who found himself in a position with Wiley that he didn't know how to get out of. So yeah, you're probably right about him setting Wiley up because he couldn't see his business going under and probably because of how he felt about the girl, too. He came up with this plan that you have to admit was pretty damn clever and there was still an element of chance. Wiley might have survived and that probably justified in Farmer's mind that it wasn't the same thing as murder. On the other hand, when you were both in danger he felt he had to do something. I don't think he intended to get himself killed; that was just bad timing. Hell, I don't know; maybe it was Fate or some kind of fucking poetic justice, but I wouldn't spend too much time trying to figure it out."

Bev rubbed the back of her neck. "I don't know Chief, maybe that was it, and I'm damn glad he took those bullets instead of me, but it's pretty hard to make sense of it."

The Chief almost smiled. "You try too hard to make sense of things sometimes, Bev. People do a lot of things that are hard to understand and those are the ones that are supposed to be normal. Let it go; you're a goddamn heroine and you'll be all over the news for a few days. Why don't you just enjoy it?"

Bev sighed. Christ, she was tired! The euphoria and adrenaline were waning and she was torn between wanting a hot shower and sleep and a stiff drink.

"Not to mention that after you've stopped being a headline item, you'll have to help break in the new detective," the Chief said and sucked on the cigarette until it glowed bright red.

She leaned forward and kept her face still. So that was it. The Chief had made his decision about bringing someone in without any further discussion with her. Son of a bitch! "I see," she said quietly.

The Chief actually grinned at her and if she didn't know better, she'd think there was mischief in his eyes. Mischievous was not a part of Chief Taylor.

"I doubt you do," he said. "The new guy has maybe five years until retirement and he's looking to move here from Tallahassee to start winding down. He'll pull his weight, but he doesn't have a problem with letting you be the head detective and I'll tell you it wasn't easy for me to find a seasoned guy who would agree to that."

Bev stared at him. Had she hear him correctly? Maybe she was hallucinating from the stress of the day.

"Are you serious?" she asked without thinking. "You're going to put me in charge?" She struggled to hold back a grin. *My God, he was! He was going to do it!*

The Chief lit up again and blew a stream of smoke directly toward her. "At the risk of your dad telling me I've lost my mind and probably taking a load of shit from the mayor, yes I am." He coughed and lowered his voice.

"Look Bev, I'd be more comfortable if you were in your forties or at least if Jim had hung for another few years, but things are what they are. You deserve this and I'm giving you your shot at it," he said and held his hand up in his familiar gesture. "This doesn't mean you'll have a free hand, though. I'll snatch you up short in a heartbeat if you let it go to your head."

Bev pursed her lips to keep from laughing out loud. "Chief, I never thought otherwise, but you don't have to worry. I know it's a gamble for you and you won't be sorry. Is it okay for me to ask when it's official?"

He pointed the cigarette to his outbox. "As soon as I send that piece of paper in. I'll wait and make the announcement tomorrow; we've had more than enough hubbub for one day. Besides, you need to get the hell out of here and get some sleep."

Bev stood and was surprised when the Chief rose, came from behind his desk and put his hand on her shoulder. "Bev, it might be kind of tough on you tonight when it all finally sinks in. Don't set your alarm in the morning and you sleep in if you need to. The rest will do you good."

Bev was touched. This was virtually a torrent of sympathy. She smiled in response. "Thanks Chief, I may do that."

She returned to her own office and looked around. The Chief was right, she needed to leave and get away from everything for a little while. She had had enough of crowded rooms, but she didn't particularly want to be alone with the barrage of emotion that was beginning to break through. She was going to have a couple of drinks and get something to eat. Sleep could come later after she had a chance to relax. Lorna was still at work, although she'd said she would turn the shop over to her assistant and come by if Bev needed her.

The truth was that she wanted to be with Kyle. She moved her hand to the telephone to call him and stopped. What kind of signal would that give him? It might seem like she was looking for a strong shoulder to lean on. She was, but would that imply that she couldn't emotionally handle tumultuous events without some guy to turn to?

That was silly, wasn't it? Kyle would have stayed around

if he'd been able to and then he'd probably have suggested they go for a drink. Yes, but if she picked up the telephone and asked him to come be with her, then that might make her look vulnerable. She withdrew her hand from the telephone and found her purse. Oh hell, she'd go to the Fish Hut, have a drink or two and then make her mind up.

She walked out of the office and stopped in surprise when everyone stood, gave her a round of applause and formed a loose gauntlet between her office and the exit. She smiled in embarrassed appreciation and shook hands on her way out the door.

Bev drove to the Fish Hut, but she went inside to the darker, nearly empty bar rather than taking her usual spot alongside the canal. A man she didn't recognize was at the end of the bar and a couple was at one of the tables. She had bourbon on the rocks instead of beer and enjoyed the taste as it slid down her throat. She rarely drank hard liquor, but whiskey seemed more appropriate.

The lingering smells from lunch set her stomach rumbling and she ordered the Fisherman's Sampler Basket. She drank the bourbon quickly, downed one more only slightly slower and switched to beer when the bartender set the seafood laden basket in front of her. She pulled a shrimp from the mound of crisp seafood, blew on it and blotted everything out for a few minutes while she savored the food.

When her stomach was full she wiped her mouth and poked the small pile of fries and calamari that remained in the bottom of the basket. She eyed the telephone in the corner and tapped her finger against the side of the beer mug. Call Kyle? Don't call Kyle?

"I know you might want to be alone, but I'd be happy to oblige if you'd like some company," Kyle's voice said behind her.

Bev swiveled the barstool to her left and felt a smile before she could hide it. "Hi," she said quietly.

Kyle pointed to the stool next to her and she nodded. "I called the office and they said you'd left and I got your voice mail at your apartment, so I thought about what I would do in your shoes. I figured booze and/or food and started here first," he said and motioned for a draft. "I can leave if you'd rather be by yourself," he offered when she hesitated.

Bev shook her head rapidly and pushed the basket between them. "No, I'm glad you're here," she replied and searched his face. Had he taken her admission as a sign of weakness?

His eyes were steady and caring without so much as a hint of condescending male ego. They were nice eyes; eyes a girl could trust. Eyes a girl could get lost in if she wasn't careful. *And would that be such a terrible thing?*

Kyle popped a piece of calamari in his mouth and touched his beer mug to hers in a simple gesture. Oh hell, she didn't want to worry anymore about what he might or might not be thinking.

In less than forty-eight hours she'd solved an incredibly difficult case, shot two men, damn near been killed, stopped a murderous spree and was on the verge of a career leap years ahead of when she'd expected. She needed someone as a sounding board and that had nothing to do with weakness.

"I'll be more than happy to sit here for as long as you'd like," Kyle said. "But I do have cold beer at my place and you could kick your shoes off."

Bev rubbed an imaginary spot from her mug and then looked back into Kyle's eyes. "Are my shoes all I can take off?"

He grinned, reached out and stroked the back of her hand. "I certainly hope not," he said. "But I didn't want to presume, plus you've got to be exhausted."

Bev drained the last of her beer, slid off the stool and swayed slightly from the effect of no sleep and the alcohol.

She motioned for Kyle to lean forward and when he did, she whispered in his ear. "Okay, I am tired and I'm on the way to getting drunk, but I bet I can stay awake for another hour or so."

Kyle stood, dropped some money on the bar and slipped his arm around her waist. "In that case," he said softly so he couldn't be overheard, "how about if I start you with a nice hot shower and then we'll go from there?"

Bev nodded and as they walked out of the restaurant into the warm sunshine, Kyle pulled her close. It felt good and that was exactly what she needed at the moment. It was time for her to let go and lean against someone else for at least a little while.

Shades of Murder is the second novel for Charlie Hudson who is a retired military officer. She and her husband, Col. Hugh Hudson, currently reside in Alexandria, Virginia. They are both avid scuba divers. Ms. Hudson works part time for a major Army Head Quarters as a logistics analyst.